P9-DGO-177

HANNAH MASSEY

Catherine Cookson

CORGI BOOKS

HANNAH MASSEY
A CORGI BOOK 0 552 13715 4

Originally published in Great Britain by
Macdonald & Co (Publishers) Ltd

PRINTING HISTORY
Macdonald edition published 1964
Corgi edition published 1990
Corgi edition reprinted 1991
Corgi Canada edition published 1992

Copyright © Catherine Cookson 1990

The right of Catherine Cookson to be identified as author of
this work has been asserted in accordance with sections 77
and 78 of the Copyright Designs and Patents Act 1988.

Conditions of sale

1. This book is sold subject to the condition that it shall
not, by way of trade or *otherwise*, be lent, re-sold, hired out
or otherwise circulated without the publisher's prior
consent in any form of binding or cover other than that in
which it is published *and without a similar condition
including this condition being imposed on the subsequent
purchaser.*

2. This book is sold subject to the Standard Conditions of
Sale of Net Books and may not be re-sold in the UK below
the net price fixed by the publishers for the book.

This book is set in 11/13pt Times by Kestrel Data, Exeter

Corgi Books are published by Transworld Publishers Ltd,
61-63 Uxbridge Road, Ealing, London W5 5SA, in Australia
by Transworld Publishers (Australia) Pty. Ltd, 15-23 Helles
Avenue, Moorebank, NSW 2170, and in New Zealand by
Transworld Publishers (NZ) Ltd, 3 William Pickering Drive,
Albany, Auckland.

Printed in Canada.

UNV   10   9   8   7   6   5   4   3   2   1

LAUDER

Catherine Cookson was born in Tyne Dock, the illegitimate daughter of a poverty-stricken woman, Kate, whom she believed to be her older sister. She began work in service but eventually moved south to Hastings where she met and married a local grammar-school master. At the age of forty she began writing about the lives of the working-class people with whom she had grown up, using the place of her birth as the background to many of her novels.

Although originally acclaimed as a regional writer – her novel *The Round Tower* won the Winifred Holtby award for the best regional novel of 1968 – her readership soon began to spread throughout the world. Her novels have been translated into more than a dozen languages and Corgi paperback editions have sold more than 40,000,000 copies. Three of her novels – *The Fifteen Streets, The Black Velvet Gown* and *The Black Candle* have been made into successful television dramas, and more are planned.

Catherine Cookson's many bestselling novels have established her as one of the most popular of contemporary women novelists. She and her husband Tom now live near Newcastle-upon-Tyne.

OTHER BOOKS BY CATHERINE COOKSON

Contents

The print was a brown ... She passed this without looking
in the window, but by the butcher's shop next door she
paused ... came to a ... for a moment before going on. She paused
again in front of a chemist's shop, but ... she should
not stop until she ... ... purpose until as
side end of the block. ... again she paused and scanned
the contents of the window before entering it ...

The Arrival

As she came slowly through the doorway into the
snow-covered street she paused for a moment and put
her hand against the wall near where the cards that gave
the names of the flat-dwellers reposed in three slots one
above the other. But, as if becoming aware of the
proximity of something dirty, she snatched her hand
away and put it in her coat pocket, then went slowly
down the street.

She was a tall girl with very long legs, a flour-white
face topped with thick, dark auburn hair, which had been
cut to bouffant style but which now fell from jagged
partings over each side of her high cheek-bones. She had
large, slightly slanted grey-green eyes, and a wide
straight-lined mouth, but what could have been a set of
perfect features was marred slightly by her nose which
was a little too long and a little too thin. Altogether she
looked rangy. She was wearing a knee-length brown coat
with a broad belt that swung loosely below her buttocks,
and she carried in her hand an open-woven basket; she
didn't look adequately dressed for the weather, she
looked like a young woman who had slipped out
hurriedly to do some shopping. And this was apparently
her intention.

Walking slowly past four Victorian houses, similar to
the one she had just left, she came to a row of shops.

The first was a baker's. She passed this without looking in the window, but by the butcher's shop next door to it she paused for a moment before going on. She paused again in front of a chemist's shop. But thereafter she did not stop until she reached the large all-purpose store at the end of the block. Here again she paused and scanned the contents of the window before entering. Her journey down the street had been slow, even leisurely, and her whole attitude, if judged by her back, could have been one of boredom; yet immediately she was within the store her manner changed. She did not pause at any counter, but walking hastily around the perimeter of the store she made for a side exit, and having gained the street once more she took to her heels and ran.

The street opened into a main thoroughfare thick with traffic, but she made for the other side of the road with the assurance of someone used to London's traffic. Once across, she left the main road and cut down another side street, not running now but hurrying at the point of a trot. Ten minutes later she stopped outside a small pawn shop and stood for a moment inhaling deeply before entering.

There was no-one in the shop except the man behind the counter. He was in his fifties and looked unusually spruce to be in a pawn shop. Pawn shops were dusty places, even those like this one that sold new stuff such as silver and rare china. Men who worked in pawn shops seemed to take on the patina of their surroundings and it usually gave off a dull sheen, but even this man's smile looked clean and bright.

'Good morning, madam,' he said.

'Good morning,' she answered. Her voice sounded

rough, almost rasping, as if she had a bad throat or her mouth was dry.

'What can I do for you?' He inclined his head towards her, as if he had known her a long while and wanted to be of service to her.

She groped into the single deep pocket of her coat and brought out a ring, which she placed on the counter.

He did not immediately touch the ring but looked at her. He watched her swallow twice, then waited for her to speak.

'Could you . . . could you give me ten pounds on it?'

'Ten pounds!' His eyebrows moved up slightly towards his smooth hair. He picked up the ring and reached out for a small black eye-piece. After a moment he looked at her again; his expression had changed. It could have been the expression of a man who had found something out, something detrimental about someone he loved. He said again, 'Ten pounds?' His words were a question, and in answer she moved her head.

He looked at the ring once more; for an eternity he looked at it, and she grew old the while.

'Yes.' He let out a long breath. 'Yes, I can give you ten pounds on it. Yes. Yes. Well now, would you like to sign?' He pulled a book towards her and offered her a pen. As it passed from his hand to hers it fell to the counter and he apologised, saying, 'Oh, I'm sorry,' although they both knew it wasn't he who had dropped the pen. When she had signed her name he turned the book towards him. 'Rose Massey,' he read aloud, then glancing up at her he proffered gently, 'You have forgotten the address, madam.'

She stared at the book for some seconds before writing

in it again. When the pawnbroker turned it towards him he studied it a moment before saying quietly, 'Eight Brampton Hill . . . Brampton Hill?' He put his head back on his neat shoulders and, looking up towards the age-smoked ceiling, said musingly, 'I can't quite recollect . . . Brampton Hill?'

'It's on the outskirts, Lewisham way.'

'Oh. Oh, Lewisham way.' He was nodding at her. Then he smiled, and picking up the ring he placed it behind him on a piece of glass, and from a drawer he took a bundle of new notes from which he pulled off the elastic band and counted ten out to her.

She folded the notes twice, then again, until they were a tube squeezed in her fist. 'Thank you. Good morning,' she said.

'Wait . . . you will want a ticket.'

'Oh, yes.' There was another eternity while she watched him write out a ticket, and when he handed it to her he smiled again as he had done when she came in.

'Thank you.' She did not return his smile but inclined her head.

'Thank . . . you.' There was deep emphasis on the words.

She was conscious of him watching her walking to the door, and her legs shook and her feet in the high stiletto-heeled shoes wobbled slightly. In the street she hesitated a moment, looked to the right, then left, then once again began to hurry towards the main road, but when, at the corner, she saw a taxi coming towards her, the 'For Hire' sign up, she hailed it.

'Can you take me to King's Cross?'

'Certainly, miss.'

'I mean could you get me there for about ten to one? The train leaves at one.'

'Ten-past twelve now . . . I don't see why not, if the traffic jams are kind to us. Hop in.'

In the taxi she sat bolt upright, gripping the handle of the basket on her knee with both hands.

When they were stopped by traffic lights for the third time she leant forward and asked, 'Will it be all right?'

'Eh?' he said.

'Will it be all right? Will there be plenty of time?'

'Yes, yes, we'll make it and likely twenty minutes to spare.'

She sat straight again, staring unblinking at the constant movement ahead.

'There you are,' said the taxi-driver. 'What did I tell you? Just two minutes out.'

Standing on the kerb she hesitated on his tip, whether to give him a shilling or two shillings. . . . She could make it two shillings, she'd have enough. Yes, she'd have enough.

She had just crossed the pavement towards the entrance hall when the taxi-driver's voice hailed her, and she turned towards him. 'You've left your basket, miss.' He jerked his head towards the back of the cab. She glanced downwards before running back, pulling open the door and grabbing up the basket.

At the ticket office she said, 'A single to Newcastle, please.'

She ran again, weaving in and out of the throng towards the platform. At the barrier she said to the ticket collector, 'How long before it goes?'

'Ten minutes,' he replied.

She withheld her ticket. 'I won't be a minute.' She turned from him and, running once more, went into the ladies and to the lavatory. She did not sit down but waited a few seconds before she left the basket at the side of the pan, then hurried out.

She was crossing the waiting room when a voice hailed her from the door. The attendant stood there with a large duster in one hand, the basket in the other. 'You forgot this,' she called.

Her eyes dropped again before she moved towards the woman, and taking the basket she said, 'Oh, thanks.'

As she approached the train she held the basket at an angle so that its emptiness would not be noticed.

After walking the length of the train she stood in the corridor. She had known she wouldn't get a seat, not this late. It didn't matter, it didn't matter. With the first shuddering movement of the train she leant against the partition and, her lids slowly closing, she allowed her muscles to unwind.

When a voice said 'Excuse me,' she opened her eyes and pressed herself back to allow a man with a suitcase to pass her, and when he looked at her and smiled his thanks no muscle of her face moved in response, but as he put down his suitcase and took up his stand against the door she moved slowly away. Walking down the corridor she crossed over the jangling connecting plat- form, and stood in the corner of the next coach.

It wasn't until the train reached Doncaster that she found a seat, and when she placed her basket on the rack it drew the attention of the two men and the woman sitting opposite. Time and again her eyes would lift to

12

the basket, incongruous between the suitcases, before dropping automatically down to the girl with the bright hair and the white face and the long legs, which she kept pressed close to the seat. She didn't look the type to travel with a basket.

When at Durham she was left alone in the compartment with one passenger, and he a man, she went into the corridor and stood looking out into the whirling darkness.

Before they reached Newcastle the man came out of the compartment, and as he passed her he looked at her with open curiosity. A girl was travelling with an empty basket and without a hat or a handbag . . . no girl ever travelled without a handbag.

Just before the train reached Newcastle she tore up the pawn ticket and put it down the lavatory, and when she left the train she left the basket on the rack.

Again she was hurrying, now into the main thoroughfare of the city. All the shops were still brightly lit, but most of them were closed, even the one that advertised late closing on Friday night was about to shut its doors when she entered.

'It's five to, we're closing, miss,' said the doorman.

'Please.' She looked up into his face. 'I won't be a minute, I just want a case.'

'All right,' he said, 'go on.' His voice was kindly, and broad and thick with the northern inflection, and told her she was home.

On a counter to the right of her were some suitcases. An imitation crocodile, priced at twenty-one shillings, brought her hand to it, and handing the money across the counter she said, 'I'll take this. Where are the hats?'

'On the first floor, miss.'

They had covered up most of the millinery in the hat department, but, glancing swiftly around her, her eyes alighted on a grey felt. Pulling it on and with hardly a glance in the mirror she said, 'I'll take this one.' The price was twelve and eleven.

As she turned to go down the stairs she saw a notice proclaiming 'The Bargain Counter'. A model with wire arms extended towards her showed a three-piece suit in charcoal edged with dull pink braid. It looked exotic, and therefore wasn't everybody's buy. The price had been slashed three times. The tag hanging from the lapel showed thirteen guineas in large red letters. This was scored out and underneath was ten guineas, then eight guineas, and now the black figures stated that the garment had been reduced to five guineas.

She said to an assistant who was watching her as she looked at the suit, 'What is the waist?'

The girl said, 'Oh, the waist? The hips are thirty-four.'

Before the assistant could pull the tag from the inside of the skirt to ascertain the size, she said, 'I'll take it.'

'There's no time to try it on.'

'I know.'

'You won't be able to get it changed, not at this price.'

'I know.'

The assistant was smiling as she whipped the suit from the model. 'I'm sure it'll be all right; you'll be able to carry it.' She smiled a complimentary smile.

After she had handed the girl the money, she took the parcel and put it into the case, and when she passed out of the shop the doorman said, 'I see you've got what you wanted, miss.' He smiled at her as men mostly did.

'Yes,' she nodded, but without answering his smile.

Once again she was walking back to the Central Station, without hurrying now. In the restaurant she bought a cup of tea, and from the bookstall a paper; then going to the booking office she asked for a single to Fellburn. Out of the ten pounds she had received for the ring and the pound she had in her pocket when she entered the pawn shop she had only a few shillings left, but it didn't matter, it didn't matter; she was nearly home.

Half an hour later she stepped out of the train on to the platform at Fellburn Station, and edging her way through the crowd in the station hall waiting for the buses she went out into the driving, skin-searing sleet. She had one more thing to do before she could go home.

She went down Marlborough Road. This cut off the main part of the town and the new shopping centre, for even at this hour the street would be thronged, it being Friday night and pay night for both the pits and the factories. Even if the shops were closed the coffee bars would be doing a trade, and the clubs . . . the clubs roared on a Friday night, and who knew who she would run into.

She came out near the park and past the road that led to Brampton Hill; Brampton Hill where the élite of Fellburn lived, those that were left of them; Brampton Hill, the name she had put on the pawn ticket. Why had she put 'Eight Brampton Hill' on the pawn ticket? Perhaps because she had heard of 'Eight Brampton Hill' since she had heard of anything. She passed by St Vincent's Catholic Church and the Convent, and next to the Convent the school at which she had attended until she was fifteen. Then she crossed the road and went down a dark alleyway. She had always been afraid of going down this alleyway, even as recently as two years ago; now she was afraid no more. What was it? It was just a cut between a factory wall and a railway siding. And the dark? The dark was no longer terrifying; it was something that you could lose yourself in . . . sometimes.

The alley led her into an open plane. Once or twice she slipped, her high heels slithering over the snow; but all the time she was making her way towards the faint blur given off by a lamp in the far distance. When she had almost reached the lamp she stopped and peered at the white-capped hills of builders' rubble. Stopping, she picked up a stone, weighted it in her hand, then discarded it as being too light. Then selecting a rough, chipped-edge house brick she laid it near her feet and searched until she found a similar one. When she found it she opened the case and took out the newspaper, and wrapping the bricks in it she put them in the bottom of the case, placing the bag containing the new suit above them.

The sleet, nearly all rain now, was full in her face and almost blinding her, but had she been blind she would have known the way to Grosvenor Road.

The houses in Grosvenor Road were large terraced houses; they were all old and looked respectable and dignified, even crowned with dirty melting snow as they were. Age alone had not brought these qualities to them; these had been built into the façade at the end of the last century. Each house had an iron-bound square of garden and the front door was approached by four steps, and number forty-nine, the third house from the top, was unique in that its steps were made up of red and ochre-coloured tiles.

As she reached the top step she leant against the framework of the door for a moment. She wanted to get her breath, gather her wits together, say all the things she had rehearsed in the train. When there came to her the buzz of voices beyond the door, loud harsh voices, and the deep roll of laughter, she knew indeed that she was home. She straightened up and rang the bell.

PART ONE

ROSIE

Friday

When the door opened and Rosie saw her brother Jimmy standing there she did not move or speak, and he, for a moment, did not recognise her, for being six foot two the lights in the hall beyond him diffused its rays from the back of his head.

'Aye?' he asked. 'Who . . . ?' then bending forward he exclaimed in a quick, breathless whisper, 'Name of God! Is it you, Rosie?'

'Yes, it's me, Jimmy.'

She was in the hall now; Jimmy had one hand on her shoulder, the other still grabbing the door. As his voice, spurting up his long length like steam from a geyser, yelled, 'Ma! Everybody! Look who's here. Just look who's here,' he shook her.

'What is it? What's up?'

'No, no, begod! 'Tisn't true.'

'Rosie!'

'Where have you sprung from?'

'Rosie . . . Rosie.'

The hall was packed now, filled with men, all big men; and one woman, a big woman too. She came forward towards her daughter like a sleepwalker, her eyes wide and unblinking, and when she was a yard from her she flung her arms wide and gathered the girl into her embrace, crying, 'Rosie! Rosie! Aw, Rosie!'

Had Rosie wanted to speak she would have found it difficult for the breath was being squeezed out of her, but she, too, clung to her mother, hiding her face in her thick, warm, fleshy neck until she was pushed to a distance as Hannah Massey, looking round at her four sons, cried at them, 'Well, what are we standing here for like a clutchin' of dead ducks? Come on with you and into the room where it's warm. . . . But lass' – her hands were moving over her daughter now – 'you're wringin', absolutely sodden. In the name of God, have you walked all the way from the station?'

'I missed the bus.'

'Then why didn't you get a taxi?'

'I wanted some air; it's a long journey.'

'Aw, child . . . just to hear your voice again, it's lovely lovely.' Once more she enfolded her daughter in her arms; and now there was a derisive cry from one of the men.

'Away to the room she said, away to the room where it's warm. . . . Go on with you; go on, old 'un.' He put one hand on the massive back of his mother and one on the thin shoulder of his sister and pushed them amid laughter and chaffing out of the hall and into the sitting-room.

'Here, get that coat off you.' Hannah was behind her daughter, and when she had pulled the coat off her she stopped and surveyed her with surprise, as did the men.

As Rosie stood self-consciously pulling down the skimpy jumper over the tight skirt a trace of colour came into her face and she said, 'There was no time to change. I made up me mind on the spur of the moment. My other things are being sent on.'

22

'You haven't got enough on you to keep a rat warm, either in clothes or flesh.' Hannah was standing in front of her again, feeling her arms. 'And you're as white as a sheet, girl. Tell me, are you all right? I've never seen you like this in your life afore.'

'I've had the flu.'

'I can see you've had something, for begod! you look like a ghost. A puff of wind would send you flyin'. Come, sit yourself down here by the fire until I get you a meal.' She led her forward as if she was old or an invalid, then asked, 'How long you down for, lass?'

'Oh, a . . . a week or so.'

'You'll be longer if I get my way. . . . Just wait till your da sees you. Oh, begod! he'll be over the moon, over the moon he'll be.'

Hannah Massey now pressed her daughter into the easy chair by the roaring open fire, and with her hands resting on its arms she bent above her, her big broad face stretched and softened in tenderness, and she stared at her silently for some moments. Then reaching out and gently patting the white face she turned away, overcome with her emotion.

When their mother had left the room the four men who had been standing at a distance like spectators now gathered around Rosie and they chipped and teased her as they always had done; and to one after the other she put out her hand and touched them, and each of them returned her touch with a gentle pressure of their big rough hands, and their open affection blocked her throat and dimmed her gaze.

Of her nine living brothers Rosie knew these four the best. Jimmy, the eldest at home, who had opened the

23

door to her, was thirty-three. He was tall and black and handsome. Arthur was thirty. He too was tall but had not Jimmy's bulk or looks. His hair was the colour of Rosie's, only a darker hue. Then there was Shane. Shane was twenty-eight and six foot, big boned and thin, and he took after his father.

Barny was the youngest of the eleven sons born to Hannah Massey; he was twenty-six but could have been twin to Rosie herself, who was three years younger.

As she looked at these men, the lads as she thought of them, the warmth that emanated from them became almost unbearable. Up to two years ago they had teased and petted her . . . and had been proud of her. Yes, they had been proud of her. But two years ago they had not appeared to her as they did now. Then she had secretly seen them as big, blundering, narrow-minded bigots. Then she had longed to get away from their deep laughter, laughter that the weakest joke could elicit. Then, God forgive her, she had looked upon them as common and coarse, men without a thread of refinement among them. How dared she have thought that way about them! . . . How dared she!

Barny, touching her wrist with his blunt, hard fingers, said, 'By, you've lost weight; you're as thin as a rake.'

'Well, you couldn't say she was ever fat.' Arthur pushed his fist gently against the side of her head. 'All thoroughbreds are lean, eh, Rosie?'

'Why didn't you let us know?' put in Shane, peering at her through narrow, thick-fringed lids out of a face that looked as Irish as his name. 'You been bad or something. . . . I . . . I mean afore you had the flu?'

'No. It was just the flu.'

'Just the flu,' said Jimmy, strightening up and adjusting his tie while he looked down at her. 'Just the flu. It's enough for, begod, it pulls you down. I should know: I had it, an' that bug, diarrhoea and sickness. It's been going mad round here. It was only four days I was down, but Christ!'

'Not so much of your Christing.' Hannah came marching in to the room with a laden tray. 'I've told you, our Jimmy, we're going to have less blasphemy round here . . . now mind, I've said it.'

The four men looked at their mother, a wide grin between them ,then turning to Rosie almost as one Barny and Shane cried simultaneously, 'Hear that, Rosie?' while Arthur put his head back and laughed; and Jimmy, bending above Rosie again, said in a mock whisper, 'Talk posh now; that's the latest. Live up to our best shirts.' He pulled at the front of his well-cut nylon shirt. 'Bloody and bugger and Christ's taboo . . . abso-bloody-lutely.'

'Jimmy!'

'All right, Ma, I'm only having you on.'

'Well don't.' Hannah Massey's back was straight, as was her face; her head was high, which brought it almost on a level with Shane's, who stood near her, and as she allowed her gaze to rest condemningly on Jimmy she spoke in an aside to Shane, saying in a tone of command, 'Fetch the dish out of the oven, you, and don't spill it.'

'OK, captain.' Shane pressed his shoulders back, made a salute with a wavering hand, winked broadly at Rosie, did a smart about-turn and marched, knees up, feet pounding the floor, towards the kitchen. This act brought great gusts of laughter from the others and a

25

compressed smile to Hannah's lips. Then as she moved towards Rosie her face broke up as it were, and fell into soft warm folds, and she said, 'You see, they don't get any better, do they? They won't learn, not one of them. Brawn, that's all they've got. Could anybody on God's earth refine this lot? I ask you. . . . Now could they?'

'Oh, Ma.' Rosie smiled faintly and shook her head, and Hannah said, 'Come away, sit up; it's just something to be going on with. If you'd only let me know you were coming I'd 'ave had a spread for you.'

'Aye, begod you would at that.' Arthur nodded at her, his brown eyes twinkling. 'And we'd all 'ave been on our toes. Spit and polish it would have been for every one of us, an' sitting here like stuffed dummies waiting for your entry, like last time. Do you remember, Rosie?' He laughed at her. 'The house full of us all, like Madame Tussaud's we were, all set up. Here's one that's pleased, anyway, you've come on the hop.'

'Where's your things, Rosie?' said Barny now. 'If they're at the station I'll get Phil next door to pick them up in the car.'

'Aye.' Hannah, pressing Rosie into the chair at the table and, bending over her and looking into her face, said, 'I was just going to mention your things. Are they at the station?'

Rosie picked up her knife and fork. 'They're going to be sent on. I, I came on the spur of the moment, and just threw a few things into a case.'

'But . . . but that in the hall; that isn't your good leather case. Why did you travel with that thing? They'll bash the good one to smithereens on the railway, you know what they are. . . .'

'. . . And after meself paying nine pounds ten for it.' Arthur was leaning across the table imitating his mother's voice. 'You'll not get another present out of me; begod, you won't.'

Hannah struck out at her son; then cried at them all, 'Go on, the lot of you, and get going; you were almost on your way.'

'She's pushing us out,' said Shane. 'She's got our money.' He nodded to the other three. 'Friday night; she's got our packets and now we can get to hell out of it. She's got Rosie, so she doesn't want us. She wouldn't care if she never saw a hair of our heads . . . except on Friday nights. On Friday nights you're as welcome as the flowers in May to Hannah Massey's home.' He touched his trouser legs and went into a little jig, which his brothers applauded.

Hannah, ignoring the by-play, seated herself at the corner of the table opposite Rosie and heaving in a great breath she squared her lips as she said, 'Begod! I could cover with spit the amount I make out of you lot.' She nodded towards Rosie now. 'Rump steaks, fresh cream on their puddin's, suits at fifteen to twenty guineas a piece. And take their shirts now. Two pound twelve and six apiece I've to pay so's the sweat won't show at the oxters. Wouldn't you say now there's a fat lot left out of a pay packet when the bills are cleared?'

The four men, following a signal, now walked solemnly towards each other, and putting their heads together began to sing, 'Tell us the old, old story.'

The satirical chorus was broken up by Hannah remarking caustically, 'Aw, you're all flat, there's not a note right atween you. The only time you lot can sing together is when you're three sheets in the wind. . . . Now' – her voice held a note that Rosie knew from experience could put a damper on the lads' rough humour – 'you've done your piece so get yourselves along with you. I want to talk to me girl here.' She winked at Rosie.

'Aw, there's no hurry, Ma. Me da should be in any minute now.' Jimmy looked at his wrist-watch. 'I want to see his face when he spots her.' He smiled towards her and Rosie, with an effort, smiled back.

'Aye, me too,' said Barny. 'He'll be over the moon. Aye, we'll all wait; so settle yoursel', old woman.' He flapped his hand at his mother, which caused her to shake her head widely as she lowered it to her chest like a bull about to charge. Then before she could make any further remark there came the sound of the back door opening; and Shane, darting to Rosie, pulled her to her feet and whispered, 'Get behind the door, go on.'

'Yes, yes, go on.' Hannah, her face alight once more, signalled to her as she pulled herself up from the chair.

'Hannah!' The voice came loudly from the kitchen, and she called back to it, 'Aye, I can hear you.'

'Where's them blasted slippers?'

'Coo! Mrs Massey.' Barny was whispering as he poked his head towards his mother. 'Listen to him, Mrs Massey; he's swearin'. He said blasted, Mrs Massey.'

'You wait, me lad, I'll give you blasted afore you get out of the house the night. . . . Ssh!' She silenced them all. 'Move round, don't look so guilty like, push yourselves about.' She pressed the door back, hiding Rosie, then called, 'Have you found them?'

'No, I haven't, an' I'm not lookin' for them.' The heavy padded footsteps came towards the living-room,

28

and Broderick Massey entered, growling, 'If you want me to wear blasted slippers then have them out for me.'

Hannah had her back to him and she busied herself at the long table in the middle of the room. She took a glass bottle from out of a large cruet and, shaking it, held it up to the light, ascertaining the amount of pepper in it, as she said, 'If I had three wishes in the world, do you know what I'd wish for?'

Broderick stopped dead on his way to the fireplace. He looked around his sons, all self-consciously doing nothing, then towards his wife's bent back and her great expanse of buttocks pressing her skirt up into a point above her thick calves. A sly twinkle came into his eye and a smile slithered over the grey dusty grime of his face, and he cast his glance towards Jimmy and winked. Then making his way to the chair by the side of the hearth, he sat down, saying, 'Begod now, let me think. The last time I heard that sayin' it pushed us all back over a hundred quid for the suite. You remember, boys?' He rolled his head backwards on his shoulders, taking in the amused glances of his sons. 'An' the time afore that it was spin-dryer, remember?' He jerked his chin upwards and his Adam's apple danced under the loose skin of his neck. 'And the time afore that, the time afore that was an electric mixer. An electric mixer, begod! You remember the schemozzle about the electric mixer? She couldn't mix another spoonful, rheumatics she had in the wrist you remember?'

The men were all laughing now; and Hannah, from the table, her back still towards her husband, said calmly, 'If I had three wishes, Broderick Massey, the first one would be to see my daughter in this very room. . . . And the second one would be . . .' She straightened up and took a large knife and sawed off a thick slice of bread before continuing. 'The second one would be to see me daughter in this very room this very night. And . . .'

Before she reached the third wish Broderick was on his feet, and now he looked at her as she swung round, her face one large beam, crying, 'And the third wish would be to see me daughter . . .'

'Stop it, woman! Tell me.' He was walking toward her. 'She's comin'? Rosie's comin' home?'

The men were laughing out aloud now like lads at the climax of a joke they had prepared.

'She could be at that. Aye, she could be at that; she could be on her way.' She looked at him, at his thin, wiry body which looked puny against her breadth. She lifted her hand to his shoulder and turned him round to face the open door, and then silently she pointed.

He flashed his glance wide now towards her, then slowly he padded to the door and pulling it forward he looked at his daughter; and then they were in each other's arms.

After holding her for a moment in silence, words tumbled out of him. 'Aw, Rosie. Begod, Rosie. Aye, three wishes, three thousand wishes and every one that Rosie would be in the kitchen the night. Aw, lass. Aw, lass.' He held her from him and looked at her for a moment, then turning to Hannah who was standing to the side of him he said in awed tones, 'She's as thin as a lath.'

'She's had flu.'

'Flu, begod!'

'Aye, it's pulled her down.' They were talking as if

she was a child, a child who could not speak for herself. They murmured over her as they walked back to the middle of the room, and when Broderick sat down in his chair he still had hold of her hand and cried, 'Come and sit down on me knee, come on.'

'Don't be silly, Da.' Rosie shook her head. She was smiling more easily now but not laughing.

'Come here.' He pulled her on to his knee, and after holding her tight for a moment he pushed her upwards and looked at Hannah, saying, 'She's not the weight of a feather; you'll have to do some fatten' up here, missus.'

'Who wants to be fat?' Rosie touched his rough cheek, tenderly, lovingly, and he caught her hand and held it, his face crumpling almost as if he was going to cry, but he shouted, 'Who wants to be fat? Better than lookin' like death on wheels; you haven't a pick on you.' He felt round her ribs. 'Not a pick. Aw, we'll soon alter this. How long are you here for?' He squeezed her tightly now.

'A week, or so.'

'Make it . . . or so, eh?' He was about to go on when his attention was drawn to where Hannah, once again at the table, was now speaking to Arthur, but harshly, saying, 'You goin' to the club?'

'Aye,' said Arthur; 'of course I am.'

'Well then, wait for the others.'

'Aw, Ma.'

'Never mind aw ma-ing me. I told you what I'd do; and I mean it mind.'

'God in Heaven!' Arthur turned away and dashed out of the room, leaving the atmosphere changed.

As Jimmy and Shane exchanged glances, Hannah said

31

to them, 'You keep an eye on him, 'cos mind, I'm tellin'
you as I told him, if I see him with her once again I'll
go to her place an' pull her out and rub her nose in the
gutter. I will, so help me God. If anybody's going to
bring disrespect on me family it'll be meself, an' that's
the way I'll do it. But I'll take good care as long as I've
got breath in me body none of me own blood's goin' to
show me up.'

'If you'd let up, Ma, it would likely peter out.'

Hannah turned on Barny. 'Peter out, you say? It's been
going on for nearly a year now, and if her man comes
back from sea we'll have him at this door wantin' to
beat his wife's fancy man's brains out.'

'He's left her, Arthur's told you.' Barny's voice was
low. 'He won't come back.'

'Aye, he's told me an' I don't believe a word of it.
He'll be back when his ship's in. Women like that are
as bad as drugs to a man; they should be horse-whipped,
her kind.'

'Now, now, now! No more of this.' Broderick looked
towards his wife. 'Let the child get acclimatised again
afore you start. . . . Eh, Rosie?'

Rosie made no answer, but, pulling herself from her
father's arms, got to her feet, saying, 'I'll go up and have
a wash, Da.'

'You didn't finish your tea.' Hannah came quickly
towards her now, her face once again smiling. 'Look,
I'll get some more hot, there's piles of fish pie.'

'It's all right, Ma; I'll have something later. I'd rather
have a wash and tidy up. I feel filthy.'

'All right then, lass, all right.' Hannah stroked her
arm, then pushed her towards the door.

32

'I'll take your case up.' Barny followed her into the hall, and Rosie said, 'It's all right, Barny; it's quite light.'

'When did you carry a case upstairs?' Barny smiled at her over his shoulder.

'Aye when!' Hannah exclaimed from the doorway now. 'An' put on something nice,' she added. 'That rig-out you have on isn't you at all.' She wrinkled her nose, then smiled.

'Which room am I in?' Rosie turned from the foot of the stairs.

'Oh, aye, begod, yes. Well, look.' Hannah pointed. 'Jimmy's on the landing now but I'll throw his things back into the attic in two shakes when I get your da settled.'

'No.' Rosie stepped down into the hall again. 'No, please leave Jimmy where he is, Ma; I'd rather be up in the attic. You know I always liked the attic; it's big, and, well, I'd rather be there.'

'You mean that?'

'Yes. Yes, I'd rather be up there.'

'Aw well then, for the night. I'll make the bed up later. And, Barny, you take up an oil stove now an' we'll fix everything good an' proper the morrow.'

Rosie followed Barny up the stairs and on to the first landing. It was a big landing with four doors going off it and another flight of stairs leading from the far end. They went up these and on to another landing with three doors, and before they mounted the attic stairs Barny stopped, and after switching on a light, said in a whisper, 'Notice anything?'

Rosie looked around her, then down to the carpet on

the landing. And glancing up at Barny, she smiled slightly as she said, 'A new carpet up here.'

He jerked his head. 'Oh, you don't know the half. All the bedrooms have fitted cord carpet now; no lino, not a bit of lino anywhere in the house except the living-room. She said she would do it, and she has.' His head jerked again. 'By, she's the limit, isn't she?' He laughed.

In the attic, Barny put the case on the floor, then stood looking at Rosie. 'It's nice to have you back, Rosie.'

'Thanks, Barny.' She turned towards him but didn't look at him.

'Are you all right?' he asked quietly. 'Nothing wrong?'

She lifted her eyes quickly to him. 'Wrong?'

'Well, you don't look yourself you know, nor sound yourself. I noticed it when you first come in. But the flu does pull people down. One of the fellows in our shop had it; he came back as weak as a kitten. He could hardly handle his machine.'

When she did not answer he strained his neck out of his collar, adjusted his tie, and said, 'They're over the moon down there, the pair of them. There'll be no holding her for days. You'd better put on your best bib and tucker to give her something to brag about. Jessie MacFarlane will know you're here within the next hour. And the Parkmans and the Watsons' – he nodded his head first to one side of the room and then to the other – 'will be advised' – he was now mimicking his mother's manner – 'of your arrival in very refeened tones to-morrow morning.' He pushed her gently as he laughed, then added, 'But I don't know about the Watsons, she'd had a do with them 'cos they rapped through about the

34

noise we made last Friday night. You should have heard her. Oh, she's a great lass.' He laughed again. 'Bye-bye then. See you later, Rosie. . . . Oh, I must get the stove.'

A few minutes later he came up with an oil stove, and when he had lit it for her she said, 'Thanks, Barny.'

'That's all right. Anything to oblige me beautiful sister.' He punched her playfully, then ran down the stairs whistling.

She was home. She sat down on the side of the single bed, the bed she had slept in in this room that had been hers from the time they had moved into the house when she was fifteen. They had come to it the same week that she had left school, and the grandeur of forty-nine Grosvenor Road had taken away some of the humiliating sting of not having got to the High School. She had failed her eleven-plus, and again the examination when she was twelve, and then at thirteen. Apart from her own disappointment about this, it was the blow to her mother that had affected her most. Only she and Barny had had the opportunity to try for the High School, but in Barny's case he didn't bother, for he was wise enough to know that he was destined for the pit the minute he left school. Dennis was the only one of the boys who had achieved scholastic distinction. Dennis was now a schoolteacher, but he had achieved this on his own and with the help of the Army. Her mother, Rosie had always maintained secretly to herself, had been hard on the lads, but she couldn't say she had been hard on her . . . never, for it had been the open desire of her life to see her only daughter get to the High School . . . and she hadn't. Yet this failure of her own to achieve success had not daunted her mother for long. She had not dragged her young family from a three-bedroomed bug-ridden hovel in Bog's End at the bottom of Fellburn, to a four-roomed cottage, then to a five-roomed house, from which she had jumped a great social gulf and landed them all triumphantly in Grosvenor Road, to be daunted by such a small thing as the failure of her daughter to pass an examination.

Rosie remembered the morning when Hannah had suddenly got into her hat and coat and said, 'Get your things on, I'm taking you to the Secretarial School. That's what you'll do; take a course and become a private secretary, and likely you'll end up running the firm; secretaries do.' She had smiled a conquering smile which effectively dissolved all protest. So they had gone to the Principal, and within a fortnight of leaving school Rosie found herself at school again, but with a difference. Instead now of wavering near the top of the class she was soon pushing towards the top; she knew she was . . . cut out for this. When at the end of the three-year course she came out top of her class both in typewriting and shorthand her mother had been borne skywards with pride. For days she floated, enveloped in a cloud of sagacity which had had its birth – so she told her family in her own words – the day it was revealed to her what her daughter was to be. And when the great moment of prizegiving came and Rosie was presented not only with certificates but with a medal, Hannah, sitting in the front row of the audience, made no outward or coarse show of her pleasure, but passed herself like a lady, born to see honours bestowed on her family. As she said cryptically later, 'When the thunder is rolling you don't get to your feet and shout, ''What's that noise?'' ' The world knew that her daughter, besides being beautiful and with a figure that had none its equal in Fellburn, or any other town for that matter, was also a brilliant scholar.

And so said the papers the following morning. *Fallburn Weekly* had shown a photograph of Rosie being handed her medal by no less a person than the mayor. Hannah had bought half a dozen copies of the paper, and immediately despatched one to her eldest son Patrick who was in Australia. One to her next son, Colin, who was in Canada, and one to Michael, who lived in Cornwall, which could have been as far away as Australia or Canada for all she saw of him or his family. And she had thrust one at her schoolteacher son, Dennis, when he had paid her one of his infrequent visits just to let him see he wasn't the only member of her family with brains. And she had told him to show the paper to his Godless lady wife.

As the not-so-distant past came back to Rosie she twisted round and dropped her head on the pillow. It was all so ordinary, her past, at least the past that held its place in Fellburn. Nothing had really happened to her here; she had just been part of a large family, of which her mother was ruler and pivot.

Even the business of Ronnie MacFarlane seemed of little account now, although at the time she had thought it the worst thing in the world that could happen to anyone. For a man to go mad and tear the clothes off your back when you were just sitting with him holding hands on the fells on a Sunday night was shocking . . . and him a Catholic. That had made it worse. It had seemed the most horrifying thing at the time, that a

Catholic could be so full of lust as to lose control. How simple she had been. How naïve. And she knew now that if she had cared anything for Ronnie MacFarlane he wouldn't have had to pull the clothes off her. But you live and learn. The awful part of it was that you had to live before you could learn. And she had made Ronnie the excuse to leave home and find out about living. And she had done just that. The thought brought her teeth clamping into the pillow, and when the tears forced themselves from between her closed lids she pulled herself up straight and rubbed her hand over her face, saying to herself, 'Don't start now. Later . . . later. Take things quietly; it'll all work out. Go and get a wash and put on the suit.' Oh, the suit. Would it fit her? It would have to.

She went down the two flights of stairs again and into the bathroom. It was cluttered with cups, toothbrushes, toothpaste, hair cream, after-shave lotion and towels. It was a man's bathroom. But it was warm and it was . . . it was home. She had the silly feeling that she wanted to embrace it and ask it to forgive her, ask the whole house to forgive her. After she had washed herself her face looked whiter than ever. She had no cream, no powder or make-up, not even a lipstick, nothing. She smoothed her skin with her hand, she looked awful, then she stared at herself in the mirror as she thought there would be plenty in Karen's room. But no, she couldn't use her things without asking her.

Karen. She hadn't thought much of Karen. If she was to stay home there would always be Karen. Karen and she had never hit it off. Barny had often referred to Karen as a little bitch, and that's what she was, a little bitch.

It was difficult to realise that she herself was Karen's aunt because there was only two years between them.

Ever since she was a child Rosie had heard of Moira – her sister Moira. Beautiful, vivacious, fascinating Moira, who had been her mother's first child, and who, at the age of twenty-four, had died giving birth to Karen.

Even when they were children together Rosie knew that Karen resented her and the affection displayed towards her by the men of the family. So the dislike between them grew, and there was no-one Rosie knew happier than Karen when she had left home for a position – a grand position, in her mother's words – in London.

In the attic again she unlocked the case, and lifting out the wrapped bricks she went to the far corner of the room, and sliding back a piece of loose floorboard that gave access to a junction box she pushed the bricks far back between the beams. They had served their purpose; they had taken the emptiness from the case.

Now she tried on the suit. The skirt proved to be a little large but the rest fitted her as if it had been made for her.

Before going downstairs she locked the case, but stood hesitating with the key in her hand, then dropped it into a china trinket bowl. Her mother was not likely to go rummaging around until tomorrow, by which time she would have given her a reason why the case was empty.

On her way downstairs she went into the bathroom again and brushed her hair with one of the men's brushes, taking it upwards and back from her brow; then bit on her lips and pinched her cheeks. And when she entered the living-room her father and mother turned and gazed at her in open-mouthed admiration.

'Aw, that's more like my Rosie.' Hannah came towards her, pride wreathing her face. 'That's new, isn't it?' She touched the short coat. 'By, it's a smart set; I bet it knocked you back something.' She poked her head towards Broderick. 'Look at it, Brod.'

'Aye, it's real bonny. But it's the bonny lass that's in it that makes it out, isn't it? . . . I tell you what.' He sounded excited. 'We're not goin' to waste you on these four walls the night. You'll come along to the club with us. Just let me get meself changed and we'll all go and make a night of it.'

'Aye, that's the ticket,' cried Hannah. 'The very thing.'

As they looked at Rosie for approval the smile left their faces and Hannah said, 'You don't want to go, lass?'

'Not tonight, Ma; that's if you don't mind. I think I'll get to bed early. I . . . I still feel a bit shaky from the flu, and the journey was tiring.'

'Aye. Yes, of course.' Hannah nodded understandingly. Then almost dreamily she pushed her hand backwards towards her husband, saying, 'You away to the club on your own; I'm going to have a natter with me girl.'

'No, no, Ma, you go on. You always go on a Friday night.'

'Well, I'm not going the night and that's flat. Now that's settled. . . . Yet' – she held out her arms in a wide dramatic gesture – 'it's a shame to waste you, it is that, and you so bonny. Doesn't she get bonnier, Brod? Doesn't your daughter get bonnier with every year that's on her?'

'Aye indeed; but I'll like her better when she gets a bit more fat on her. I likes 'em plump.' He slapped at Hannah's buttocks.

As they laughed loudly Rosie smiled, and the front door bell rang and Hannah cried, 'That'll be Karen.' She nodded towards Rosie. 'She's doing a late turn at the exchange. I'll go and open it. She's been coming the front way 'cos it's shorter.

Rosie heard her mother's voice from the hallway extra loud and hearty, saying, 'I've a surprise for you. You'll never guess. Who do you think's come?' The next minute Karen was standing in the doorway.

'Hello, Karen.'

There was a pause.

'Hello. What's brought you?'

'What's brought her?' Hannah's voice was high. 'Doesn't matter what's brought her; here's one that's mighty glad to see her.' Her voice dropped now to a soothing tone. 'She's had the flu, she's come to convalesce.'

Karen made no rejoinder to this, sympathetic or otherwise. She moved forward but not near to Rosie. She never stood near to Rosie, to do so emphasised the difference between their heights and their figures, for Karen was five foot four and tubby. If she'd had a beautiful mother there was no sign of it on her. She looked over her shoulder towards her grandmother and said, 'I don't want any tea, I'm going to a dance.'

'You can't dance on an empty stomach,' said Hannah, still in a conciliatory tone.

'She doesn't dance on her stomach she dances on her feet, eh, don't you?' Broderick thrust out his hand playfully towards his grand-daughter's cheek, but she ignored him and, turning slowly about, went out of the room.

Broderick, taking his pipe now from the mantelpiece and grinding his little finger around the empty bowl, said, 'Begod! I don't know who that one takes after; it's none of us, yet she was me own child's.'

'Oh it's green she is. Always has been, you know yourself, of Rosie here. An' the lads make more fuss of her when she's on her own. Yet she won't trouble you.' Hannah looked towards Rosie. 'She's never in the house five minutes, in and out like a gale of wind. She's going steady, I understand, though he's not much to crack on by all accounts. He's on a job on the new estate but has never reached more than fourteen a week yet. One of them that doesn't like overtime. Still, it's her choice.'

Rosie had always been puzzled at her mother's attitude towards her grand-daughter. She had never bothered about finding her a job, nor had ever timed her comings and goings as she had those of herself. With regard to intelligence, or having it up-top, as her mother would say, Rosie knew that Karen had much more 'up-top' than she had. With very little trouble she had got on to the switchboard at the telephone exchange. The criterion for such a job might not be brains, but Rosie doubted whether she herself would have been able to achieve this without her mother behind her; she wouldn't have had the nerve to canvass a councillor and to go round asking for references as Karen had done. Karen had the quality she herself lacked – initiative.

When Broderick went upstairs to change and they were alone, Hannah beckoned Rosie with a curl of her finger as she whispered, 'Look, I want to show you something. Come into the front room, come on.'

Rosie followed her mother into the hall and across it, and when the lights were switched on in the front room she gazed at the new suite almost in awe before she murmured, 'My! What made you get this, Ma?'

'Well, I saw one like it in a shop in Northumberland Street in Newcastle after the war and I said to meself, "Hannah, you'll have one like that some day," an' there it is. I told 'em, the lads and him, it was just over a hundred pounds, but guess what?'

'I don't know.' Rosie was shaking her head.

'A hundred and forty-five.'

'No!'

'God's me judge.'

'Oh, Ma, a hundred and forty-five!'

'It's what you call a Parker-Knoll. Look.' She whipped off the cords that held the drop sides of the settee to the back. 'Look, they go flat. Isn't it magnificent?'

'Beautiful, beautiful.' Rosie's eyes narrowed as she looked into Hannah's beaming face, and for the first time since coming home a touch of humour came into her speech. She said seriously, 'What do the lads wear when they come in here, Ma?'

Hannah, smothering a gust of laughter, dug her in the ribs with her elbow. 'That'll be the day when I let them sit on that, or the chairs. They've been in once, but I had it covered over, every inch of it.' She ran her hand along the pale green tapestry and said almost reverently, 'There's never a day goes past that I don't come in and just stand and look at it. . . . Oh begod!' She flapped

43

her hand at Rosie. 'You should have been here the day it was delivered. Oo . . . h! The curtains. Every curtain in the street had the tremors. There they were, with their faces behind them, their eyes sticking out like pipe shanks. As for Jessie' – she thumbed in the direction of the wall – 'the green's still sticking on her yet. Oh, she's a bloody jealous old sod, that one.'

Somewhere deep within Rosie there trembled a quirk of genuine laughter – no swearing in the house she had said. Oh, her ma, her ma.

'It's always been the same since the days we were in place together. Determined to rise she was, and I said to meself, "All right, Jessie, for every step you take I'll take a jump," and begod, I have.' She nodded solemnly at Rosie. 'With the Almighty's help I have done just that. An' I'll go on doing it until the day I die. . . . But whist a minute.' She lifted her finger to Rosie's face as if admonishing her for interrupting. 'Wait till she hears me latest. I've got something up me sleeve.' She stretched the cuff of her woollen cardigan without taking her eyes from Rosie. 'An' she won't be the only one that'll be knocked off their feet with surprise this time. Aw, me lass. . . .' With mercurial swiftness her attitude changed yet again, and her big arms dropping to her sides, she stood before her daughter as if in supplication as she went on, softly now, her words hardly above a whisper, 'There's a saying, and true, that frock coats are not to be found on middens. That was true years ago but more so the day, for who gives a damn for you if you've got the wisdom of Christ and his parables but are living in Bog's End; who would listen to you from there, I ask you? No, you know yourself I've always said a man is judged by the cut of his coat an' a woman by the front of her house.'

As Hannah paused as if to allow her oratory effect, Rosie, shaking her head slightly, said, 'You're not going to move again, Ma, I thought you loved this place?'

'I am, we are, and I did.' She smiled widely now. 'But I'm going to move, girl. At least we are. And I did love this house, but everything has its allotted time and its place. . . . What have I been aiming for all me life since the first day I married? What's the place that's ever been in me mind? Think back, think back, Rosie.' She dug her finger into Rosie's arm. 'What did I tell you stories about as a child? Didn't I tell you about the fine rooms and the splendid furniture, and the luscious food that I meself cooked many a time?'

'But, Ma' – Rosie's eyes were stretching – 'you don't mean . . . ?'

'I do, I do. Number eight itself. Number eight Brampton Hill.' There was unmistakable reverence in her voice now.

'But the money! It'd be huge. You could never . . .'

'Hold your hand. Hold your hand.' Hannah held her own hand up warningly. 'They couldn't sell it outright, they wanted too much for it. Then speculators took a hand, and God so planned it that who should be one of them but Councillor Bishop.'

'You mean Mr Bishop from the church?'

'Aye, Mr Bishop from the church. That was another thing I learned many years ago. The more friends you have at court the deeper will be your carpet to walk on. Well, what are they doing but turning it into flats? When I first heard this it nearly broke me up. It was for all the

45

world as if a picture in me head had been smashed into smithereens. How, I said to meself, could I think of the old place and all its grandeur if it was in flats? And then the idea came to me, and I went along and I had a talk with Mr Bishop. . . . I was very good to his wife during the war, you know, when things weren't easy to come by, and he hadn't forgotten. ''Cast thy bread upon the waters.'' There was never a truer sayin'. Well, as I was sayin', I went to him and got the inside information. Four flats they're turning it into, all with a separate entrance. And the two bottom ones have good bits of garden. It was the conservatory side I was interested in. There's seven rooms goes with that side. He showed me the plans. There they were set out afore me eyes. The drawing-room that was, together with the dining and breakfast-room, they're making into seven fine rooms, and the long conservatory thrown in. Oh, it's a fine sight, the conservatory. And a strip of garden, he says, a hundred feet wide and twice as long. Now what do you think?' She spread out both her hands, palm upwards, as if upon them lay the entire flat and she was offering it for her daughter's inspection and admiration.

But Rosie's face was serious. Not only serious; there was pity in it too. Pity for the restless ambition that was her mother's life force. 'But the money, they'll want the earth for it, and up on Brampton Hill! And then – Oh, Ma. . . .' She put out her hand and touched Hannah's. 'The lads, they'll never, well, you know them, they'll never fit in up there.'

The smile seeped from Hannah's face, and in its place came the defensive steely mask that Rosie knew well. Before the opposition to every move she had planned to

46

a different house her mother had donned this mask, because before every move, someone, perhaps Dennis, or Michael, or even a neighbour, had dared to suggest, 'The lads won't fit in.'

'My sons will fit at Brampton Hill, Rosie, as they've fitted in to Grosvenor Road. There's no better dressed nor finer set up men in this town.'

They were staring at each other now, a veil of hostility between them. Rosie knew she had said the wrong thing, also that her mother spoke the truth, at least about one thing, for it would be hard to find better dressed men in Fellburn. But that fact would hardly count on Brampton Hill, for the lads had only to open their mouths and their measure was patent. They were working men; they would never be anything else but working men; and this woman, her mother, who would have died defending the fact that she loved her family, every single one of them, had made them working men and kept them working men.

It dated back more than two years ago since Rosie had discovered that her mother's thinking was slightly crooked. Her mother wanted prestige, and she went for it in the only way open to her, a bigger and better house. Truly she believed that a woman was known by her front door. That her ambition could have been achieved by the educational betterment of her sons she refused to acknowledge, and she had a reason for this particular way of thinking.

Rosie knew it was this fanatic and fantastic ambition of her mother's that had added just that weight to her decision to leave home in the first place. The term 'Keeping up with the Joneses' could hardly be applied in her mother's case, for Hannah did not desire to keep up with her neighbours but to march ahead of them, miles ahead of them. In fact, to walk in step with the Peddingtons who had lived in number eight Brampton Hill.

As her mother had said, she had been brought up on the stories of number eight Brampton Hill. They had been her fairy tales, and they had all begun with the day her mother had first set eyes on the house. It was in nineteen-fourteen, when Hannah was eleven, that she had come with her mother straight from Ireland. They had only the clothes they stood up in, but her mother had got a . . . position. She was to be kitchen-maid in the Peddingtons' establishment and to receive the vast sum of four shillings a week, living-in, of course. Her daughter, Hannah, was boarded with a distant relative in Bog's End. Her mother paid two shillings a week for her, until, in nineteen-fifteen, when labour was scarce, Hannah was taken into training . . . in the beautiful mansion. It was on her twelfth birthday, the fifth of May.

Hannah did well at the Peddingtons', until she fell for a soldier and on one half-day off became pregnant by him. She was not yet sixteen at the time. The man was a distant relation of the people she had stayed with. His name was Broderick Massey; he was a Catholic and therefore an honourable man. He married Hannah, and to the present day he considered it the best day's work he had done.

The Peddingtons, being broad-minded and aware that they had a good loyal servant in Hannah, took her on daily after her first child was born, and she stayed in their service, on and off between giving birth to babies, until nineteen-twenty-three when her fifth child was born dead. This Hannah took as a personal insult, and her spirits were very low until she became pregnant again. When her next child, too, was still-born, Hannah, who had decided years earlier that her main job in life was to bear children, realised that if she was to carry out this purpose she must go steady. So reluctantly she was available no more to the Peddingtons. Yet at times she visited . . . me lady, and her old friend Jessie Mulholland, the housemaid – who was now Jessie MacFarlane – and on each visit she sorrowed at the diminishing fortunes of the house. The scanty staff and the over-run garden touched her nearly as deeply as it did the owners.

So this was Hannah's life story, and Rosie had been brought up on it, and although it had been presented to her almost in the form of an Arabian Nights' story she had for many years assessed the tale at its true worth. Had her mother told her, two years ago, of her determination to live on any part of Brampton Hill, she would have greeted the proposal with, 'Oh Ma, you're mad; you'll be a laughing stock.' Yes, she would have dared say this, although it would have brought the house down about her ears. But now she was older, oh, more than two years older, twenty years older inside, and she had more understanding of everything and everyone. More pity for the mad things life led one to do. So she said softly, 'You would love to live there, wouldn't you, Ma?'

Hannah's face crumpled; it looked for a moment as if she was going to cry. 'Love it?' She shook her head. 'Lass, I would die of happiness.'

'It'll be very difficult all round.'

'Leave that to me.' Hannah was patting Rosie's cheek now. 'Leave everything to me.'

'What are they asking for it?'

'Hold your breath. Four thousand five hundred.'

'Oh, Ma!'

'Look . . . look at it this way. We paid seventeen for this house. 'We'll get three thousand for it like a hundred shot.'

'But houses are not selling, Ma. There's so much unemployment now; you know yourself the lads are lucky to be all in work.'

'I tell you, just leave it to me. There's a buyer for everything. But you're right. Houses are not sellin' the day; that is the two thousand pound ones are not sellin', for most of them go in for that price are finding it tight. . . . And don't tell me about the unemployed. I've had me share and I'm not goin' to cry over those whose turn it is now. Nobody cried over me when I was stretchin' a penny into a shilling. We'll sell this house, never fear, and what we get from it will be put down for the other. Then there's another thing, I'm not on me beam end either, I've got a bit put by.' She poked her finger into Rosie's arm. 'I'll show you the morrow; you and me'll have a crack. You leave all this to me. I don't suppose . . .' She paused and dropped her head slightly towards her shoulder and screwed up her eyes to pin-points before going on. 'I don't suppose you'd think of stayin' home, lass, would you, and gettin' a job here? Oh, me cup would overflow to have you home.'

Rosie was looking straight down towards her feet while moving her lips hard one over the other.

'Oh, all right, all right. It was only a suggestion like.

Mad I am at times with me plans. It's all right, lass. Now don't fret yourself, it's all right.'

Rosie lifted her head slowly. 'I've . . . I've been thinking about it, Ma, but – but there's Ronnie. I couldn't bear that to start up again.'

'Oh, but it wouldn't lass, it wouldn't.' Hannah's whole body expressed her excitement. 'I'm positive of that. He's married an' his wife's going to have a bairn. He hardly ever comes into Jessie's – well at least just pops in at the weekend to see her. . . . Aw, lass, would you? Would you?'

'Then there's Karen. She hates me being at home.' Rosie was looking into her mother's face now.

'Karen will have to take what she gets if she wants to stay here.' The aggressiveness slid from her voice and she murmured, 'As I said, she's goin' strong, and I'll do nothing to stop it, I'll help it on. Aw, lass, you mean it? You could get a job in Newcastle and be home at nights and I'll see your face every day.' She was upping Rosie's white face between her two brown-blotched, vein-traced hands, and as she stared at her daughter the expression on her own face was changing yet again. Her lips parted and her brows moved into enquiring points and she became still. Her expression rigidly fixed now, she gaped at Rosie, until, her eyes springing wide, there came over her face a look that could have been taken for terror, that is if the emotion of fear could have been associated with Hannah Massey. 'It's just struck me,' she said in an awesome whisper. 'You wouldn't . . . wouldn't be in any sort of trouble? Name of God! You comin' home on the hop like this, it's just come to me . . .'

'No, Ma, no. . . .'

51

'You're not goin' to have a bairn or anything?'

'I'm not going to have a bairn, Ma.' Rosie's words were cold but without any touch of indignation in them, and Hannah, breathing deeply, bowed her head for a moment before saying, 'I'm sorry, lass, I should've known not to say such a thing to you. You'd be the last creature on God's earth. . . .' She put out her hand. 'Oh, don't turn away from me, lass, I didn't mean it. But there's so many of them at it these days, the town's peppered with them. And some of them still at school. Aye, it's unbelievable but they're at it afore they leave school. Two cases in the papers last week. I said why don't they do the thing properly and have rooms set up for them in their playtime.'

'Oh, Ma!' Rosie sounded shocked; and Hannah put out her hand and pulled her around to face her, and with head lowered she said, 'I'm a rough, coarse-mouthed old woman and I beg your pardon for besmirkin' you with me thoughts.'

The humility was too much. It brought Rosie's hands to her face to press her tears back, and her voice sounded like a whimper as it came from between her fingers, saying, 'Don't, Ma. Oh, don't, Ma.'

'Aw, don't cry, lass.' She was enfolding Rosie now, pressing her between her wide breasts, stroking her hair. 'I can humble meself to you. I couldn't do it to any one of them, but I can to you, the last of God's gifts to me.'

Rosie felt her flesh shrinking away from her mother's. How would she be able to bear it? The circumstances of the last few days had made her obsessed with a longing for home and now she was here there was the

52

old fear rising in her, and the fear was of her mother. This woman who loved her; this strong irrational, masterful and childish woman.

Hannah said, 'Aw, but you're shivering, and me keepin' you in this cruel cold room jabbering.'

'Have you got a hankie, Ma?'

Hannah groped in her jumper, saying, 'No, I haven't one on me but go up to me drawer, you'll find plenty there. . . . But wait.' She put her hand out tentatively now. 'I'm not keepin' on, don't think that, me dear, but it's just come to me you hadn't your big bag with you, you hadn't any handbag. . . . Look, Rosie, there's something not quite right.' She bent her head forward. 'Tell me.'

Rosie took one long deep gulp of air. 'Can we leave it till the morning, Ma?'

'Then there is something?'

'Well . . . yes. But I'll tell you in the morning. All right?'

For a brief second Hannah's face wore a dead expression, then she smiled and said, 'All right, it'll keep; we'll have a long crack in the mornin' when we have the house to ourselves. Go up now and get what you want out of me drawers'.

Rosie went slowly up to her mother's room. Once inside, she stood with her back to the door and looked about her, but without seeing anything.

The room held an ancient brass bed with a deep box spring on it that cried out in protest at the modern biscuit-coloured bedroom suite. But the bed was one thing Hannah would never change. The reason for her clinging to the brass bed was usually gone fully into after a visit to the club, then Hannah, a few double whiskies down her, would inform her family yet again, and almost word for word, the reason why she meant to die in the brass bed. Rosie's skin had never failed to flush on these occasions, but the men grinned or laughed or, when bottled up themselves, went one better than their mother. Anyway it was all like 'God bless you' to them, for hadn't they been brought up to the sound of slaps and laughter, and groans and grunts coming from their parents' room? And hadn't some of them slept on a shake-down for years at the foot of their parents' bed? What was there to hide? Silently they agreed with their mother; if God hadn't wanted it done he wouldn't have provided the implements.

The stark vatality of her mother, almost like male virility, pervaded the atmosphere of the room, and Rosie found her flesh shrinking again, as it had at one time been wont to do from things . . . not nice. As she crossed the room to the dressing-table she glanced at the little altar perched on a wall bracket in a corner to the right of the bed. There were two half-burnt candles on it. When the thought came to her that her mother was putting in overtime on the Brampton Hill project, she chided herself for her caustic comment. Her mother meant well; she always meant well.

Out on the landing, Karen was knocking on the bathroom door, calling, 'Granda, hurry up, will you! I want to get in.' Karen glanced at her as she passed. It was a calculating glance, raking her from head to foot, but she didn't speak.

Downstairs, as Rosie entered the living-room from the hall there came into the room from the far door leading out of the kitchen a man carrying a plate in his hand. When he looked at her with his mouth half-open before exclaiming in amazement, 'Why, Rosie!' she knew that her mother hadn't loudly acclaimed her presence to Hughie, Hughie being of no account.

The man put the plate, which held a portion of fish pie and peas which didn't look hot, on to the table without taking his eyes from her, and again he said, 'Why, Rosie.' Then, 'When did you come?'

'Oh, just an hour or so ago, Hughie.'

Still looking at her, he went to the corner near the fireplace and picking up a chair he brought it to the table and sat down; then lowering his glance towards his plate he said, 'Nobody told me you were coming.'

'They didn't know, Hughie; I made up my mind all of a sudden. They all got a gliff when I walked in.'

'Oh, I bet they did.' He was smiling up into her face.

She went to sit down and face him across the corner of the table, but hesitated, while he, looking at his plate again, took a mouthful of the fish pie before saying, 'Your ma's just gone along to the MacFarlanes. I saw her as I was coming in.' Still eating, he added, 'How are you keeping?'

'Oh, all right, Hughie.' But as she answered him her mind was on her mother running to tell Jessie MacFarlane she was home. That was cruel really.

Hughie lifted his eyes to her where she sat opposite to him now. They were dark brown and round and quiet looking, and seemed at variance with his long, thin, mobile face. He looked at her for a moment before beginning to eat again, but he made no remark whatever on her appearance.

She said to him now, 'And how are you getting on, Hughie?'

'Oh . . .' He smiled, a self-derisive smile. 'Oh, you know me.'

She looked at him softly, kindly. Yes, she knew him. She had for years thought this man was her brother, for there never had been a time when she hadn't seen Hughie in the house. She was seven when her mother said to her, 'He's no brother of yours, he's a waif.' And her father had put in quickly, 'No. Now, Hannah, he's no waif. If the lad gets on your nerves so much let him clear out. He's big enough to stand on his own feet. . . . Nineteen . . . he's a man.' Nor had there been a time when she didn't realise that her mother disliked Hughie, even hated him. Nevertheless, she also knew that twice, when he was just turned fifteen and had tried to run away, she'd had him brought back. Once he had stowed away on a ship. She had never been able to understand her mother's attitude towards Hughie. That day her father had told her Hughie's story.

Hughie was twelve in nineteen-forty when his mother was killed in an air raid; his father had died a year earlier. His mother and Broderick Massey had been half-cousins. Broderick had said, 'We must have the lad.' And Hannah had said, 'Of course. What's one more or less. And the child with no-one in the world.' This wasn't strictly true because Hughie had an elder sister whom he could only remember faintly. She had gone to America as a private nurse before the war. So Hughie had been taken into the Massey household, and his shy nature had blossomed in the warm, rough atmosphere, until he was fourteen . . . well just coming up fifteen, when Broderick remembered that Hannah had turned on the boy. Why, he couldn't get out of her. But from that time he could do no right. Yet when he had run away she had gone to great lengths to get him back. Aw, Broderick had said to Rosie, there was no understanding her mother's heart. It was so big a man would need a couple of lifetimes to get into its workings.

Rosie had always liked Hughie, perhaps because he was so diffefrent from the other men in the family. Yet she liked her brothers too. But Hughie was different, thoughtful. She felt he was clever in a way. Perhaps this was the reason her mother didn't like him. But no, the reason went farther back, before Hughie could have proved his cleverness in one way or another. The lads took Hughie for granted; he was part of the fittings of their home. They chaffed him about the women he had never had, and Miss Springer who lived down the road and who had had her eye on him since they first came to live here. One year he had received a Valentine, and they all declared it was from Miss Springer. But he had never passed more than the time of day with the trim but not unattractive woman who worked in the drapery department of Bailey's store. To Rosie, Hughie was . . . comfortable. He had no male virility oozing out of him, sparking off disturbances. He was a sort of cushion one could lean against, if one dared; but her mother had always checked any friendly contact between Hughie and herself. If she had come across them talking, the subject being nothing more than the weather, she would divert them into separate ways, and to Rosie herself she would speak sharply but with no real reprimand behind it but her voice, when she spoke to Hughie, thrust him back into his place, and his place was a wooden chair in a recess near the door, away from the warmth of the fire. This, when Rosie thought about it, seemed significant of her mother's whole attitude towards Hughie, pushing him away, always pushing him away yet never letting him go beyond the wall, so to speak.

'It's nice to see you back, Rosie,' he was saying.

'Thanks, Hughie. It's nice to be back . . . for a time.' She dared say that to him.

He did not, as the others had done, exclaim about her white, peaked look; but after swallowing the last mouthful from his plate he straightened his shoulders against the back of the chair and repeated her words thoughfully: 'Yes, for a time.' Then glancing round the room and towards the two doors, the one leading into the kitchen, the other into the hall, he brought his head forward towards her and said under his breath, 'I might be making a move soon meself, Rosie.'

'Really Hughie?'

He nodded slowly. 'I haven't told any of them; that is except Dennis. He knows. But it's likely I'll be on me way soon.' He nodded again.

'But where to, Hughie?' She was leaning toward him now, interested, even slightly excited for him.

Again he looked from door to door, then said, 'Another time. I'll tell you all about it another time, only keep it to yourself, will you?'

She nodded back rather sadly now. Perhaps it was only wishful thinking on his part. From time to time over the years she could remember him saying, 'One day I'll make a break, I'll be away, you'll see, you'll see.' When she came to think of it now they were like the words of

58

a prisoner threatening to make a run for it. There were lots of things about Hughie she couldn't understand. Jimmy, who was nearest to Hughie in age, being only three years younger, always said Hughie was the type of fellow you couldn't get to the bottom of, close, tight-mouthed about things. And working in a cobbler's shop by himself for years hadn't tended to open him out.

She had at one time asked her mother, 'Did Hughie want to be a cobbler, Ma?' And Hannah had replied, 'He's damn lucky to have a job at all; he's fallen on his feet. If he's got any gumption in him he'll make a business of it.'

This was at the time when her father, who had tried to scrape a living for years as a cobbler, was turning his back on it to go into a factory. But the cobbling business was still to be kept going, and by Hughie, whom Broderick had trained from a boy.

The cobbler's shop was an eight by ten foot room with a small cubby hole leading off the back. It was placed at the end of twenty similar workshops, all peopled by men striving to make a go of it on their own. When Hughie had worked with Broderick, part of his job had been to collect the boots and shoes for mending, and later to return them. Another part of his job was to solicit orders; but Hughie was no salesman, so when Broderick got the chance of a nine pounds a week job in the factory he jumped at it. And so Hughie was left . . . with the business. Rosie remembered saying to him at the time, 'Wouldn't you like to go into the factory, Hughie, and earn big money?' and he had smiled at her and said, 'I would sooner be on me own, Rosie.'

From the day Hughie had taken over the little shop her mother had forbidden her to go near it.

With the sound of the back door opening Rosie got to her feet and moved from the table, and she was sitting near the fire when her mother entered the room.

Hannah came in blowing her lips out, saying, 'Whew! It's enough to cut the nose off you out there. I've just been along to Jessie's.' She smiled towards Rosie but said no word to Hughie, and he, rising from his chair, gathered up the dirty dishes from the table and went towards the kitchen. But as he passed from the room he turned his head over his shoulder and, looking towards Hannah, said, 'Can I speak to you a moment?'

'Speak to me?' She didn't even bother to look at him. 'Well, I'm here, amn't I? Spit it out. There's nobody in the house but Broderick and Karen upstairs, and Rosie here, and she's me daughter.' She smiled at Rosie as if she had said something extremely witty, and on this Hughie turned about and went into the kitchen.

Hannah bending towards Rosie whispered low, 'There's a sod if ever there was one; deep as a drawn well, he is. Do you know what I learnt the day?' She pressed her lips together, pulling her mouth into a tight line. 'Him and our Dennis are as thick as thieves. He's been over to their place.' She nodded quickly. 'And it's not the first time he's been there. Oh, I could spit in his eye. And our Dennis. Wait till I see him. Five weeks it is since he darkened this door.'

'It's the weather likely, the roads are –'

'Don't you start makin' excuses for him. If you took a tape measure from door to door it would be three miles. But I know who I've got to blame for it. Oh, begod!

60

Yes. Oh, we're not up to the standard of his lady wife. But wait, just you wait; I'll show them or die in the attempt.'

'I think you should know something.' Hughie was speaking from the doorway. He never addressed Hannah by her name or with the prefix of aunt, which would have been natural. He had for the first three years of his sojourn in the house, and at her own request, called her Mam, but this endearing term had come to an abrupt end.

'Well, what should I know?' She was standing facing him, aggressiveness emanating from her.

Hughie, looking straight back at her, said quietly, 'Teefields are putting on a search for stolen parts.'

The shiver that passed over her body seemed to sweep the aggressiveness from it and leave her without support for a moment. Her mouth closed from its gape, then opened again, and in a much mollified tone she asked, 'Where did you hear that?'

'Dave Hewitt went out of his way to call in at the shop.'

'Hewitt? Then the polis is on to it. Name of God!' She jerked her head round and looked at Rosie, who was standing now; then turning back to Hughie, she asked, aggressiveness back in every inch of her, 'You're not just putting the wind up me, are you?'

'Why should I take the trouble to do that?'

It was not an answer Hannah expected from him. The quality of his voice, which touched on indifference, brought her eyes narrowing, and she said, 'Why should Hewitt go out of his way to help me?'

'I don't think that was his intention; but he was a

61

friend of mine, and still is in a way, and he knew that I wouldn't want Barny to be caught red-handed.'

Rosie was staring at Hughie; she had never heard him speak so boldly to her mother before. It was as if he didn't care a damn for her mother's reactions any more, as if he was freed from something. That his attitude was also puzzling her mother was very evident. She hoped it wouldn't arouse her anger against him still further.

But Hannah had something more serious on her mind at the moment than to dwell on Hughie's attitude. She said rapidly, her words running together, 'How've they got on to Barny? He's not the only one; every man jack of them's at it.'

'They're on to a number. As far as I understand they're going to make a house search.'

'They could come here, you think?'

Hughie didn't answer, he just stared at her. And she put her hand over her mouth as she exclaimed, 'God in Heaven!' Then she asked, 'When?'

'I don't know for sure. It could be tonight or tomorrow morning, I don't know.'

'Jesus, Mary and Joseph!' Again her body shivered; but now with strength and purpose, and flashing her eyes to Rosie, she said, 'Go and get your da down.' It was as if her daughter had never left the cover of her domination. Then turning to Hughie she ordered, 'Get down to the club and get Barny back here as fast as his legs'll carry him.'

As Rosie went from the room she saw Hughie still standing in the doorway. He hadn't moved, and her mother was staring at him. Then Hannah's voice came to her, still loud but in the form of a request, saying, 'Well, will you go for me?'

Rosie heard the back door bang before she reached the bathroom, and there she called, 'Come quickly, Da, me ma wants you.'

'She can just wait.'

'No, Da, there's trouble; come quickly.'

As she ran downstairs again Broderick was on her heels, drying himself and exclaiming loudly. And when he entered the kitchen he demanded to know what was afoot, but Hannah silenced him with 'Less talk and more action, that's what we want in the next hour or so. The polis is on to Barny and the wireless bits.'

'Good God! . . . Who told you this?'

'Hughie; he got it from Dave Hewitt.'

Broderick looked frantically around the kitchen, as if searching for hiding places; then turning to Hannah, he cried, 'But there's no place where we can stick that stuff, woman. We can't bury it in the garden, the ground's like flint underneath the slush.'

'I wasn't thinking of the garden. Only a numbskull would think of the garden. We'll have it upstairs in the box mattress.'

'The box mattress! Oh, aye, begod. Aye, yes.' Broderick nodded his head. 'That's the place for it. But will it stand it? Those bits are a sight heavier than tea and sugar and clothes and the like.'

'We'll have to take that chance. But don't stand here wasting breath, let's get down to the shed and get as much loose stuff up as we can. An' we've got to do it with as little nuration as possible or else Nebby Watson'll have her nose hanging over the wall sniffing like a mangy retriever. And Alice Parkman is not above lifting the blind on the other side. So I'm telling you.'

The shed at the bottom of the garden was fitted up as a workshop. When her mother switched the light on Rosie stood gazing above her at the pieces of electrical equipment and half-finished wireless and television sets that took up every inch of the bench that ran the length of the shed, and overflowed on to the shelves beneath and those above it. Barny had started at Teefields factory before she had left home, and she hadn't been able to close her eyes to the fact that the stock in the shed had rapidly mounted, or that Barny made quite a bit on the side making wireless sets. But if it had troubled her, she had thought along the lines of her Catholic training – well, what Barny did was between him and God. It was a nice easy way to prevent herself from thinking of Barny as a hypocrite, one who wouldn't miss Mass on a Sunday, nor his duties once a month.

'Here now!' Her mother thrust a box of valves into her arms, hissing, 'Get up with them. Be careful how you go, and don't spill them. Leave them on the bedroom floor; we'll attend to the bed when we come up.'

They had made some inroad in the transportation when Barny came pelting into the house. He looked not only worried, he looked frightened, very frightened. 'This is a to-do, isn't it?' His voice was hoarse. 'I'm for it if they find this lot.'

Hannah had met him in the hall, her arms full. 'Less crack,' she said, 'and get going. Take that big set down there to pieces, and do it quicker than you've ever worked in your life afore. Go on now.'

As he went to run from the hall she shouted, 'Where's Hughie?'

'He's gone back to the shop.'

'He would, the sod, knowing how we're fixed for an extra pair of hands. Oh, I'll see me day with that one. Yes, by God, I will.'

She was mounting the stairs when Barny, dashing back into the hall, cried at her under his breath, 'Don't be so bloody vindictive, Ma; you're always at him. But the night you should go down on your knees and thank God for him givin' us the tip, for if he wasn't a pal of Dave Hewitt's we'd have known nowt until they were on top of us.'

'An' they likely could be that at any minute, and you standin' there defending him. Get going, you young fool!'

In an hour the shed was clear except for a few tools and some garden implements, but Hannah's bedroom looked, as she put it herself, like Paddy's market. The mattress from the bed was standing up against the wall with the top of the box spring leaning against it. The box resting on its iron support should have been full of springs, but these had been disposed of many years ago; in nineteen-forty to be exact when Hannah went into the black market. Now the bottom of the box was covered with wireless parts, on top of which were spread blankets, and into the hollows and dales of the blankets went further pieces, until the floor was clean of every last piece that had been brought up from the shed. Then the lid was screwed on again. The lid had attached to it an overlapping padded cover, and it would have taken a very clever detective to realise it was detachable from the box itself. On top of this the two men lifted the mattress, and then, Hannah, at one side, and Rosie, at the other, made the bed up.

'There, let them find that if they can. . . . Now away downstairs, the both of you.' She looked towards her husband and son. 'And get yourselves to the club, for if they should come on the hop, it's better they find you spending the evening normally.' She nodded at Broderick.

'Spendin' the evening normally!' Barny said. 'I've got the jitters. But if I'd had any bloody sense I'd have known somethin' was going to happen, for every man jack in our shop's been at it lately; all except creeping Jesus.'

'You mean Harry Boxley?'

Barny nodded at his father.

'It wouldn't be him who's given the show away?' said Broderick.

'No, no; Harry wouldn't do that. Come and give you a sermon on the quiet about the evil of covetin' thy neighbour's goods. . . . Neighbour's goods, be-buggered! An' that firm makin' millions a year profit. Keeping old Lord Cote sitting pretty in his marble-floored mansion on the Riviera. Even the bloody manager's got a yacht. . . . Thy neighbour's goods!'

They were in the living room again when Hannah said, 'Where's Karen in all this? She must have known we could do with help. . . . Where is she?'

'Aw, she went out a few minutes ago; I saw her on her way downstairs,' said Broderick.

'And never a word.' Hannah bristled. 'She'll have the back of me hand across her lug one of these days, will that madam. Well now, get yourselves off' – she waved

66

at the men – 'an' I'll deal with anybody should they come. But I pray to God –' her voice dropped now, 'aye, I do sincerely pray to God we'll have no-one comin' to search the house, because it'll be down the length of the street afore they are over the step. . . . Go on, get yourselves off.'

When the men had gone, Hannah turned to where Rosie was sitting staring into the fire, and going slowly towards her, she said apologetically, 'Aw, lass, I wouldn't have had your first night home spoiled for the world, but it was an emergency; it had to be done; you could see for yourself.'

'It's all right, Ma.' Rosie's voice was reassuring. 'It's all right, don't worry. I only hope Barny doesn't get the sack.'

'The sack! Why should he get the sack?' Hannah was bristling again. 'He'll get no sack. They'll find nothing here, not so much as a nut.'

Rosie, looking back at her mother, did not answer. She had worked for eighteen months in the London office of a Midland firm. From that distance men were just numbers. When an order came to cut down, numbers one, two and three were the same as four, five and six to an executive who had never seen the man behind the number. She remembered, too, that their firm – she still thought of it as their firm – stood to lose twenty thousand pounds a year through pilfering. They made allowance for that sum, yet every now and again they would clamp down on the general practice, as Teefields were doing, and there would be dismissals, sometimes followed by lightning strikes. . . . 'Thou shalt not covet thy neighbour's goods.'

Hannah, now pulling a big leather chair towards Rosie's, seated herself in it before leaning forward and saying, 'There now, we're settled. Let's forget all that's happened. Isn't this nice, just you and me and the house to ourselves?' She kicked off her slippers and held out the soles of her feet towards the blazing fire. 'You know, when I got up this mornin' I had the feeling it was going to be a good day. I always go by me feelin's first thing in the mornin' an' I said to meself, "Hannah, you're going' to get a surprise the day," and what better surprise in the world than seeing you, lass.' She stretched out her hand and squeezed Rosie's knee; then leaning back, she said in a casual tone, 'We mightn't get another opportunity like this to have a crack, the morrow mornin' Betty'll be in with the bairns; she always drops in on a Saturda' mornin' as you know. So when we've got the chance, let's have our chin-wag now, eh?' She hunched her thick shoulders up around her neck in a questioning attitude.

Rosie turned from her mother's waiting glance and looked towards the fire. A heat came surging up through her body and showed in moisture on her upper lip. She dabbed it with her mother's handkerchief and said, 'Aw, well.' Then went on, 'There's no much to tell, not really. Well, you see, I had words with a girl in the office. It . . . it was about promotion, but she had been there longer than me. And anyway things got unpleasant and I gave me notice in.'

'When? When was this? You never said a word in your letters.'

'Oh . . . oh about three months ago. I – I didn't ask for a reference; because I had had words I didn't like to go back, sort of climb down, you know. And it's difficult to get set on anywhere, at least in a good job, if you haven't a reference.'

'Was that why you haven't written for weeks? I was worried sick at times. An' gettin' your da to write is as hard as gettin' him up in the mornin's. . . . Was that why you moved to the new address?'

'Yes . . . yes, Ma.' Rosie was looking into the fire as she spoke. 'I couldn't keep up the rent of the flat and so I went into rooms . . . with a girl I knew. We . . . we shared everything; she was to pay the landlady. Then about three weeks ago she went off without a word and I found she owed a lot of back rent and the landlady said I was responsible for it. Well . . . well I had the flu as I told you and I ran·out of money altogether, all I had saved, and the landlady said she was entitled to keep my things until I could pay. And so' – Rosie turned towards her mother but didn't look at her – 'there . . . there was nothing for it but to come home.'

'Aw, lass.' Hannah was gripping her hands now. 'The heartless bitch of a woman, she should be spiflicated. All your beautiful clothes and your cases. Your fine dressing-case an' all, with all the bottles and things in, she's kept the lot?' Her voice seemed to be pushing up her arched eyebrows and raising her thick grey hair from her scalp.

'Yes. Yes, Ma.'

'Well, the morrow mornin' you'll send what you owe her and she'll send those things on or else me name's not Hannah Massey.'

'No, no, Ma; I don't think I'll do that. I'd rather buy new clothes and cases than write to her. I . . . I don't want anything more to do with her, or London. I just want to forget everything. I . . . I'll get a job and soon stock up again.'

'Well, I for one wouldn't let her get off with –'

'Oh, Ma, just leave it. . . . Please. I'm tired of it all, London and everything.'

'Aw, all right, all right, lass, have it your own way. As long as you're home that's all that matters to me. But I'll say I wish her luck with your things; I hope she falls down an' breaks her blasted neck, I do so. What will she do with them, do you think?' She peered at Rosie through narrowed lids.

'Oh . . . oh, I think. . . . Well, she's my build, perhaps she'll wear them. It . . . it doesn't matter.'

'No, no, it doesn't matter.' Hannah was shaking Rosie's hands firmly between her own, each movement being accompanied by a word. 'But listen to me. Don't let on about a thing you've told me to any of them. Do you hear me? An' tomorrow we'll work somethin' out. You said your stuff was coming on. Well, it'll have to come on. We'll go into Newcastle and get you rigged out, two or three rig-outs for that matter.' She winked. 'An' some cases, one exactly like the other I bought you. And when we get off the train we'll put them in a station taxi and say we've collected them on our way. How's that for strategy?'

Rosie smiled faintly. 'It's marvellous, Ma.'

'Oh, I'm a good liar.'

As Hannah shook her head proudly at herself, Rosie thought sadly, But not such a good one as your daughter.

Saturday

Rosie was sound asleep when her mother brought her breakfast up to her room. 'That's the ticket,' Hannah said. 'The rest will do you the world of good.'

'Oh, what time is it, Ma?' asked Rosie.

'Well, turned nine. You've slept the clock round, me girl.'

Rosie hadn't slept the clock round. It had been five in the morning when she had finally fallen into troubled sleep.

Hannah sat with her, demanding that she ate every scrap of food on the tray, and before she rose to take the tray away she nudged her, saying, conspiratorially, 'Don't forget we're goin' out this afternoon, hail, snow or blow.'

'I'll pay you back, Ma.'

'Who's talkin' of payin' back? Aw, lass, I get paid back with interest every time I look at you.' She lifted the rumpled mass of gleaming hair between her fingers and felt it. 'Like spun bronze, it is,' she said. 'I've never seen the like.'

The shiver went through Rosie's body again. Such admiration was fear-filling, terrifying.

'Look,' said Hannah now, excitedly. 'Get into your things an' come down to me room when we've got the house empty, for it won't be that for long, an' I'll show you somethin'.' She paused; then bending over the tray and bringing her face down to Rosie, she said, 'Your mother's no fool.'

As Rosie looked up silently into her face, Hannah winked broadly. Then walking sideways towards the door, the tray balanced on one hand, she said, 'Come on down with you now, and look slick. Get into anythin'.' She paused, then added, 'Put on your new suit; the other things are not you, not you at all, at all.'

Slowly Rosie got from the bed and put on the new suit. All her movements were slow and laboured. She felt very tired, not only from the lack of sleep but from the reaction of the whole of yesterday. She went down the stairs, and as she was going into the bathroom her mother opened the bedroom door and called, 'Let that wait a minute, come on in here.' And when she entered the room Hannah locked the door behind her, and pointing to the bed, said, 'Sit yourself down there.' Then she went to a short chest of three drawers that stood in a recess.

The chest did not match the modern suite. The edges of the drawers were all scarred, and the bottom and deepest drawer and the bulbous legs showed the imprint of hard toecaps. It was not a chest at all but an original Charles the Second walnut desk with flat top which Hannah had picked up forty years ago for two pounds ten. The sum then was a small fortune and she thought she had been done; she was unaware of its present-day value, but the chest held something even more valuable than itself. After pushing her hand down inside her jumper she brought out a small key and, unlocking the bottom drawer, she lifted it right out of its socket and carried it to the bed. Dropping it down next to Rosie she sat at the other side of it and pointed at its contents.

Rosie's wide lids hid her expression as she looked along the lines of neatly rolled bundles of notes. Line after line of them, some two deep, covering the bottom of the drawer. Then her lips falling apart, she lifted her eyes to her mother, and Hannah, whose every feature was expressing triumph, said softly, 'Can you believe your eyes?'

'But, Ma, where. . . . Whose is it?'

'Whose is it!' Hannah pulled her chin inwards, making a treble row of flesh down her neck. 'Whose is it, do you ask? Why, it's mine of course. An' don't look like that, lass; I haven't stolen it. Oh, begod!' She put her hand up to her cheek. 'Did you think . . . did you think I'd pinched the stuff? Now, where would I be findin' a place to pinch pound notes except in a bank? An' I wouldn't be up to that.' She laughed. 'An' I can assure you, not one of me children have soiled their hands at thievin' either.'

There flashed across Rosie's mind the picture of them emptying the shed last night and what lay beneath where they sat at this moment, but she let the picture slide away.

'How much do you think is there?' Hannah dug her index finger downwards.

'I haven't any idea.'

'Go on, give a guess.'

Rosie didn't answer, 'I really don't know – tell me,' because she knew her mother wouldn't know either, at least not exactly, for this woman could count up to ten and then add three to it because she'd had thirteen

73

children. At a stretch she could put ten and ten together and make it twenty, because there were twenty shillings in a pound note, but that was as far, Rosie knew, as her mother could go, because her mother could neither read nor write. But this lack was never referred to in the house. It was like a disfigurement that was ignored, but more out of fear than pity, for her mother would have slain anyone who made reference to her deficiency. Hannah could discuss the news of the day as if she had read the paper from end to end, when all she had done was listen to the wireless. The wireless was not only her tutor, it was her face-saver.

Rosie picked up a roll of notes and, taking off the wire band, she counted twenty pounds.

'Are they all the same?' she asked quietly.

'They are all the same,' answered Hannah just as quietly.

Rapidly Rosie began to count. She liftged one layer after another, and after some time she looked up at her mother and said in a whisper, 'Roughly about two thousand eight hundred, I should say.'

'Two thousand eight hundred!' Hannah repeated. 'Well now, what do you think of that?'

'But, Ma, how have you done it?'

'Management, lass, management. I'm no fool you know, as I said.'

Rosie looked in amazement at the big smiling woman sitting at the other side of the drawer as she went on, 'Well now, for the last five years they've hardly lost a day, except Shane in the winter on the buildings, and big money they've been makin'. Jimmy could take forty pounds a week at times in the bad weather, making the

74

bridge. Hell the work was, up to his eyes in water, but the money made up for it. And Arthur still makes a steady twenty-five when he's leading from the quarries. Shane's never made much, never more than eighteen, but Barny could make his twenty with overtime. Your da . . . well, it's been twenty sometimes, but mostly sixteen. Then there's Karen and the other one, but Karen's two pounds a week hardly keeps her in the fancy puddings she likes. As for the other –' she didn't say Hughie, 'four pounds is all I've ever got off him, never more.'

At the bitter note in her mother's voice, Rosie felt compelled to say, 'Well, I don't suppose he makes much more than that some weeks. There's nothing much in the cobbling, is there?'

'There's plenty in the cobbling if he would go out an' look for it – people still have their boots mended – but no, sittin' in the back shop readin', that's how he spends his time. His room upstairs is full of nothing else but books. . . . That's where his money goes, second-hand book shops. An' what good have they done him I ask you, for he's nothing but a scug? Aw' – she shook her head violently – 'don't let's talk about him. . . . Now, as I was sayin', about the money here.' She drew her fingers gently over the rolls. 'You wanted to know how I've managed it. Well, when they all got steadily going I said to them, we'll divide it into three, I said, each of your pay packets into three. One part will be for your own pocket, another part will be for your board and your workin' clothes, and boots et cetera, and with the other part I'll buy your best suits and things and put a bit by for a rainy day. An' all said OK, Ma, it was all right by them. All except Arthur. He wasn't so keen, for even then he had his eye on that piece. But I put me foot down. You'll be like the others or not at all, I said. An' there's Jimmy. There's hardly a week goes by even now when he hasn't ten pounds on a Friday night in his pocket, but never a penny he has by the Monday mornin'. If he had twenty it would be the same with him, the big softy. I said to him he should look out for a rainy day. And you know what he said?' She leant across the drawer towards Rosie. 'I'll leave you to cope with the weather, Ma. That's what he said.'

'Do they know about this?' Rosie pointed to the money.

'Begod! No. Not even Broderick knows the amount I've got; nor is he going to. That's me drawer, Broderick, I've said, an' it's the only personal thing I have in this house. I look to you to honour it. An' don't go searchin' for the key. An' I know he never has, an' it's been locked all this many a year. When it only held a few shillings it was locked.'

'But, Ma.' Rosie shook her head slowly. 'What if someone was to break in, if someone got to know?'

'Who's to know? How could anyone outside know when those inside don't? Oh, they chip me about me stockin' leg, an' they know I've got a few pounds put by because they know who to come to when they're up against it; an' they've only got to say they want a suit and it's on their back. But I don't forget to tell them how much I spend on them; I rub it in' – she bounced her head – 'so's they won't think I'm makin' a pile out of them.'

Rosie lowered her head. You had to laugh at her ma,

76

you had to laugh or go for her and say, 'Well, that's what you're doing, isn't it, Ma, making a pile out of them?' But no-one could say that to her ma; her ma was a law unto herself, her ma had her own type of reasoning.

'Begod, listen!' Hannah had jumped up from the bed, her hand held aloft. 'Here they are already, Betty and the bairns.'

As the shouts of 'Gran! Gran!' came from down below, Hannah whipped up the drawer and, shuffling with it to the chest, put it back into place again and locked it. Then pulling the front of her jumper wide, she inserted her hand in, saying the while to Rosie, 'I have a bag pinned on me vest.' She patted her breast. 'There's no-one going to go rummagin' in there.' She laughed as she pushed Rosie in front of her on to the landing.

The three children were grouped around the foot of the stairs looking upwards with eager faces, and Hannah cried at them, 'Hello! Catherine, me bairn. And you, Theresa. Aw, an' there's me big man.' She came down the last stairs with hands extended as if in benediction and laid them on the four-year-old curly-headed boy, saying, 'An' you've still got them?' She lifted one of the curls with her finger. 'I thought you said you were goin' to have them off?'

There came a chorus of, 'He was, Gran. He is, Gran.' And from the little boy himself. ''Safternoon, Gran; I am. 'Safternoon.'

'Aw, a shame on to God it is to cut those beautiful ringlets.' Then looking from one to the other of the children she said, 'Don't you see who's here? It's your Aunt Rosie. Say hello to your Aunt Rosie.'

The children looked to where Rosie was standing on

the stair above her mother and chorused, obediently, 'Hello, Auntie Rosie.'

They had heard a lot about their Auntie Rosie whom they very rarely saw, their clever, beautiful Auntie Rosie who was in London, living among the swells. They were shy of her. She silenced their tongues and they turned as one and, scuffling, went back into the kitchen and to their mother, who was emptying a basket on to the table.

'Hello, there, Betty.' Hannah greeted her daughter-in-law, and the plump, matronly girl turned her head over her shoulder saying, 'Hello, Ma.' Then catching sight of Rosie, she turned fully round, crying, 'Rosie, you're home? When did you come?' She was smiling, broadly, kindly.

'Last night, Betty.'

Before Rosie could go on Hannah put in loudly, 'It's the flu she's had; she's as white as lint. Did you ever see her lookin' like this? Oh, I'm goin' to try and persuade her to get a job nearer home so I can look after her and fatten her up. She hasn't a pick on her.'

The two girls smiled at each other.

Rosie liked John's wife; she always had. Betty was an uncomplicated girl. From the first she had fallen like a cat on its feet into the ways of the family; and this was demonstrated in the next moment when she pointed to a large parcel she had taken from her extra large shopping bag. 'You'll be able to use that,' she said.

'What is it?' Hannah quickly undid the brown paper, then some greaseproof paper, and exposed to her glistening eyes a quarter of an eighty pound Australian cheddar cheese, and she breathed deeply as she said, 'Yes, indeed, indeed.'

'We've got a big lump an' all, Gran.' It was six-year-old Theresa speaking, as she gazed up at Hannah.

'Have you, me child?'

'Yes. Me da found it in the grab.'

'He did, did he?' Hannah was bending over the child now, looking down into her face.

'Yes. When me da pulled up the dredger there was the cheese in a wooden box, and they opened it and they shared it out; me da had half and Mr Rowland had half.'

'He did, did he? Well, that was kind of your da to share it out,' said Hannah. The child nodded and smiled before adding, 'He found some butter in the dredger last week.'

Hannah raised her eyes to Betty, but Betty was busy repacking her bag. Her face wore a deadpan expression and she said without looking up, 'They've been warned not to tell anybody outside what their da finds in the dredger. They know they would get him wrong if they did. But as their da told them, if he didn't bring it home it would only be thrown into another part of the river again where they are blocking it up.'

'That's right, that's right.' Hannah nodded now from one child to the other. Then looking at Rosie, she asked, 'Isn't it, Rosie? Isn't that right?' And Rosie nodded, and after a moment said softly, 'Yes, yes, that's right.'

'Take them into the kitchen, Catherine,' said Hannah now, 'and have two bullets each out of the tin. No more, mind, just two apiece.' She thrust her finger at each of them, and they ran from her, laughing, into the kitchen. And now she turned to her daughter-in-law and pushed her with the flat of the hand. 'Cheese out of the dredger! That's a good-un. And they could come out of the river

79

bottom at that; who's to say they couldn't? With all the boats that's sunk outside the piers, the stuff's bound to float back.' She pushed her again, and Betty, chuckling deeply, said, 'Well, you have to tell them something; it's impossible to keep the stuff out of their sight.' She buttoned her coat now. 'I'll have to be goin'. And John'll not be in the day, he says, but he'll look in the morrow mornin' after Mass.'

'Won't you stay for a cup of tea and have a crack with Rosie here?'

'I can't, Ma. . . . You see' – she glanced towards the kitchen door, then muttered under her breath, 'I've got to be at Bill's stall in the market by half past ten; he's to let me know then about a bit of bacon, an' if it's all right John'll pick it up this afternoon in the car.'

'Aw, I see, lass, I understand, I understand.' Hannah flapped her hand. 'And how's the car goin'? The lads have got it into their heads that they're goin' to club together and get one, but I have different ideas; I'll tell you about it later. If you'd had a minute we could have gone into it; perhaps the morrow. But how's the car goin'?'

'Oh, he's always taking it to bits, it's always wanting somethin' spending on it; but as he says what can you expect for forty pounds. He's got his eye on another one. A hundred and twenty they want, but it's in good condition.'

'You'll get it, you'll get it, me girl.' Hannah patted Betty's back affectionately; then turning her head over her shoulder, called, 'Come away, you lot, out of that, your mother's goin'.'

As the children came running into the room again

80

Betty, looking at Rosie, said, 'We'll be seeing more of you then, Rosie?'

'Yes, I suppose so, Betty.'

'That'll be nice. John'll be pleased to know you're back. Come round and see us, eh? What about the morrow?'

'I'll pop in sometime. I've still a bit of a cold on me, I don't want to go out much yet.'

'No, and you're wise. Did you ever know weather like this? I'm sick of the sight of snow. Come on.' She gathered the children round her, then pushed them out into the hall amid cries of, 'Goodbye, Gran.' 'Bye, Auntie Rosie.' 'Bye, Gran.'

As Betty passed her to go down the steps, Hannah pushed a ten-shilling note into her hand, saying, 'Get your hair done this afternoon, an' all.'

'No, Ma. No, Ma.' Betty made great play of pushing the note back into Hannah's hand, but was eventually persuaded to take it. Then she smiled her thanks. 'There was no need for that,' she said.

Hannah came bustling back into the living-room now, talking all the time. She was in fine fettle. She bustled the cheese off the table and into the kitchen, shouting her conversation back to Rosie, where she stood looking down into the fire.

The whole world was a fiddle . . . life was a fiddle. There was nothing honest or decent or good in it. Life was putrid. Rosie found her teeth clamping down tightly into her lower lip, and even when it became painful she went on biting. There was badness of the body and badness of the mind, and she didn't know which was worse. . . . Oh, yes, she did. Oh, yes, she did. She was

81

shaking her head slowly at herself when the front-door bell rang, and as she turned she saw her mother come to the kitchen door holding the palm of her hand to her brow, the fingers extended wide.

'There's nobody comes to the front door on a Saturday mornin', not at this time.' Hannah hurriedly crossed the room, slanting her eyes towards Rosie. 'Now if it's them, act natural like.' She glanced swiftly about her; then putting her shoulders back, she made her way to the hall, but stopped again at the sitting-room door and, turning swiftly to Rosie, said with a nervous smile, 'Better still, go up to your room. The look on your face would give God himself away.'

When the bell rang again, Hannah went forward, crying, 'All right, all right, I'm on me way.'

Since the stampede last night in getting the shed cleared there had been no more mention of the matter. When the men had come in around eleven, merry and full of talk, her mother hadn't checked them with, 'Whist now! We've got something on our plates.' She had made no mention of the transfer of the stuff nor the fact that the house might be searched, and she had warned Barny to keep his mouth shut. Rosie knew that her mother was living up to the slogan: Sufficient unto the day is the evil thereof. She had always applied this to the ways of the house, and they had been happier for it; but now, apparently, the evil had come upon them.

She was making her way towards the door when her mother's voice from the hall checked her, crying, 'Oh, begod! It's you, Father, and on a Saturda' mornin'. Come in, come in; you look froze to the bone. . . . And what have you there?'

Rosie moved back swiftly towards the fire and stood with her hand pressed across the lower part of her face. Had she been given the choice she would have preferred the men to come and search the house rather than to be brought face to face with Father Lafflin. He was kind and jolly was Father Lafflin, but he had eyes that could see through you.

The priest preceded Hannah into the room, saying, 'It's my wireless I've brought along. I want Barny to have a look at it.' At this point he stopped, and looking towards Rosie, he exclaimed, 'Why! Rosie! And they never told me you were back.' He turned his face towards Hannah. 'You never told me the child was back, Hannah.'

'You've never given me a chance, Father.' Hannah's voice was sharp and her eyes were riveted on the wireless set the priest was holding before him. She was looking at it as if at any minute it might explode, and it might too. The wireless could bring disaster on her house. She grabbed it from his arms, saying, 'What had you to bring it round for, Father?'

'What? What were you saying? Oh.' He dusted the front of his coat down. 'Well, Barny made it and I've asked him two or three times to pop in and have a look at it, but he never has a minute, and I thought to meself, well, I'll take it round, and why shouldn't I? The boy makes me a wireless and I expect him to service it, and to come out of his way to do it. And so I brought it round knowing he'd see to it. But let us forget about the wireless. How are you getting on Rosie?'

'Oh, all right, Father.'

'You don't look all right, child.' He moved slowly

towards her. 'You look . . . well —' he paused, 'sort of drained. That's London for you, I suppose. That air's no good for man or beast up there.'

'I've had the flu, Father.'

'Aw . . . aw, that's it, is it? Now that's the thing for pulling you down. I think all the fat women in the land should be injected with flu, it would save all their dieting.' He threw his head back and let out a high laugh. But it didn't reach its full height before it was checked by Hannah saying flatly, 'Father, I'm sorry to ask you so pointedly, but this is no time for gildin' the lily so to speak, but would you mind takin' your wireless back, an' I'll have Barny come down and see to it this very afternoon.'

The priest turned slowly and looked at Hannah. He looked at her for a moment before saying, 'Don't be obtuse, Hannah, what is it? Have I done wrong in bringing the wireless? Is he up to his eyes in work? . . . But I'm in no real hurry for it, although it's handy.'

Hannah bowed her head and put her hands on the side of the table for support; her silence brought the priest's eyes narrowing towards her. He looked hard at her, then at the wireless; then flicked his glance to Rosie before turning to Hannah again and saying flatly, 'What's wrong with the wireless, Hannah?'

Hannah lifted her head and looked at the priest. She had to take a chance. There mightn't be anything wrong with the wireless, there mightn't be a part of it that could be recognised as the firm's, but she couldn't tell if this was so or not, only Barny could do that . . . or them, if they came and searched the house. If she kept her mouth shut the priest would walk out of the door and leave it, and where could she hide a big thing like that? She could burn the case. Aye, she could do that. But what could she do with the innards? Even if she could take it to bits, and she couldn't, there mightn't be time to get it into the box mattress. She couldn't risk it. She looked straight into the priest's eyes and said, 'Barny gets pieces on the cheap now and again; that's how he makes them up.' She stumbled awhile. 'But . . . but the factory's got a bee in its bonnet. It's after some of them that have been helpin' themsleves too freely, not being able to restrain themselves to a bit here and there, and so, from what I understand, they're goin' to do the rounds like. . . .'

The priest looked from Hannah to the wireless. He looked at it for a long while before saying, 'All that stuff in Barny's workshop? He told me he bought it from bankrupt stock. In the name of God, Hannah' – he turned on her, his voice angry now – 'you shouldn't have done this to me. You've got me involved in more ways than one, but enough at the moment is that I'm a receiver of stolen goods! Innocent or not, I'm a receiver of stolen goods. You shouldn't have involved me, Hannah.'

Hannah's head was up, her lower lip thrust out. For the moment she forgot she was addressing the priest. She forgot . . . the cloth. Before her she saw only an ungrateful old man, and she cried at him, 'You were involved enough during the war, Father, God's truth you were. Did I ever see you short of socks or shirts? Or sugar or tea? An' throw your mind back, throw it back to the side of bacon, Father, a whole side, just to mention a few things. Involved, you say? What's black now was black then.'

'The circumstances were different, Hannah, we were in a war. They were different.'

'No, begod, Father, not as I see it.'

'I'm not going to argue with you, Hannah. This present situation goes deeper than you have the insight to realise. I know now where some of the firm's stolen goods are. Don't you see, woman? You shouldn't have done this to me.'

As he walked towards the door, not even saying goodbye to Rosie, Hannah's voice checked him with, 'What about this, Father?' She pointed to the wireless.

'What about it?' He was looking at her over his shoulder.

'You're taking it with you?'

'I don't want it any longer.'

'Look, Father.' Hannah hurried towards him, her hands extended outwards. 'In the name of God, get it out of here. Take it away with you. If Barny was here I wouldn't ask you, but as it is, the very sight of it might put the kibosh on him if they were to come around.'

The old priest drew in a breath that pushed his black coat sharply outwards. Then turning back into the room he grabbed up the wireless and made for the hall, Hannah after him. As she opened the door for him he said, 'Get yourself to confession tonight, Hannah, and make a clean sweep, be finished with it for good and all.'

'I will, Father, I will that.' Hannah's voice now held a soft, conciliatory note, and she ended as if he was leaving after one of his usual friendly and laughter-filled visits. 'Goodbye, Father. Mind how you go. Goodbye.'

In the living-room once more she went straight for a

chair and sat down, and, lifting up her apron, she wiped the sweat from around her face.

As Rosie moved from the fireplace towards the hall door, Hannah asked, 'Where are you going?'

'Just upstairs.'

Hannah made no reply to this, nor did she try to stop her by going into a tirade about the priest.

As Rosie went up the last flight of stairs to her room she was shaking her head. She wouldn't be able to stand this for long. It was the same thing over and over again. But her mother was right about one thing, what was black now was black in the war. Somehow it seemed to her that the priest had lost points in the game of morality.

Hannah was her usual self when the men came in at dinner time. To Barny's query 'Everything all right, Ma?' she answered, 'Right as rain.' She did not tell him about the priest's visit; she would wait until she got him on the quiet. Then she would warn him what to expect from Father Lafflin.

After the meal she said to Broderick, 'Will you see to the dishes for me? Rosie here and me are going out on a jaunt, just to have a look round the shops; I've never been in Newcastle for weeks. I want vests for Jimmy and some shirts for Shane. That fellow must rasp his collars with a razor blade, he goes through them so quickly.'

'Get yersels away.' Broderick smiled at his daughter. 'But I'd have thought you'd have been better in than out the day, the weather the way it is.'

'Aw, she wants to pick her things up from the station,' said Hannah. 'An' we'll come back by taxi. We'll do the thing in style, won't we, Rosie girl?' Hannah put out her hand to Rosie's shoulder and, pushing it gently, said, 'Go on up now and get ready; I'll be with you in two shakes.'

As Rosie passed her father, Broderick pulled her to a halt, saying, 'You're quiet this time, lass. There's hardly a peep out of you.'

She smiled at him, and in an attempt at jocularity she said, 'I talk when I can, Da, but it's difficult to get a word in.'

There was loud laughter at this, and Shane said from across the table, 'There's a dance at the club the night. Why don't you come along and have a fling; they do some old time ones an' all? There's high jinks on a Saturday night, and variety they have . . . the lot, just like on Fridays.'

'I'll see, Shane. Thanks.' She nodded at him.

On the first landing she met Karen dressed ready for out doors, and as she went to pass her Karen stopped dead in front of her, and looking up into her face, said pointedly, 'What brought you back anyway?'

'I . . . I told you I had the flu.'

'The flu! You can't hoodwink me, I'm not a fool.'

Somewhere in the back of Rosie's mind she was saying, She's right. Like me ma, she's no fool. But aloud she said, 'You surprise me.' The cheap quip was her only counter to the forthright attack.

The colour deepened in Karen's cheeks. Her small, full mouth pursed itself further. 'You think you're clever, don't you? Smart . . . the London lady . . . well, you don't impress me. You're in trouble, aren't you?'

No muscle of Rosie's face moved, her whole body

was still. She had the desire, and not for the first time, to lift her hand and slap the small, pert face of her niece. Her voice betrayed her anger as she said below her breath, 'You would like to think that I've come home to have a baby, wouldn't you? Well I'm sorry to disappoint you. That's the only trouble you can think of, isn't it, being landed with a baby? You would have loved it to happen in my case . . . oh, I know. But just you be careful that your wishful thinking doesn't come home to roost.'

'Well' – Karen took a step to the side as she spoke – 'I might be wrong on one count, but I'm not altogether, I know that. And I'll tell you another thing; if you've got the idea into your head to stay home, I'm going.'

'Good, you'd better look out for digs then, hadn't you?' Rosie turned from the small, bitter face and was aware, as she crossed the landing, that Karen was still standing staring at her, and she knew that her jaws would be working, viciously.

In her room she stood looking out through the small attic window at the white-coated roofs opposite. She had her arms crossed tightly about her, her hands pressed against her ribs as if giving herself support, and she stood like this until she heard her mother's voice calling from below, 'Are you ready, Rosie? Rosie! Do you hear me? Are you ready?' She did not swing round and grab up her things, but slowly she got into her coat and pulled on her hat, and when her mother's voice came to her again, calling, 'Are you up there, lass?' she clenched her hands tightly before calling back, 'I'm coming, I'm coming, Ma.'

was still. She had the desire, and not for the first time, to lift her hand and slap the small, red face of her elder. Her voice betrayed her anger as she sank below her breath. 'You would like to think that I've come home to have a baby, wouldn't you? Well, I'm sorry to disappoint you. That's the only trouble you can think of, isn't it, being landed with a baby? You would have loved that to happen in my case . . . oh, I know. But that you're careful that you won't be thinking, doesn't I come home to roost.'

'Well' – Karen rose, easing to the side as she spoke – 'I might be wrong on one count, but I'm not altogether . . . I know that. And I'll tell you another thing, if you've got the idea into your head to stay home, it's going . . .'

'God, you'd better look out for this, that, but I stop.' Rosie turned from the small, bitter face and was swung, as she crossed the landing, that Karen was still wanting, staring at sea, and she knew that her face would be working violently.

In her room she stood looking out from the small attic window at the white-coated rock opposite. She had her arms crossed tightly about her, her hands pressed against her chest, giving herself support, and she stood like this until she heard her mother's voice calling from below: 'Are you ready, Rosie? Rosie! Do you hear me? Are you ready?' She did not swing round and rush up her things but slowly she got into her coat and pulled on her hat, and when her mother's voice came to her again, calling, 'Are you up there, lass?' she clenched her hands tightly before calling back, 'I'm coming. I'm coming, Ma.'

PART TWO

HUGHIE

Sunday

Hughie was sitting in the back of the cobbler's shop. He was sitting in his shirt sleeves and wearing a pullover, and he looked at home, as he never did in Hannah's house. The little room had no window, and no light but that which came in from the shop through the half-glazed door. But it was extremely bright now, being lit by an electric bulb beneath a pink plastic shade, and the light was reflected from the rough mauve-painted walls. Along one wall was a narrow desk-cum-cupboard, above which were shelves holding books. One step from the desk and against the opposite wall stood two chairs – a straight-backed one and an old extending bed-chair. At the far end of the room was a shallow sink, with a table at its side holding a small grill, on which stood a kettle, now coming up to the boil. To the side of the sink a curtain hung from a rod, which was used to cut off the kitchen section of the tiny compartment. On the floor below the sink was a rough mat, and a piece of carpet ran the length of the room to the far wall, where stood an oil heater. The tiny room gave off an air of compact snugness, and had been Hughie Geary's real home for so long that now, when he was about to leave it, it tugged at him, saying, Don't go yet, there's plenty of time.

But there wasn't plenty of time. There wasn't all that time left, for he was thirty-five. Already there was grey in his hair; already the dreams of travelling that had haunted him for years were fading; at least they had been until a couple of months ago when they had been pleasantly startled into life.

Before him now on the desk lay numbers of travel brochures; there were dozens of them dating back for years. They had been part of his recreation; he knew every route on every map of every folder. He could have told you, without referring to the appropriate brochure, the route to Baghdad as easily as another man could have pointed out the route to the Lake District, yet never in his life had he been more than a hundred miles from Fellburn, never in his life had he had a holiday. But then there was nothing so strange about that. As Hannah had said to him on several occasions, 'Broderick and me have never slept away from home for a night,' so if Hannah Massey didn't need a holiday, why should he?

He lifted his head and looked at the blank wall before him. How much could you hate someone and still live with them? How deep could the hate go before you wanted to kill the object of it? At times he thought he could measure his hate for Hannah; it was so many inches long, and so many inches thick, and it was wedged tight within him. But at other times he knew his thin body could not be measured from his chest to his backbone, for it was stretched wide with hate, hate for the woman who had dominated him since he was twelve years old; who had for a period from the age of fifteen put the fear of God in him, and who had stripped him of his manhood as certainly as if she had performed an operation on him. And she had performed an operation on him, on his mind. But this time next week he would be away, and from the time he left the house he would never look on her again. And yet he knew that he would never forget her, for her personality was imprinted on him as indelibly as the stamp of a concentration camp. But there was one bit of enjoyment he was going to give himself before they parted; he was going to keep his eyes tight on her face when he told her about the money; he was going to draw into himself and hold, like some precious gift, her fury when she realized she had thrown away, not only the fatted calf, but the golden calf.

As the kettle began to whistle the shop door shook and the bell rang, and rising hastily, he pulled the kettle aside, pushed all the travel folders into a drawer, and went out through the shop and opened the door.

'Did I hear the kettle boiling?'

'Oh, hello, Dennis. Aye, you did.'

Dennis hurried around the counter, 'Lord, it's cold . . . ugh!' He took off his coat as he entered the room, then went towards the stove and held his hands above it as Hughie mashed the tea. And for a moment there was a silence between them, the silence of two men who were past the need to fill every minute with sound.

'It won't be a tick, I'll let it draw. Sit yourself down.'

Hughie was speaking to Dennis's back now. It was a thin back, narrow shoulders topped by a longish head with dark hair, close cut, almost black as were his eyes. There was no look of Hannah about Dennis, and very little of Broderick. They said he took after Broderick's father. His face wore a keen, sharp look, and when he turned it towards Hughie the expression was tight and the eyes hard. 'I suppose you've heard the latest?' he said.

'A bit of it.'

'My God!' Dennis shook his head as he sat down. 'What will she think of next? Brampton Hill, number eight of all places! But there's one thing about it; this time the lads are making a stand.'

'Their lines will break.'

'Yes, Hughie, as you say, their lines will break; as they've done before. The woman's mad. . . . Brampton Hill with our lot. Can you imagine it? But she's determined as I've never seen her before. The house was like hell let loose this morning. Did you know she broke the news to them last night after she came back from the club?'

'Yes, I heard the racket from up in my room.'

'Huh! She must have been well fortified and thought the time was ripe. I was flabbergasted when I went in. I was expecting to get it in the neck straight-away for not calling in and for what I had to tell her, but that came later. You know, the atmosphere on a Sunday in the house has generally made me laugh, because it's always so full of restrained holy bustle; this one getting ready for this Mass, the other coming back from Communion, and the virtue of having gone to the seven o'clock Mass oozing out of her like sweat. But not this morning. It was like going into a house where a bomb had exploded, and the worst thing they could have done they did, I mean the lads, they appealed to me. What did I think of it? You can imagine how she took that.'

Hughie jerked his chin as he poured out the tea. 'I can imagine it. But how did she take your news?'

'How did she take it?' Dennis took the cup from Hughie's hand and, lifting the spoon, tapped it against the saucer. It was a nervous movement. 'You know, sometimes I want to laugh in her face, a debunking laugh, or laugh at her . . . but never with her. At times I forget she's my mother and want to slap her mouth for her. I could have done it this morning quite easily. It was during one of the lulls when the lads were coming up for more breath that I told her. We were in the kitchen alone at the time. I broke it gently, saying, 'I've got a bit of news for you, Ma.'

' ''Aye?'' she said; she didn't even turn from the sink. ''Florence is going to have a baby,'' I said. I was grinning self-consciously as I said it, I couldn't help it. You know Hughie, the way she turned around and looked at me was an insult in itself. And you know what she said?'

'I could give a good guess.'

'She kept wiping up as she turned round, and there was that tight, bitter smile on her face. ''Well,'' she said, ''you should feel much better now that you've proved yourself; in fact, you should both feel different and more normal like. It's a great stigma for a woman to bear, not to be able to have a child. She's for ever at a loss to know if the man's no use or it's herself'' . . . She's my mother, Hughie, and she said that. And then she finished, ''I only hope her body's as strong as her mind and she's delivered safe. Brains are not important to a woman in childbirth, she'll likely deliver hard''. . . . I had to come out, Hughie; I just had to come out.'

'Don't you worry, Dennis. Both you and Florence are in a position to laugh at her.'

Dennis took a long drink from his cup, and he stared at the oil-stove for some moments before replying, 'Yes,

97

I suppose we are, but you know we just can't . . . you can't laugh her off for she gets into your skin, pricking you all over like squirrel fleas . . . I don't know how you stand it day in, day out . . . I don't. Florence was saying the other night that she could understand the lads putting up with her because they were nearly all as dim as doornails. As long as they are fed and clothed and have their pocket money, that's all that matters. Like her, she said, they think God will provide, only unlike her they don't help Him with the job. And why should they when they've got Ma? But she said, she just couldn't begin to understand how you've put up with it all these years.'

Hughie smiled now, a quiet, thoughtful smile, and he looked through the glass door into the shop to a shelf where rested a row of cobbled boots and shoes as he replied softly, 'I've asked meself that many times, and given meself the answer, too. And it's very simple, I haven't much gumption.' He cast a smile towards Dennis.

'Nonsense!' Dennis gave a disbelieving jerk to his head. 'But really, why didn't you just walk out?'

'I did. You know I did, twice, and she had me brought back.'

'But that was when you were a lad. I've bever brought this up before, it seemed too pertinent. But what really kept you? I can't believe it's just what happened years ago and the hold she had over you. As I see it, there was nothing to stop you just walking out, any day of any year as far back as I can remember . . . just walking out.'

Again Hughie looked through the door to the line of

shoes, and his expression took on a sadness that buried itself deep in his brown eyes. 'You belong to a family, Dennis, and anybody who has a family can't really understand what it's like not to be a member of one. When I first came into the house I felt I was one of you lads, because she was kind, but there were still times when, in a temper, she would say, "As for you, I've got enough to put up with from this horde, you'll go into a home." She'd forget it the next minute, but not me. I was terrified of this thing called . . . a home. I was terrified of not being a member of a family. And you know, on the two occasions she had me brought back I was glad. Moreover, your da was good to me when we worked together here. We could laugh and be easy, and he would make excuses for her, mostly first thing in the morning, saying, "Don't mind, Hannah; all she says is just like God bless you. She's a great woman, a great woman." I often wondered what he would think about me if she had told him the truth, as she threatened so often to do.'

'Just the same as he does now. But the fact that he didn't know, that she kept mum about it all these years, makes her more formidible still, don't you think?'

'Yes, I suppose so. The reason she gave me for not telling him was that he would kill me, in fact they would all kill me if they knew. And then I felt I owed her something after what happened. And as the years went on it wasn't too bad. I had the shop on my own, and this.' He spread his hands out to indicate the little room. 'I had my books; and then the last few years I've had' – he leant his head forward and his voice dropped as he ended – 'you and Florence. That's meant a lot to me, more than you'll ever guess, Dennis. And the pastime you opened up for me.'

'Oh, that was Florence's doing, not mine. She saw immediately that you were a natural writer and would make an essayist.'

'Huh! A natural . . . an essayist who couldn't spell more than a four-letter word.'

'You can spell better than me, it was never my strong point either.' They laughed at each other now. Then again there was silence between them, until Dennis exclaimed, 'Oh, by the way, what I meant to say when I first came in was, what do you think about our Rosie coming home?'

'Oh . . . Rosie.' Hughie got up, took Dennis's cup and went to the stove to refill it, saying, 'Well, I don't really know. What's your opinion?'

Dennis shook his head. 'Well, since you put it like that I feel there's something not quite right. She says she's had the flu. That could account for her being thin and white, but . . . well, I might be imagining it, but she looks sort of scared to me.'

'She's in trouble, Dennis.'

'God, no!'

'Oh, I don't think it's that.' Hughie raised his eyebrows as he handed Dennis the filled cup. 'Yet I don't know. But I just don't want to think it's that, not with her. But there's something. You put your finger on it when you said she looked scared. The others though don't seem to have noticed anything.'

'They wouldn't.' Dennis jerked his chin upwards. 'But if she's in trouble it'll drive the old girl barmy. That would be the end of it, because she's the apple of her eye, as you know. It's a wonder she isn't a completely spoiled brat, yet she isn't. . . . I've always had a soft spot for Rosie.'

'Me too.' Hughie again went to the sink, filled the kettle and set it on the stove, but did not light the gas. And Dennis, looking towards him, was about to say something further but withheld it. Then he bit on his lower lip as if to suppress the question, after which he drained the last of his tea at a gulp and stood up, saying, 'I'd better be making a move or I'll be late for dinner. You'll be along this afternoon?'

'Yes. Yes, Dennis, I'll be along this afternoon.'

They went through the shop in single file, and when they were near the door Dennis turned towards Hughie and said quietly, 'We're going to miss you, you know.'

'It won't all be on one side, Dennis. I'll never forget the pair of you.'

'Will you ever come back this way, do you think?'

'I doubt it; not the way I'm feeling now; but you never know. There's one thing I'm certain of. Wherever I come to rest there'll be room for you and Florence and' – his face spread into a grin – 'the bairns.'

Dennis put out his fist and punched him in the chest, then opened the door, saying, 'So long. See you later.'

'Yes, Dennis. So long.'

Back in the room again, Hughie sat down before the narrow desk. There was half an hour before he need go back to the house. He reached up and took down some sheets of paper from the shelf where the books were, and after thinking for a moment, he began to write from where earlier he had left off. But he had only written a few lines when he stopped, and staring down at his thin,

101

scribbly writing, he thought to himself, an essayist. It was a wonderful word, essayist, and Florence didn't say things for the sake of saying them. He had started scribbling years ago, but hadn't dared show his efforts to anyone, until by chance Dennis had picked up something from the desk here. That's how it had started; and with it his friendship with them both. Dennis had said, 'You're a deep one; I never even thought you thought – I forgot you weren't one of us.' They had both laughed. Now, if he wanted, he could spend all his days just writing. Going carefully, he had enough money to keep him for the remainder of his life; and who knew? He might one day see himself in print. That would be worth all the money in the world. And he was going to see the world, the whole world. From his house on wheels he was going to see the world.

At this point, the shop bell ringing once more surprised him, and when he opened the door there stood Dennis again, but now with Rosie by his side.

'I brought her back to go along home with you. She'll explain.' Dennis pressed Rosie over the threshold. 'I must be off. Look' – he pulled at Rosie's arm – 'what about coming over to our place this afternoon with Hughie, eh? Florence would love to see you.'

'Thanks, Dennis, but Betty has already asked me. But I'd rather come over to you. I'll . . . I'll see if I can manage it,' she smiled at him.

'You do, you do. So long.'

'So long, Dennis. . . . Thanks.'

As Dennis turned away Rosie took a step into the shop and stood waiting, and Hughie, closing the door, said, 'Go on into the back room, Rosie, it's warm there.'

102

She kept her head slightly down as she went round the counter and into the back shop, but once inside an exclamation came from her, and she turned to him spontaneously, saying, 'By! You've got this cosy, Hughie.' She looked about her now. 'It's something different from when I saw it last.'

'Home from home.' He smiled shyly at her. 'Sit down. I'll make you a cup of tea.'

'No . . . no, don't, Hughie, I don't want anything. Thanks all the same.'

'It would warm you up. It won't take a minute.'

She was looking up at him, and he down at her, and their exchanged glances embarrassed them both. She said quickly, 'All right, all right, I'll have one,' and he turned just as quickly and went to the stove and lit the gas.

The striking of the match was like a whip's crack in the silence. It was a different silence from that which he had shared with Dennis. Aware of the strained atmosphere too, Rosie moved on the chair and turned sideways and leant her elbow on the desk and her eyes dropped to the paper lying there.

Having been trained to read quickly she took in the first paragraph of the writing almost at a glance. It read: 'March 12, looked at programme "The Cosmologist". Speakers were: Professor Fred Hoyle, Professor Sir Bernard Lovell and Professor Hermann Bondi, and Doctor Margaret and Geoffrey Burbidge. This programme interested me so much it set my mind moving, and I thought of the following when I was on the point of sleep and made myself put it down, just as I thought of it. Must extend it.'

Then followed the words: 'The word conscious is the only means we have of explaining our ability to be aware of our surroundings. Yet how do we know that unconsciousness, which now we understand as a state of unawareness, might not, when deprived of this body, be a higher form of mind which will produce another body, which will in turn take up life on a planet suited to maintain it for a span of time in accordance with the properties of that planet, where it will go through the same process – namely, what we now term unconsciousness will be a form of consciousness. This consciousness will eventually merge again into the universe as unconsciousness . . . ad infinitum.

'Unconsciousness, or the subconscious mind, could be the reality. All the universe could be alive to deeper and deeper forms of unconsciousness. The whole universe could be made up of these levels of unconsciousness, and death could be a mere merging into the universe by way of this unconsciousness.'

'It won't be a minute before it boils.'

'Oh . . . oh, I'm sorry, Hughie. I . . . I didn't mean to read it.'

'Oh, that's all right.' He smiled widely. 'It's just some of my scribbling . . . Passes the time, you know.' He sat down opposite to her; their knees were almost touching.

'I . . . I stopped you writing,' she said, 'barging in. It reads very clever. I didn't understand it.'

'There's two of us.'

They laughed together.

'But I stopped you, and . . .'

'That you didn't,' he put in quickly. 'I was on the point of going home. It's on dinner time, isn't it?'

She lowered her eyes, then said, 'I was just passing Waldorf Street when I saw Ronnie in the distance; he was going up the school cut. He stopped when he saw me, but I knew what he would do; he would come out in Baldwin Road and meet me full on. I was standing like a stook not knowing whether to go on, or to go back into the town and to take the bus to the top of our road, when Dennis came down the hill.'

'He's married now, it'll be all right.' Hughie's voice was low.

And hers was just above a whisper as she answered, 'It wouldn't, Hughie, it wouldn't.'

'Well, I suppose you know best.' He cleared his throat, then smoothed his hair back.

Rosie looked at her hands encased in the fur-lined gloves that her mother had bought her yesterday, and she began to pick at the fingers as she said, 'I half told my mother that I would stay home and get a job near, but I don't think I can now.'

He did not speak for a moment, but kept his eyes intently on her averted face before he said, 'His wife's going to have a baby, I don't think he would –'

'Oh, it isn't only him, Hughie, it's everything. . . . You change when you go away, you know, and in a way it's a good thing you do.'

'I wouldn't know about that.'

His tone held regret, and she lifted her eyes to his and said quickly, 'Oh, you don't need to change, Hughie.' She shook her head at him, a gentle smile playing round her lips.

'Huh!' His body moved in self-derision.

'Well, you don't, you've always been sensible. I mean

you've thought for yourself, an' you've got more brains than all of us put together.' She glanced towards the paper on the table which had read like double Dutch to her.

He leant towards her now. 'If I'd thought for meself, Rosie, do you think I'd still he here?' Both his look and tone were enquiring.

As she looked back at him, she had the urge to ask him questions, but found herself overcome by a sudden feeling of shyness. What she did say was, 'You said you were leaving. What's made you change your mind, Hughie?'

He looked at her a full minute before speaking. 'I've come into money, Rosie,' he said.

'Into money, Hughie? The pools?'

'No, not the pools. . . . I don't know whether you remember or not, but I had a sister; I can hardly remember her meself.'

'I seem to have heard something about her.'

'Well, she went to America just before the war as nurse-companion to an old lady. She was about twelve years older than me. And she wasn't really a nurse, not a trained nurse, and I never heard of her until two years ago, and in a really odd way. You see she wrote to the Vicar of All Souls, you know, the big Protestant church behind the market, and she asked him did he know of Hugh Geary who had been evacuated to Fellburn during the war. Now you know me, Rosie. I never put me foot inside a church, either Catholic, Protestant, or Methodist, and it's ten to one any other minister but this Mr Pattenden would never have heard of me but for the strange coincidence that he's always brought his boots here to be mended. He always did in your da's time and he still does, and he came to me with this letter. He was as happy about it as if it was affecting himself. And that's how it all started. I wrote to her and she wrote back, a long letter, telling me all that had happened to her. It wasn't much when you summed it up. She had looked after the old lady all these years, and a few months previous to her trying to find me the old lady had died and had left her a good slice of her money. She asked me if there was any chance of me coming to America, and I wrote back and said no, I was settled comfortably here. I didn't want her to think that I was on the cadge – but I told her that if ever she thought of coming to England I would be overjoyed to see her. Well, it turned out that she wasn't very well herself, apparently and wasn't up to travelling; then just before Christmas she died.' From his seat he looked out through the glass door again towards the row of shoes, before he said, as if to himself, 'She must have been bad when she tried to contact me. She likely knew she was going then and she wanted to be in touch with someone belonging to her. I know the feeling. But, you know, I'd rather have seen her than had the money.'

After a pause Rosie said, 'I'm sorry you didn't meet her, Hughie, but I'm glad for you, oh, I am. I would sooner it had happened to you than to anyone else I know of.'

'Why me?' He turned his head and looked at her intently. And she dropped her eyes from his and said, 'Oh, I don't know. Perhaps just because I was brought up with you, and . . . and I never thought you got . . . well, a square deal. And you took everything so quietly, not bashing, or yelling, or swearing as the others would have done, if . . . if me ma had treated them as she did you.'

Following another silence, during which she kept her eyes cast downwards, she asked, 'And me ma knows nothing about it?'

'Not a thing. If Nancy, that was me sister, had written to the priest he would naturally have gone to the house.'

She looked up at him. 'She's going to get a glif.'

'Yes, Rosie, she's going to get a glif.'

'When are you going?'

'As soon as they've altered the caravan.'

'You've got a caravan?'

'Yes, I bought it second hand. A Land-Rover and a caravan. I got it as a bargain an' all. The funny thing is, if I hadn't had enough cash I would never have got the chance of it at the price; I would have been asked to pay through the teeth. It's the irony of life, isn't it?'

'Yes, yes. But why are you having it altered? Is it in a bad way?'

'No, it's in fine condition, but they used it mostly for sleeping. There were five in the family and it's all bunks. I'm having a sink unit put in, and a cooker.' His face looked alight now. 'And a kind of desk-cum-drawers, and a wardrobe. It'll be like a house on wheels. I've taken the design from one I saw in a weekly, and old Jim Cullen, next door, is doing it.' He nodded his head. 'You wouldn't remember him, I don't suppose, but he's a wizard with wood. In fact he makes antiques, you know, copies, when he has orders for them. But things have slumped in his line this past few years, it's with Brampton Hill going down and all that, and so I've given him the job. And I know I won't even have to bother and look at it until he's finished. He's that kind of a worker. The only thing is, he won't be hurried too much, he's a craftsman. If he keeps at it, it should be ready a week come Monday or Tuesday, and the minute it is I'm on the road.'

'Can you drive a car, Hughie?' Her eyebrows were slightly raised.

'Oh, aye. And I've got Dennis to thank for that an' all. I've got Dennis to thank for a lot of things. And Florence, too. When they had the car a few years ago he would insist on teaching me to drive; and then when I could he said, "You go and pass your test." "What for?" I asked. "You never know," he said, "you never know." And you don't, do you Rosie?'

She shook her head.

'But now they've sold the car because they've been trying to raise the money for a deposit to put down on a house. But what they don't know as yet' – he leant forward towards her, his elbow resting on his knee – 'they're going to have a house bought for them.' He nodded slowly. 'A three-thousand pound one. But I can't do it until I'm on the road, because Dennis wouldn't hear of it. But when I'm away and he can't get in touch with me . . . well, he can't do anything about it, can he?'

His plain face looked almost handsome, illuminated as it was with the joy of being able to give. And the look did something to Rosie that nothing else had been able to do for days. It penetrated the terror that was still encased in her body, the terror that had gone beyond fear. On Friday night she had thought when once she was alone in bed she would cry and cry and ease herself,

109

but she had lain dry-eyed, staring through the terror into the blackness of the night; blackness that was disturbed only by the sounds below her; grunts, faint sighs, snores, splutters and coughs; and these had made the terror more real. All those men down there . . . MEN . . . MEN . . . MEN.

'Rosie. Aw, Rosie, what is it?' Hughie was on his feet. 'Don't cry. Aw, don't cry like that.' His hand hesitated as it went out to her shoulder; then it rested gently on it, and at his touch something cracked in her throat and she gulped and gasped and held her face in her hands, while the tears ran through her fingers.

'There, there.' He was kneeling by her side now, his hand still on her shoulder, and when, like a child, she turned her head into his neck, he stared at the wall opposite, and it looked as if he too was fixed with emotion, for his other arm hung by his side like a false limb.

Perhaps she felt the stiffness of his body, the unresponsiveness of his hand, for, pulling herself upright, she turned her face from him, gasping and spluttering as she said, 'I . . . I'm sorry, I'm sorry, Hughie.'

He was on the chair opposite to her again. 'What's to be sorry about? A cry will do you good.' His voice sounded flat.

She groped at her handbag, and taking out a handkerchief, dried her face; and again she said, 'I'm sorry.'

He did not make any remark for a moment, but when he did his words weren't put as a question but as a direct statement.

'You're in trouble, Rosie, aren't you?' he said.

110

There was no denial from her, only a downward movement of her head.

'Can you tell me?'

Now her head shook slowly from side to side.

'Well, you should tell somebody, it would ease it. Why don't you go to Dennis?'

Again she shook her head. Then raising it, she gulped for breath a number of times before looking at him and saying, 'If . . . if I could tell any . . . anybody, it would be you, but I can't.'

'You're frightened about something, aren't you?'

'Not any more,' she said.

'Isn't it anything you could tell your . . . your mother?'

She made a sound that was something between a groan and a whimper. 'My mother . . . ? I'd sooner jump in the river, Hughie. My mother? I'd sooner die than she knew. She'd want to kill me in any case. You know it's frightening when somebody lays so much stock on you as she does on me. You can't live up to it. But she'd never understand that. She frightens me with her feeling, she's so . . . so . . .' She searched for a word, moving her head the while, and he put in, 'Irrational?'

'Yes, that's it, that's the word . . . irrational. And in everything, in everything. I thought of them going to Mass this morning after the business of Friday night and yesterday morning.'

'What happened yesterday morning?'

She sniffled. 'You didn't hear . . . ? The priest came with a wireless to be mended.'

Hughie's face slowly stretched. 'The one Barny made for him?'

'Yes. He came bounding in, all chatter like he always

111

does. When she opened the door to him she really thought it was them coming to search, you know.'

Hughie bit on his lip, trying to suppress a smile, as he asked, 'And what happened?'

'He went for her because he said she had involved him. Then she threw in his face about keeping him supplied with bacon and butter and shirts and things during the war. . . .'

At this Hughie put his hand over his mouth, bowed his head and began to laugh. It was a silent laugh at first, evident only in the shaking of his body; then unable to control it any longer he gave vent to it, and as Rosie watched him her face trembled into a smile, then stretched, and the next moment she, too, was laughing, but with more than a touch of hysteria.

How they came to grasp each other's hands neither of them knew, but as their laughter subsided their hands were joined breast high between them and their heads were almost touching.

It was Hughie who sobered first. He released her hands, and, getting up, reached out and picked up a towel from a rail to the side of the desk and rubbed his face vigorously with it.

Rosie had a bout of the hiccoughs now, and between them she said, 'Oh, Hughie, hic . . . I . . . never thought I would . . . hic . . . laugh in me life again. Oh thanks, Hughie, thanks; you've done me the world of good.'

'Well, if you didn't see the funny side of some things you would commit murder. It isn't often I get a real laugh. No, it isn't often.'

And that's true, she thought. She hadn't, as far as she could remember, heard him laugh heartily before. His laughter had always been controlled, just a shaking of the body.

She rose to her feet, saying, 'Can I wash me face, Hughie, it'll be a mess?'

'Of course.' He pointed to the sink.

As she washed her face and took a lipstick out of her new bag and made up her lips, he got into his coat, and put on a scarf, and picked up his hat and stood waiting for her, all without looking at her. It was as if he was embarrassed now by her personal acts.

As he locked the shop door behind them, Rosie said, 'What are you going to do with it? I mean the shop, goodwill, and stock and that?'

'Oh,' he said, 'I'm passing it on to a fellow called Lance Briggs. He's handicapped in the legs and works in Tullets factory. He's delighted about it. He's a shy bloke . . . not unlike meself' – he laughed – 'and having a quiet place of his own will make all the difference to him. He'll do all right an' all because he was apprenticed to the boot mending until he was twenty. I'm glad he's having it.' He looked at his watch and said, 'We'll have to put a move on, we're late as it is.'

Once, when she almost slipped on the frosted pavement, he put out his hand to steady her, but before he touched her she had righted herself.

After this they covered most of the distance home without speaking. The intimacy that the room behind the shop had created with its snug smallness was gone, and they walked apart, intent on picking their way over the humped frozen snow that covered the pavements.

It was as they rounded the corner of the school that they came face to face with Ronnie MacFarlane.

113

MacFarlane was a tall man, six foot two and broad with it. He was handsome in a rough-hewn way, with strong Celtic features, large blue eyes and a full-lipped mouth above a heavy jaw. He stood one foot on the kerb and one in the gutter, his right shoulder in line with that of Rosie's. His skin looked ruddy and warm as if he was blushing. 'Hello, Rosie,' he said.

She paused only for a second before answering, 'Hello, Ronnie.'

'Hello,' put in Hughie. This brought Ronnie's eyes flicking reluctantly from Rosie as he answered, 'Hello there, Hughie.'

'Awful weather.' He was looking at Rosie again.

'Yes.' She nodded her head.

'Are you home for long?'

'No, no, not long.'

'I'll be seeing you then?'

'Yes,' she hesitated. 'Be seeing you.' As she moved sideways to pass him, he stepped back into the gutter and watched her.

'So long, Rosie.' Her name came soft to his mouth.

'So long, Ronnie,' she answered.

'So long,' said Hughie. And for reply Ronnie nodded to him, but his eyes were still on Rosie.

She didn't speak until they had turned the next corner, and the trembling of her body came over in her voice. 'He . . . : he must have been hanging about. You see, it's as I said, I won't be able to stay; not in the town anyway.'

'Don't worry.' Hughie was walking close to her now. 'He can't do anything. Perhaps he just wanted to have a word with you.'

'A word? Huh! I know what he wants.' She put her fingers to her lips. 'I'm sorry, Hughie.'

'Why be sorry for saying what you think, and the truth.'

'It sounds so awful, but . . .' She turned and looked squarely at him. 'You know something, Hughie? There's worse than Ronnie.'

'Yes, I believe that, and by a long chalk; but I'm sorry you've found it out.'

She was looking ahead as she said, 'So am I.'

Again there was silence between them. Yet now it wasn't so strained. But the same thought was in both their minds as they neared the house. Should they go in together?

Rosie knew she should say, 'You'd better go round the back way, Hughie.' But she couldn't. It would be an insult to say that to him. She would rather brave her mother's wrath than hurt him. She said, 'We'll go in the front way, it's nearer.'

He made no protest, but stood with her on the step as she rang the bell.

The door was opened by Hannah herself, and as soon as she saw them together her face darkened. But it was to Rosie she addressed herself, saying, 'Where've you been in all this, the dinner's been on the table this last twenty minutes? The Mass was over at twelve and it's now nearly half-past one. Where've you been?'

As short a time ago as yesterday Rosie wouldn't even have thought of making a reply like 'Do I have to account for every minute to you?' but now she almost voiced it, yet as she took off her coat and hat and hung them on a peg of the hall-stand without answering, she reminded herself of how kind her mother had been to her, and that she owed her for every stitch of clothing she was now wearing.

'You heard what I said.' Hannah was close behind her.

'I . . . I went for a walk, Ma.'

'You went for a . . . !' Hannah glanced to where Hughie at the far end of the hall was disappearing into the kitchen, there to hang up his coat and hat on the back door, the place allotted to him, and coming close to Rosie now, she hissed, 'Don't tell me you've been walkin' with him!'

Rosie shook her head; then turning and facing her mother, she said, 'I went down by the river.'

'In this weather?' Hannah brought her brows together. 'An' answer me, was he along of you?'

'I met him in the street, Ma.' Rosie closed her eyes for a moment. She only hoped that Hughie was listening and had not gone straight through the kitchen and into the living-room so he would know what to say if he was questioned.

Hannah, after giving her one long look, said, 'Well, come an' have your dinner, what's left of it.'

The men had nearly finished their meal when Rosie sat down at the table, and their greeting of her was not boisterous, as it had been on her arrival, for they were still shuddering from the impact of their mother's new venture, which the Sunday beer hadn't been able to show up in a more favourable light.

When Hannah put the dinner plate in front of her with the remark, 'It's kizzened up to cork, so it is,' her father put in placatingly. 'Aw, she'll get it down, won't you, lass? This weather would make a mare eat its foal.' She smiled at him. She liked her da. Her da always wanted peace. Somehow he was like Hughie, or Hughie was like him. As she glanced at Hughie sitting now at the farther end of the table, his head bowed, she thought that, although they did not look alike, they were like enough in nature to be father and son, more so than the other four men at the table.

Karen, too, was at the table, seated next to her grandfather. She hadn't spoken to Rosie, she hadn't even looked at her, that is until Shane asked, 'Did you come out early from eleven o'clock? I hung about waitin' for you, but I didn't see you?'

'What?' Rosie fluffed the question as one taken off her guard, then said, 'Oh, yes . . . I came out early. I was at the back. It was stuffy. I came out just before the end.' It was now that Karen looked at her and spoke. She said, 'I was at the back an' all; I didn't see you. And it wasn't stuffy; the heating had gone wrong, it was freezing.'

The men all looked from Karen to Rosie, and for the first time she had come home they saw colour in her face. She was red to the ears.

'You weren't there, were you?'

Rosie thrust the chair back as she rose hastily to her feet, and looking down at Karen, she said, 'No, I wasn't there, Miss Mischief-maker. Now are you satisfied?'

'You didn't go to Mass? Then why did you say you did?' Hannah was standing with her arms held stiffly some distance from her sides. It was an attitude of surprise, which made her look ludicrously like a cowboy waiting to draw.

117

Rosie turned to her mother, and the restraint sounded in her tone as she answered, 'Because I thought it would save being asked a number of questions. I am tired of being peppered with questions.'

'Who in the name of God is peppering you with questions? What has come over you, girl? What I want now is just a straightforward answer to a straightforward question. Why didn't you go to Mass?'

'I can't give you a straightforward answer, Ma, it would be too involved.' There was that word again, involved. It would seem that everything was involved with something else; you couldn't speak or move unless you involved someone.

'Involved?'

'Oh, be quiet. Be quiet.' Broderick thrust out his hand and pulled at Hannah's skirt. 'Leave the lass be. She didn't want to go to Mass and that's that.'

Hannah tore her skirt from her husband's grasp and, turning on him, she cried, 'There's no child of mine goin' to miss Mass unless I know the reason why.'

'I think I'll go to bed,' said Jimmy, rising to his feet. 'Where's the papers?'

'And me along o' you,' put in Shane.

As their chairs scraped back from the table Hannah swept her glance over her entire family, and cried at them, 'What's this house comin' to anyway, that me wishes are flaunted by every damn member of it? I work me brain, body and guts out from Monday mornin' till Sunday night tryin' to further the lot of you, and what's me thanks? Hair raised because I want to move you to decent quarters, and now lies thrust at me when I ask an ordinary question.' She flicked her eyes reproachfully at Rosie, and, her voice dropping suddenly to almost a pathetic whimper, she ended, 'I didn't deserve it, lass, I didn't deserve it.'

Rosie, putting her hand tightly across her mouth, lowered her head and hurried from the room, and Hannah stood looking towards the open door for a moment before her voice, no longer holding the pathetic note, bawled at them, 'There's something radically wrong in this house. Radically wrong, I say.'

'There always is when she's home.' Karen's thin voice had hardly finished this statement when Hannah was upon her. With one hand gripping her shoulder, she pulled her from the chair as if she was an empty paper bag, and swinging her round she brought her other hand with a ringing slap across the girl's face.

'Here! Here!'

'My God, Ma!'

'Let up, Ma. Hell! What's come over you?'

'There was no call for that.'

All except Broderick and Hughie, one after the other, the men reproached her, but Broderick looked at his wife, a look that brought her to her senses quicker than all reasonable talk could have done. He drew Karen towards him and, putting his arms about her stiff body, said, 'There, there, your grannie didn't mean it.' He had no need to say, 'Don't cry,' because Karen wasn't crying.

Hannah now, looking from her husband into the accusing faces of her sons, swept her eyes over them as if they were of no account, and her gaze came to rest on Hughie, where seemingly unperturbed he was still eating, and as she moved up the table towards him, pushing Shane aside from her path, she addressed his bent head, crying, 'And you! Why don't you do somethin'? Why don't you protest in some way and tell me what a wicked woman I am an' to keep me hands to meself? No, no, you couldn't could you, you gutless sod, you!'

Slowly Hughie rose to his feet. His face very white and strained, he looked at Hannah. All the eyes in the room were upon him, and the men without exception were wondering how he would react to this last insult. He had stood something, had Hughie. Then all of them saw his reaction. It was silent yet yelled aloud. They saw his lip moving upwards leaving his teeth bare; it was as if he were looking upon something repulsive.

No-one moved as he turned from her and walked out of the room, but he was hardly through the door when she lifted up the plate which still held most of his pudding and hurled it after him. It went right through the open door and hit the far wall of the hall. The impact was the only sound in the house before Hannah rent the place with her screaming.

Monday

On Monday morning, the house to themselves again, Hannah, standing before Rosie, said 'I'm sorry,' and the humility in her voice was real, at least momentarily, she believed, but there was something almost obscene about it, something that caused the stomach to tense, the lids to droop, the head to bow. She couldn't look at her, but she said, 'It's all right. It's all right.' Then quickly she added, 'I'm going to Newcastle to see about a job, there's an agency there. And . . . and I'll pay you back when . . .'

'Aw, don't say that, don't keep on about the money, lass, it'll only make me think you're still mad at me. I don't want no payin' back; you know I'd give you the shirt off me back. All I want you to do is to do well for yourself and not take up with riff-raff, not even to walk the length of the street with them. You look a lady, you are a lady, all I live for is to see you in your right settin' and actin' like one.'

'Oh, Ma, be quiet.'

'I needn't be quiet on this point, lass.' Hannah's voice was moderate. 'I can talk as long as I like this way because it's true, and it's from me heart. All I live for is to see you marry well, with a position you can be proud of. It . . . it was that lass' – she put her fingers out tentatively towards Rosie's hand – 'it was that that made me go off me head yesterday, thinking of you walkin' in the same step along of him.'

'Hughie?' Rosie thrust her head up and to the side as she asked the question.

'Aye . . . Hughie.'

'But, Ma, I was brought up with Hughie; what have you against him?'

'Aw, you'll know some day, I suppose. But in the meantime it angers me to see you drawin' in the same air. Keep away from him, that's all I ask you.'

'But what has he done, Ma, that you should go on at him like this? I've never known Hughie say a wrong word, I've never heard him even swear.'

'You don't have to swear, me lass, to be bad.'

'But Hughie's not bad, Ma.'

Because of the defence in Rosie's voice Hannah was unable to control her natural aggressiveness, and she cried now, 'You know nothing about it. And another thing, don't keep defending him or I can't be responsible for me tongue. Aw, lass' – her voice dropped – 'all I want is your well-being and to be proud of you. Is it too much to ask?'

Rosie shook her head helplessly; then turning away said, 'I'll be going, Ma. I'll get lunch in the town.'

'All right, lass, all right.' Hannah patted her arm affectionately. 'I'll have something tasty made for you when you come back. About what time will you be in?'

'Oh . . . I don't know. If there's anything on the books I'll go after it.'

'Now don't take the first thing they offer you, mind. With your qualifications you can pick and choose, you can that.'

'Jobs are not so easy to get here, Ma.'

'They are for somebody like you.' Her mother smiled fondly at her, so fondly it was unbearable.

As she left the house, with Hannah bidding her a loud farewell from the top step, the third door to the right of them opened and a woman came out. She was wearing a cheap fur coat and a blue felt hat, and Hannah hailed her with, 'Oh, there you are, Jessie. You haven't seen Rosie here since she was back. Are you away down the town? So's she. You can go together. Where are you off to?'

The woman paused on her step, and looking over the railings, she answered Hannah in a voice prim and tight-sounding by saying simply, 'Hello there, Rosie.'

'Hello, Aunt Jessie.'

'Where you off to?' Hannah called again. And Jessie MacFarlane replied in a tone edged now with superiority, 'The ladies of the bazaar committee are having a coffee morning.'

Hannah's natural retort to this should have been, 'Are they, begod! There'll be some throats cut there this mornin',' but what she said was, 'Oh, that's nice, that's nice. Enjoy yourself.' And now she turned her attention to Rosie again, saying, 'Away you go now, Rosie, an' have a grand day, an' have another look at that fur stole. You know. . . .' She pointed her fingers down the steps at Rosie's back. 'The one you were admiring on Saturday. Go in and try it on.'

Rosie did not bother to ask her mother 'What stole?' but she went down the street towards the plump-faced woman, who was waiting for her, and said, 'Isn't it cold, Aunt Jessie?'

'Yes, it is,' said Jessie MacFarlane. And with this they walked down the street side by side.

At the corner Jessie MacFarlane said in a tone she attempted to make light, 'And how long are you here for this time, Rosie?'

'Oh, I don't know, Aunt Jessie,' said Rosie; 'I may get a post nearer home.' As she said this she felt the woman pause in her walk, but she didn't look towards her and she added kindly, 'But not too near; Fellburn seems to get smaller every time I see it.'

'Yes, yes, we're rather a backwater.' It was a statement without bitterness.

Again they walked on in silence, until Jessie MacFarlane could contain herself no longer and she began to talk rapidly under her breath. 'Ronnie's settled,' she said. 'He's got a good wife, she's not my choice, but she's a good girl and she's going to have a child. Things are going smoothly. I . . . I would sooner have had you than anybody, Rosie, and I think you know it, but you saw it otherwise. My Ronnie was a man when he was going with you and he's still a man, although now when he's got responsibility he'll be different. Yet men are men, you know what I mean?' She was staring ahead, her lips scarcely moving as she spoke. 'What I'm trying to say, Rosie, is you . . . you'll not get in his way?'

When Rosie answered she, too, looked ahead. 'I can promise you, Aunt Jessie,' she said quietly, 'I'll not get in his way.'

'Thank you, lass.' The voice was no longer prim, it was ordinary and thick with the North Country inflection. 'When your mother rushed in on Friday night full of the news that you had come home it was as if she was pushing a knife in me, and she took the same pleasure in it. Your mother's a queer woman, Rosie. I've said it to her face, so I'm sayin' nothing behind her back. You were hardly indoors but she had to come and tell me. It was the same when you came home last year. And after knowing all the trouble that there was, and the lads fighting like maniacs in the lane after they had all been brought up together. Ronnie could hold his own with any two of them, but with the four of them it's a wonder they didn't murder him.'

Rosie could have said at this stage, 'It's a wonder he didn't murder me,' but her Aunt Jessie, like all mothers, wouldn't think along those lines. Again she said, 'You needn't worry; if I get a job anywhere near, I won't live in the town, I'll live well away. . . .' She turned quickly and looked at the older woman. 'But don't tell that last bit to me mother, she . . . she thinks I'll be living at home?'

Jessie MacFarlane stopped; a thin smile spread over her features and she nodded at Rosie. 'Never fear, I won't. I've got to leave you here,' she said, 'the café's just down the road. You were always a good lass, Rosie. I wish things could have been different.'

'Me too, Aunt Jessie.'

'Goodbye, Rosie.'

'Goodbye, Aunt Jessie.'

The world seemed full of worried and troubled people. She wasn't the only one with things to hide. Her Aunt Jessie had always hidden the fact that there was something raw and ravenous about Ronnie. She had hidden the fact that he had attacked a girl when he was fifteen, in much the same way as he had attacked her, in a blind fit of lust.

It had started to snow again when she reached the main road, and as she stood waiting for the bus she could see, between two rows of houses, the rising fells, snow spread, clean, beautiful, untouched by the slag heaps that decorated both sides of the town, where at one end stood the Phoenix pit and at the other the Venus pit. She hadn't been on the fells for years, not since that Sunday when the two men had pulled Ronnie from her and he had fallen on to the grass, crumpled and sobbing like a whipped child, while she had crawled and stumbled like some terrified animal up the dell, and then had run until she came to the first house, where the woman who had been working in the garden caught hold of her and took her indoors and covered her with a coat. And she and her husband had taken her home in their car.

Then Ronnie, driven by his love for her, that was a thing apart from his desires, had come to say he was sorry and the lads had attacked him like a pack of wolves. It had happened in the back garden. If Ronnie had not been of the size and stamina he was, and if her father had not intervened with a pick shaft in his hand, there would have been murder done that day.

Her mother had really been glad that it was finished between her and Ronnie, for, as she had said comfortingly, she was worth something better than a miner. That was until she had heard she was leaving home, and then she would have given her sanction to the dustman to come courting her daughter, if it meant keeping her within sight and sound. . . .

When she reached the agent's in Newcastle it was to

126

find that there were a number of typists required but all for junior positions, and these at a wage rate that made her raise her brows. Did she want to try for them? asked the clerk.

No, she said, she would wait. She had two years London experience working in a big office. Her shorthand speed was one hundred and twenty words a minute and her typing speed eighty words a minute, and she had been used to working with an electric typewriter.

The clerk's nostrils had dilated as he said, 'Well, we've got electric typewriters here an' all. We're not still in the Dark Ages, you know.'

She had apologised and said she hadn't meant anything, but the facts were she had started in London at nine pounds a week and had risen to twelve, and she had been next to the head in her department. She thought there was no need to explain that the staff in her particular department numbered four.

'Well,' said the clerk, 'there might be something in your line in the new factory they're building yon side of Jesmond. It's a way out from the centre of town though.'

'I'll try it,' she said.

It took her half an hour to get to the factory and another fifteen minutes walking around frozen humps of brick and machinery before she found an office with someone in it. The man was busy and abrupt. He said they were interviewing people for the clerical staff on Wednesday afternoon. She could come back if she liked. She thanked him and returned to the town, outwardly freezing with the cold, and inwardly feeling so lost, so alone, that she could have leant her head against the wall and cried.

Since yesterday morning when she had broken down in front of Hughie, the tears had never been far from her eyes. She seemed to be crying inside all the time now and wanting to give vent to it. Her body and mind felt sore, so sore that she recoiled from human contact. A man sat down beside her in the bus, and her body shrank inside her clothes and she was fearful that it would be evident and the man would look at her and say scornfully, 'You needn't move away, Miss, I'm not lousy.' He would have said something like this because he was wearing greasy working clothes; a mac that had once been fawn and was now black, a cap that had lost its shape under grease and dirt. Nevertheless, it was an enviable uniform, one that signified he was at work in some yard.

When she reached the city she was too late for lunch, so she went into a café and had a cup of tea and a sandwich. Afterwards she walked round the stores until the light faded. She had no desire to hurry home, at least not before the men came in; she didn't want to be alone with her mother again. . . .

It was half past five when she entered the house, and the brightness and the smell of fresh baking brought its own comfort. Hannah greeted her with, 'By lass, I thought you were never comin'. Everything all right?'

'Yes, Ma.'

Hannah was placing plates, piled high with bread, on the table. Her father, Arthur and Shane were already in the room, and it was Shane who said, 'Any luck, Rosie?'

128

'No, Shane; but there may be on Wednesday. They're taking on clerical staff at the new factory.'

'Come and get yourself warm.' Her father held out a crooked arm towards her, and when she went to him he pulled her into its circle and squeezed her waist. 'By, you're cold, you're froze. Just feel your hands.' He took her hands in his and chafed them together, rubbing warmth into them.

'I've made your favourite,' Hannah called over her shoulder as she went towards the kitchen, 'apple puddin'. Did you have a nice lunch?'

'Not bad, Ma.'

'Aw, you can't get a decent bite in them cafés and places. I've done you some plaice cooked in butter, t'would melt in your mouth.'

'Begod!' Broderick bounced his head at Rosie in mock anger. 'Plaice done in butter, t'would melt in your mouth, and apple pudding, at tea time at that. She never puts herself out like that for us, does she?' He appealed to his sons, and they grinned at her and Arthur said, 'Bread and scrape, that's us.'

It would seem that they had all regained their good humour, that there was no issue about Brampton Hill, and that the incident at Sunday dinner had never happened.

'Lucky if we get the bread sometimes from the old faggot.' Shane spoke loudly so that his mother should hear, and he pulled his head into his shoulders and slanted his eyes towards the kitchen like a child waiting for a clout.

'I can hear you in there; I've got me ears cocked to your slanderin'.'

Rosie looked at her father, and he smiled warmly back, and leaning his face in an endearing gesture against hers, he whispered the familiar phrase, 'She's over the moon, over the moon to have you back to do for.'

'Now if Jimmy and Barny will put their noses in the door, we're all set.' Hannah came marching into the kitchen carrying a great soup dish of stew, and as she placed it on the table the sound of the back door opening made her turn her head, and she cried, 'Is that you?'

Barny's voice answered her, saying, 'Aye.'

'It's Barny,' she said. 'Jimmy won't be far behind. Come on!' she called. 'The tea's ready.'

Hannah was dishing out the stew when Barny came into the room, and it was the way Arthur's face screwed up as he looked at his brother that made her turn towards her youngest son. In a glance, she took in trouble. She placed the ladle in the dish and, facing him, said, 'What's up?'

He passed her without speaking, and he passed Broderick, with his arm still round Rosie's waist, and he went to the fire and held his hands out to the blaze before saying, 'I've got the push, a week's notice.'

The whole room was alerted, and there were exclamations from them all, except Rosie, but Hannah's was the most strident. Questioning and commanding at the same time, she cried, 'Turn yourself about and tell us what's happened. They didn't come here. Did they find anythin' on you?'

'No.' Barny was looking at her.

'What then?'

'Somebody must have croaked.'

130

'So that's it!' Her jaws pressed themselves through her thick skin, and as she nodded her head Broderick asked Barny, 'Do you know who?'

'It's one of five. Well, you could say four. Creeping Jesus wouldn't split. But he's been kept on with the other four.'

'Twenty-five of you got it then?' It was Arthur asking the question, and Barny nodded. 'Aye, the whole shop's closed. They've been talkin' about reorganizing for months now, and they've taken this opportunity to do it.'

'You can't be sure, man,' said Broderick. 'They might be re-forming the shops at that.'

'Aw, hell, Da.' Barny shook his head impatiently. 'Every man-jack that got his cards was in on it.'

'Did they find anythin' out?' asked Hannah.

'They searched two places. Old Riley's, him whose son-in-law has the wireless store in the market.'

'Did they find anythin'?'

'Plenty, but nothing that Riley couldn't prove he had bought as seconds.'

'How was that? You made up and sold him sets yourself,' said Hannah.

'Aye, but all that stuff is packed away in a little warehouse he's got down near the docks.'

'It's as well for him.' Broderick nodded slowly.

'Well, it hasn't saved him or any of us,' said Barny bitterly.

'What are the others doin' about it?' asked Hannah now. 'Aren't they standin' by you?'

'Huh! Don't make me laugh. The other shops have all become so bloody virtuous of a sudden they make

131

you want to retch. Two years ago, even a year this time, an' they would have been out to the last man if one of us had got our cards, but now,' he pulled his chin into his neck and finished scornfully, 'They're so bloody scared of losin' their jobs, it's who can suck up the hardest and fastest.'

'What about Fred Ward? He's your shop steward, isn't he?' asked Shane, and for answer Barny turned round and spat into the heart of the fire. 'That's for him,' he said, 'him and his parables, I'll push one down his bloody throat the first chance I get. "You weren't content with tiddlers," he said, "but must try to ram carp into your jam jars." I'd like to carp him, begod! I would.'

'Is that all you got out of him?' Hannah's voice was bitter.

'That's all.'

'Well.' Broderick had loosened his hold on Rosie, and now he looked down at the hearth-rug and swung his head from side to side before saying, 'You couldn't expect the chap to do much more about it, could you now?' Then lifting his eyes to his son, he asked, 'And what did Mr Nicholas say?'

Barny looked away from his father before he answered, 'He said nowt to me, but he told Harry Brown that if the boss hadn't been a fair-minded chap who didn't like trouble we'd have been up in court, every damned one of us.'

'So they were on to it really?' said Arthur.

'What do you think?' Barny replied bitterly. Then squaring his shoulders he added, 'Aw, to hell! It might be the best thing that's happened to me. I've had an idea in me head for some time, and now I'll likely do somethin' about it.'

'What is it?' said Hannah. Then turning to the table again she picked up the ladle, saying, 'You can talk while you eat, there's good food being wasted. Come, sit up all of you.'

When they were all served and Hannah herself had sat down, she looked at Barny and asked, 'Well, now, what's this idea of yours? Spit it out. Unlike me family, I welcome new ideas.'

Barny did not pick up this last remark but said simply, 'It's Leonard's shop, you know round in Brookland Street, just off the market.'

'The electric shop you mean?' said Arthur.

'Aye.' Barny nodded. 'Well, he died about three months ago, and since then his wife's been trying to sell. It would have gone like hot cakes a few years ago but now things are tight. And there's another thing, most people who take on places like that know damn all about the inside of the things they sell, but me being able to make most of me own stuff, well I've always felt if I had the chance I would make a go of it. I know I would.' He turned and looked at Hannah, and Hannah looked at him for a moment before dropping her eyes to her plate and beginning to eat.

'You don't think much of it, Ma?' Barny's voice was nervous, quiet.

'Well, I know nowt about it yet, do I? But a shop. Aw, shops are tricky businesses.'

'But people make good livin's out of them. Look at them in the main thoroughfares with their fifteen hundred pound cars changed every year, and their trips abroad.

Look at the Parnells that started just after the war with that little furniture shop; they're rolling in it now; they've got a chain of over twenty of them.'

'We're far past the war, boy.' Hannah went on eating steadily.

'I think it's an idea.' Broderick wagged his fork towards Barny. 'I do indeed. There's no-one cleverer than you with the innards of wirelesses and televisions.'

Barny smiled at his father. 'It's only a small place, but it's got a good stock. I've been in once or twice lately, just looking round.'

'How much do they want for it?' asked Arthur.

'Well, the shop's on lease.' Barny swallowed. 'The rent's four pounds a week and rates.' Again he swallowed.

'But what will she want for the stock?' said Shane.

'Five hundred pounds.' It was a bald statement.

'Five hundred pounds!' The sound seemed to shoot from the top of Hannah's grey hair.

'It's not a lot really, not to get a start.' Barny's voice was low and his tone slightly on the defensive. 'Anyway, I could raise a bit, I dare say, if it's necessary. How much have I got put by, Ma?'

'How much have you got put by!' Hannah screwed up her eyes at him as if she didn't quite take in the question.

'Aye.' His tone was sharp now. 'How much have you saved for me?'

'Oh that . . . that. Well now, I can't tell you off-hand, I don't reckon it up every day, but I should say on the spur of the moment something between fifty and seventy-five pounds.'

134

'WHAT!' Barny pushed his chair back from the table and the sound on the linoleum was like a stone rasping glass, and it affected them all. Except perhaps Barny himself, for he was being affected in another way. 'Aw, come off it, Ma. You pulling me leg or summat? I've been in steady work for over three years now and never earned less than fifteen a week, and a damn sight more most of the time.'

'Now look here, look here, me lad.' Hannah, too, had risen from the table, the knife in her hand, and she wagged it at him. 'What was the arrangement, tell me that? Divided in three, we all said. One part for your keep and your working clothes, another for your pocket, and t'other to put by and to buy your good things out of.'

'I know all about that, Ma. But what working clothes have you bought me, I ask you that?'

'Two pairs of dungarees you've had, and the oilskin overalls for your motor-bike.'

'Aw, my God, that's over two years ago, Ma.'

'And then out of your savings as you call them, you've had two suits, fifteen pounds a piece they were, two pairs of shoes to go with them not counting a number of shirts and other odds and ends.'

'All right, all right, Ma.' He was holding himself in check now. 'Say I've had fifty pounds worth of clothes . . .'

'Fifty pounds! Begod, you're a cheap jack. Make it a hundred and you'll be nearer the mark.'

Barny closed his eyes and thumped his forehead with his fist, and still with his eyes closed and his fist to his head, he said, 'All right, say a hundred pounds. Take a

135

hundred pounds off two hundred and fifty and that leaves a hundred and fifty. And that's for only one year. You've been saving for me for three years; I reckoned on four hundred pounds up there.' He thumbed the ceiling. 'Or nearer five.'

'God Almighty and his Holy Mother!' Hannah collapsed with a thud on to the chair. 'Four hundred pounds . . . nearly five!' She appealed from one face to another of her family, but when she looked at Rosie, her daughter had her face turned away. And now with her arms across the table, her hands out-stretched, supplicating, towards them, she asked, 'Who's paid for the fine new furniture we've got, and the carpets that are in every nook and cranny of this house bar this room? And who's paid for the new bedding?'

Barny shouted back at her, 'I know, I know all that, but we've all had to fork out towards them. It wouldn't all come out of mine, would it? . . . Now look here, Ma.' His voice dropped. 'I should have a few hundred up there.'

Rosie, being unable to stand any more, picked up her plate from the table and went into the kitchen, there to see Hughie standing by the stove. It was evident from the look on his face that he had heard a good deal of what had happened in the living-room, also that in the hubbub his entry had gone unnoticed.

As Rosie put her plate on the table she whispered, 'Oh, Hughie!' and the words were laden with shame. At this moment she was not only ashamed of her mother, she felt she disliked her, even hated her. Nearly three thousand pounds in that drawer upstairs, and denying Barny his bit of savings. Surely she couldn't think the lads were so stupid. But apparently she did. She had just to yell and shout and point to what she had bought and she could convince them of where the money had gone.

'Don't let it trouble you,' Hughie was whispering back at her now.

'But, Hughie, she's got it.' She did not feel that she was giving her mother away to him by saying this.

'I know, I know.' One eyebrow moved up. It seemed to tell her that he knew as much as she did.

As Hannah's voice reached a blaring peak, he pushed Rosie gently from the table, saying, 'Go on in, go on.' And she turned quickly from him and did as he bade her. She knew he didn't want her mother to come in and see them together. As she entered the living-room Hannah was again appealing to the family as a whole, crying at them, 'I want the few pounds saved to get us out of this. We can't move up the Hill on goodwill.'

'Who the hell wants to move up the Hill?' Barny was squarely confronting his mother now. 'Here's one who doesn't. I've told you afore I don't want to leave here, and I'm not going to; we've made enough moves up the ladder I think to satisfy you.'

When he stopped speaking there was a quivering, uneasy silence in the room. And then Hannah, her voice now quiet but intense, said, 'Of all the ungrateful sods in this world, I've bred a bunch of them. For years I've slaved the living daylights out of meself, and what for? What for, I ask you? To make you respected, looked up to.' The tone was rising, and as Rosie passed from the room through the hall on her way upstairs the crash of her mother's fist on the table and the sound of the jangling dishes caused her to start and shrink as if from a blow.

Up in her room, she looked at the evidence of her mother's generosity. The two new cases, the two dresses, the shoes and stockings and underwear, not to mention the coat she had worn today. She had spent forty-seven pounds as if they were pennies, and joyed in doing it. Yet there she was downstairs denying Barny his savings, and all because she was determined to have her way and buy the flat on Brampton Hill. There wasn't a doubt in Rosie's mind but that Barny would make a go of a wireless and television shop if he got the chance. But what prestige would there be in such a shop in a back street for her mother? There would be nothing to show off or brag about in that.

There was an easy chair in the room that hadn't been there when she left this morning. Her mother must have humped it up at least two flights of stairs. She sat on the side of her bed and looked at it; evidence of a reasoning she knew now that had sent her eldest brother, Patrick, to Australia, and Colin to Canada, that had made Michael leave a good job here for one in Cornwall at half the wage. The same reasoning that had frustrated Dennis for years and made him bitter, the reasoning that had scorned his intelligence. The reasoning that pointed the finger of sin at Arthur's association with a married woman and which had intimidated him so much that he was really afraid to do what he desired, and go and live with her. The reasoning that was now determined to deprive Barny of making a living in the way he wanted to. The reasoning had not yet touched Shane or Jimmy

138

simply because, as yet, they had made no protest against her. The reasoning that made fiddling almost a virtue every day in the week except Sunday.

Then there was Hughie and Karen. Her mother's reasoning, Rosie thought, had made very little, or no impact, on Karen, for Karen had in her a great deal of Hannah herself. Added to this, she had a sharp intelligence. This advantage had, it was supposed, been inherited from Karen's father, a mysterious figure, who was never mentioned, and who had been known only to Moira.

And Hughie? The one person in the house who had always borne the weight of her mother's spleen, derision and unreasonable reasoning. And in his case one had to ask, Why? Why?

Now and again over the years she had wondered, but just vaguely, about Hughie. Why, for instance, did he stand her mother? Why did he always take a back seat? Why did he scarcely open his mouth in the house? To a stranger in the house he must have appeared like a numbskull. But Hughie was no numbskull. She had always known it, and that had been made evident in the back shop yesterday morning. Look at that piece of writing. Who would think Hughie could work things out like that? Certainly no-one in this house.

What, she thought now, would be her mother's reaction when she learned he had come into money? She could almost feel the bitterness and rage that the irony of the situation would arouse in her at a time when she needed money, real money, to further the ambition of her life, when the last person in the world she could have relied on to further that ambition was now . . . rolling in it. . . . Well, if not rolling in it, he must have come into enough to set him on his feet.

Rosie rubbed her hand up and down her cheek. She only hoped she wasn't in the house when he told her mother. For no matter how she felt about her she wouldn't be able to bear watching her reaping what she had sown.

Tuesday

But Rosie was in the house when, later on Tuesday, Hughie told her mother.

In the lull that followed the exodus of the men to work Hannah was busying herself with the washing-up and tidying of the rooms. When Rosie came downstairs Hannah just bade her good-morning and asked how she had slept. Her manner, tellingly quiet, forbade any questioning at this point, so nothing concerning last night's row or the bottom drawer of the chest was mentioned until sometime later in the morning, when, dressed for outdoors, Rosie went to her and said, 'I'm going into Newcastle, Ma, to have a look round.'

'You're going out in this?' Hannah was in the kitchen hacking at a large shin of beef, and wiping the blood from her hands, she added, 'It's snowing again, lass. I thought you said Wednesday.'

'Oh, there are plenty of other places to try.'

As Rosie went towards the back door Hannah said appealingly, 'Aw, come out the front, come out the front, lass.' As if it made just that difference which way her daughter went out, she led the way into the hall; then, with her hand on the front-door latch, she turned to her and said quietly, 'There's no hurry, you know, lass; there's no hurry. In fact, I don't see why you want to take a job outside at all. You could give me a hand in the house, and we would come to an arrangement.' She nodded knowingly. 'There I am, paying that Mrs Pratt a pound every Friday to do down, and begod, there's never a time I haven't to go behind her after she's gone.'

'Thanks, Ma, but I . . . I couldn't . . . Anyway, I couldn't stay in the house all day. You see, I've been used to going out, and I want to earn my own living.'

Hannah, her face unsmiling now, but her expression disarmingly soft, said, 'You're not holding it against me about last night, are you? You see, I know Barny. Lass, if I'd given him the lot it would've been blued one way or another within a few months. . . . Aw, I know me lads; they haven't got the sense they were born with, not one of them, where money's concerned anywhere. . . . And women. Although I've got nothing to say against Betty.' The inference was against Dennis's wife, and the mercurial change that came over Hannah's face for an instant expressed this fully.

'But, Ma.' Rosie looked straight at Hannah. 'As Barny said, his share must go into a few hun –'

'Now look here!' Hannah was flapping her fingers within a few inches of Rosie's face. The action was annoying in itself, and Rosie moved her head to one side away from their contact as her mother exclaimed again, 'Now look, lass, leave this to me, I know how to deal with me family. Barny won't go short, you needn't worry about that, but he's not going to throw money down the drain. He may be out of work for weeks – he has been afore and I've never thrown it up at him.'

As Rosie turned away she thought, No, but you took every penny of his dole.

142

Opening the door, Hannah said under her breath, 'You understand me, lass, now don't you?'

Rosie nodded, saying, 'Bye-bye, Ma.'

'Bye-bye, lass. . . . But look' – she blinked at the falling snow – 'you can hardly see your hand afore you, you shouldn't be going out in this.'

'I like the snow. I'll be back by tea. Bye-bye.'

'Bye-bye, lass. Bye-bye.'

You understand me, lass, her mother had said. She had thought that the experience she had endured these last few months had stretched her mind so that she could now understand all the intricacies of human behaviour. Badness, she had discovered, was relative. Everything was relative to something else. She understood that now. But even so she couldn't understand her mother. Her mother was too subtle. Yet some would say she was simple because she was ignorant – but her mother wasn't simple.

As Rosie said, she liked snow, but not to wander about in it all day, and not wanting to return home before the others were in, she spent the time during the afternoon in going to see a film. So it was just on six o'clock when she alighted from the bus in the market place. There were a number of men waiting to get on the bus. They weren't queueing orderly but standing in a bunch, and as she made her way through them a hand came out and caught her arm; not roughly, yet the action almost made her scream. In the driving snow and dim light she did not recognise Ronnie for a moment, and when she did she dragged on her breath, filling her lungs with short gulps of air . . . and also with relief, for she had thought . . . she had thought . . .

'I'm sorry, Rosie, I . . . I didn't mean to startle you but you didn't see me.'

'It's all right,' she said. And then turning her head towards the bus, she pointed: 'It's going, you'll miss it.'

'It doesn't matter. I'd rather have a word with you.'

She stood silent, waiting, while he looked at her, an undying hunger and ever-present remorse in his look. 'Don't be frightened of me, Rosie,' he said.

'I'm not frightened.' Her voice was soft, reassuring; and she meant what she said, for she wasn't afraid any more of Ronnie. At one time she had thought he was bad, but now she knew there was badness and badness, and if she had been forced to choose between the types of badness she knew she would take Ronnie's kind gratefully. Yet when he went to touch her, her whole body recoiled from him, and he stood, his hand half-outstretched, stiff, as was his voice when he said, 'You're not frightened of me but you're wary. That's it, isn't it? I'm not safe, can't be trusted.'

'Oh, Ronnie.'

'Oh, I don't blame you. But Rosie –' He moved, almost imperceivably, nearer to her. 'I've got to tell you. I . . . I can't get you out of me mind. I can't for one minute. I thought getting married an' that. . . . But it was no use. I'm in a hell of a mess inside, Rosie . . . Rosie, I've got to see you.'

'No, no.' Her voice was harsh, even grating. 'You're married and that's that.' She stepped aside from him. 'I said no, Ronnie, and I don't want any more trouble.'

'Just to see you now and again to have a word . . . ?'

'I said no.' She was some feet from him now. 'I'll be

144

leaving the town shortly, anyway, and I won't be coming back.'

As she watched his head slowly move downwards she darted away and ran across the open market square to where a bus was standing that would take her to the top of their street. She was trembling as she sat down. She was still trembling when the conductor came for her fare. 'Enough to kill a horse, this,' he said. 'It's no wonder there's nobody out. You look froze.'

She said she was. She wished he would leave her and go down the bus; men could always find excuses to talk.

When she entered the house her mother's voice did not greet her tonight, but she heard it coming from the living-room, saying, 'I don't believe a word of it.' She took off her wet things and hung them on the rack behind the kitchen door, and she was stroking her damp hair from her forehead when she entered the living-room.

Only her father addressed her immediately. 'Some night, isn't it, lass? Are you froze? Come to the fire.'

As she made her way to the fire her mother turned from the four men at the table, saying, 'Have you heard anything about this?'

'About what?' asked Rosie.

'About him, Hughie, buying a car and a caravan? Shane here's just come in and told us that he's bought a car and a caravan . . . Hughie. Did you ever hear the like of it?'

'I tell you, Ma,' said Shane, 'it's a fact.' He looked around his brothers now. 'It was as I said, up came Robbie Gallagher and he said, "Your brother" – he thought Hughie was me brother – he said, "Your brother's done well for himself with our Paul's car and

145

caravan." And like I said, I told him he'd made a mistake, and he said, "Your brother keeps a cobbler's shop, doesn't he? And his name is Hughie, isn't it?" "Aye," I said. "Well," he said, "he's bought our Paul's Land-Rover and caravan for five hundred quid. He bought them just two years ago but there was still some to pay off. Your brother saw to that and gave him five hundred for the two. But he's still got a bargain." '

Hannah was looking from one to the other but she wasn't seeing them, 'The swine's been cocky this past few weeks.' She looked at her husband now and asked, 'Does he do the pools?'

'How should I know, woman? I've never been with him this last ten years.'

'Well, does he?' She turned to her sons, and one after the other they shook their heads.

'Not that I know,' said Jimmy. 'I asked him to go in the club syndicate, but he said he hadn't the cash.'

'Five hundred pounds! FIVE HUNDRED POUNDS!' Hannah was blinking. 'And anybody who spends five hundred pounds on a car an' caravan has more than five hundred pounds. It would be just like him to have a win and keep it to himself. . . . But what would he be wanting a car and a caravan for?' She was now addressing Shane.

'Search me, unless he's goin' touring. Aye, likely that's what he's going to do. When I come to think about it, he used to be always sending away for travel catalogues. You remember?' He jerked his head at Jimmy.

Jimmy said, 'Aye. Aye, come to think of it, the back shop used to be full of 'em.'

'Well, if he's had a win,' said Broderick, knocking

146

the dottle from his pipe against the bars of the fire, 'good luck to him. Aye, I say good luck to him. I only hope it will be my turn next. And if it is' – he straightened up and thrust out his hand towards Rosie's chin – 'I'll take me daughter to Paris and we'll do the sights. Begod! We would, wouldn't we, Rosie?'

'Stop talkin' sheelagin, Broderick, for Christ's sake! . . . Now what I'd like to know is where that 'un's got the cash from. And how much. Because . . .'

'Because what?' Broderick was looking at Hannah steadily.

'Never you mind. I'll keep it to meself until I see which way the wind's blowing. In the meantime, sit you all down and get your teas; it will be as cold as clarts in a minute if it isn't already. Oh, lass' – she forced a stiff smile on her face – 'I've left yours in the oven. Would you be goin' gettin' it?'

Rosie went into the kitchen, and as she opened the oven door the back door opened and Hughie entered. With a swift glance towards the other door she went towards him and muttered hastily under her breath, 'They know, Hughie, about the money. Shane heard about the caravan and car.'

Hughie had his cap in his hand and he turned and hung it on the hook on the door next to her coat before looking at her again. His smile was quiet; his whole attitude seemed serene to her, while she herself was feeling strung up and nervous; first from her encounter with Ronnie, and then from the feeling her mother's attitude towards Hughie aroused in her. She went hastily back to the oven and was taking out the plate when again the back door opened, with a thrust this time, which almost knocked Hughie off his feet, and Karen exclaimed as she came in, 'Well, you don't expect me to see through it, do you?' He straightened the sleeve of the coat he was hanging on the door as he said, 'No, I don't.'

Karen was pulling her outdoor things off now, and, looking at Rosie's retreating back, she said, 'It's not a night to linger on the doorstep; it's all right for some people who can stay put all day.'

Rosie hesitated; then glancing quickly over her shoulder said, 'I've just come in.'

'Poor soul! Have you had to battle against the elements an' all? It isn't fair, is it?'

As Rosie went on into the living-room without retorting to this, Karen turned to Hughie staring at her from across the table in a peculiar way, and she asked, 'What you looking at me like that for? I don't happen to be a man so I'm not in love with her. Men are fools . . . formless idiots.' She flounced her body around, but turned it back as swiftly again, saying, 'As for you, you haven't got the gumption you were born with.'

'No, I haven't, have I?'

The admission was disconcerting, and all Karen could say to it was, 'Oh, my God.'

When she entered the living-room, Hannah spoke to her across the room, saying, 'Who is that out there?'

'Hughie, of course. Who else would it be, you're all here?' The sharp, round eyes swept the table, and the voice with which she had answered her grandmother bore no resentment for the blow she had received yesterday. She did not blame Hannah for that. She knew who was to blame.

148

Hannah knew it was Hughie in the kitchen. She had asked a voiceless question of Rosie when she had come back into the room – she had done it with the jerk of her head – and Rosie had answered with a single nod, her eyes downcast.

And when Hughie came in, he came in as he always did, quietly, his whole manner unassuming, not looking towards the table, not looking at anything really.

They were all seated except Hannah. She stood to the side of her chair and she stopped him when he was opposite the fireplace – he was going, as he always did, to bring his chair from the corner to the table. She stopped him by saying, 'Well!'

'Well what?' He was looking straight back at her.

'What's this I'm hearing?'

'I wouldn't know. You don't often tell me any news.'

'Have you or have you not bought a car and a caravan?'

Rosie was looking at Hughie now. She had an odd feeling inside of her, a racing, excited, odd feeling. Whereas yesterday she felt that she wouldn't be able to bear seeing her mother vanquished, now she knew that if Hughie were to come out on top her mother would have to be brought low, and, she wished, oh, she even prayed, that he would show her, show them all what he was really made of, and he could only do that by talking. Oh, if he would only talk as he had talked in the back room of the shop. . . . Talk as he wrote.

And he did. 'Yes, I've bought a caravan and a car.' Hughie looked from Hannah around the staring faces at the table. Jimmy's, Arthur's, Shane's, Barny's, Broderick's, and lastly Karen's. He looked longer at

Karen than at the rest; he did not look at Rosie. And then he was staring at Hannah once more.

'Where did you get the money?'

'I came into it.'

'You – came – into it?'

'That's what I said.'

'Was it a win or something, Hughie?' Broderick's good-tempered tone tried to bring a lightness into the proceedings.

'No, it wasn't a win, Broderick.' Hughie was smiling gently down on the elderly man, who alone in this house had ever gone out of his way to show him a kindness. 'It was a legacy, Broderick.'

'A legacy!' Hannah had grabbed at the lead again. Her eyes screwed up, her brows beetling, her chin pulled in to the deep flesh of her neck, she repeated, 'A legacy! Who, in the name of God, have you got to leave you a legacy, I ask you that?'

'I happen to have had a sister. Perhaps you've forgotten about her.'

'Your sister! But she was no better than . . .' Hannah prevented herself from adding, 'meself'; instead she turned it into 'the rest of us. She went to America as a servant if I remember rightly.'

'She went as a nurse-companion if you remember rightly,' corrected Hughie. 'And she was left some money. But unfortunately she didn't live long enough to enjoy it, and before she died she remembered me.'

Hannah, her eyes still on Hughie, groped at the back of her chair. She wanted very much to sit down but she remained standing.

'When did this happen, Hughie?' It was Arthur on his feet now, coming round the table.

'Oh, some weeks ago, around Christmas time. It takes a while for these things to get settled.'

'By! You're a deep 'un.' Shane, too, had risen to his feet. 'An' keepin' this to yourself all the time,' he said.

'How much did she leave you?' It was the first time Barny had spoken.

'A bit over twenty thousand. Round about twenty-four I should say when everything's settled up.' His tone was quiet but self-assured. He spoke of twenty-four thousand as if he was quite used to thinking in thousands.

For a full minute no-one in the room moved or spoke a word. Each of them was digesting this news, and most of them were wondering what was in it for them, if anything. Strangely it was the two girls who were the exceptions. Karen knew she would get nothing out of Hughie's legacy, for there had always been a mutual dislike between them. She had become aware of it as a small child and reciprocated the feeling in full, but, thinking along the lines of her grandmother, she was saying to herself, God, it would be someone like him who would come into money, a mutt who won't know how to enjoy it.

If Rosie was thinking of the money, it was to the effect that it had put power and courage into Hughie. It had also endowed him with a dignity. His back was straighter, his look even bold, he was no longer afraid of her mother, that's if he had ever been afraid of her. But he must have been, because for some reason or other he had always knuckled down to her.

Rosie saw that her mother was utterly flabbergasted,

but she also saw that she was determined not to show it.

Sitting herself slowly down, Hannah again took charge of the situation. She jerked her head up towards Hughie and said, 'Well, sit down, and tell us what you're going to do.'

Hughie sat down, after going and picking up his chair and bringing it to the table. No-one had said, 'Stay where you are, I'll get it for you.' As much as they would have liked to they hadn't the face to do that, it would look too much like sucking up.

Hughie sat down opposite to Jimmy and Karen. Jimmy's expression was eager, bright. He looked as if he wanted to say something but was withholding it with difficulty. Karen still looked surly. She had the intelligence to know when it was fruitless to beat a dead horse. Shane and Arthur had sat down again, and now they were all around the table like a family. Again Hannah said, 'Well?'

Hughie moved his knife and fork to one side and surveyed them for a moment before looking along the table towards Hannah. 'You want to know what I'm going to do, is that it?' He stared at her while waiting some response from her; but receiving none, he went on, 'As soon as the caravan's ready – I'm having it all rebuilt inside. Jim Cullen's doing it for me.' He turned his head now and addressed himself to Broderick. 'He's a good craftsman, as you know.'

'Oh, you'll get a good job out of old Jim,' said Broderick, nodding his head quickly. 'He's a grand fellow when dealing with wood; you'll get a good job out of him.'

152

'I know that, Broderick.' Hughie turned his gaze slowly back to Hannah again and unhurriedly went on, 'Well, when it's ready, and it should be towards Monday of next week, I'm starting on my travels; that's if the weather allows. Anyway, I'm going to make for the Continent and just jog along where the fancy takes me. . . . That's all.'

They had all been looking at him; now they were all looking at Hannah, their eyes brought to her by the sound of her strong short teeth grinding over each other. They watched the invective rise in her and fill her mouth, and they watched her check it and select words which had to be pressed through her lips to ask him, 'How much are you going to leave behind you?'

'How much? Nothing, not a penny.'

'Ma. . . . Ma, go easy, go easy; give the fellow a chance.' Barny had put his hand across the table towards Hughie, and he brought Hughie's attention away from his mother, saying quickly, 'I'm not asking you for anything, Hughie, but I could do with a loan. Is there any chance? I want to start a shop.'

Hughie's eyes held a kindly expression as they looked back at Barny, but he shook his head twice before he spoke. 'No, Barny, not a chance. But you could still start your shop. Your mother has around four hundred and seventy-five pounds of yours upstairs.'

Barny's hand lifted from the table; his face jerked towards his mother as she jumped to her feet. Then he looked again at Hughie; and Hughie finished evenly, 'I've had nothing much to do these last few years when I was in the house but count up. About four hundred and seventy-five I should say, Barny, would be your share.'

'You dirty sod!' Hannah picked up a knife from the table, and as her arm swung up Jimmy gripped it, crying, 'Here! Steady on. Steady on, Ma.'

'Put the knife down, woman!' Broderick was standing before her. 'Have you gone out of your senses?'

'I'll kill him! I'll kill him! The ungrateful sod that he is. And what money he's got belongs here, for haven't I looked after his offspring for years? He owes me a share of that money, he killed me daughter.'

'Stop it, woman! An' don't talk wild. Stop it! Do you hear me?'

With a jerk of her elbow, Hannah thrust Broderick aside, and because Jimmy was still holding one arm she leant crookedly over the table towards Hughie, crying. 'Do you want me to tell 'em? They'll murder you.'

'Yes, tell them.' Hughie slowly rose from the table; his face had lost it taunting expression. 'You tell them your side of the story and I'll tell them mine, and let them judge. If I hadn't been such a blasted fool that's what I'd have done years ago, and you would have had one less to suck dry then. Go on, tell them. Or will I do it without the hysterics?'

'You rat, you! You bloody mealy-mouthed rat, you!' There was froth gathering at the corner of Hannah's mouth. She turned her furious face now towards Broderick, then flashed her eyes towards her sons, and with her free arm she pointed dramatically at Hughie and cried, 'he raped me daughter, Moira, and she died with his child . . . her there!' She was pointing at Karen.

Again a silence came upon the room, and it would have been broken long before it was if the contortion of features had made any sound, for the faces of the men were twisting with amazement. They looked from their mother to Hughie, then to Karen, and then back to their mother. And it was Jimmy – big, thoughtless Jimmy – who spoke first. 'But, Ma,' he said, his face a mass of bewilderment, 'Moira was eleven years older than me; she was a woman when Hughie was a lad.'

'There you have spoken my defence, Jimmy.' Hughie motioned his head towards the big, puzzled man. 'I was fourteen, not quite fifteen, when I, as your mother put it, raped her eldest daughter. And into the bargain I was a thin, puny lad, as was pointed out to me practically every day, and was always ailing. Moira was twelve stone if an ounce. She came up into the room one night and ate me alive. Granted there was a raping, but I had very little share in it; yet there were results.' He dropped his eyes now to where Karen was staring at him, her full-lipped mouth agape. 'We've never liked each other, Karen,' he said sadly. 'It's a pity. I suppose it was my fault because I blamed you. I was held like any prisoner because of you, and also because' – he smiled wryly now – 'I hadn't, as you said a few minutes ago, any gumption. But whatever gumption I was born with and retained until I was fourteen, she kicked out of me.' He lifted his eyes again to Hannah; then they flicked to Broderick, where the old man stood, his hand to his brow, exclaiming over and over, 'God Almighty! God Almighty!'

'I'm sorry, Broderick, I'm sorry. I wouldn't have had you hurt for the world.'

Hannah gazed around her family in nothing less than blazing amazement. Their reactions were maddening her still further, and she cried at them, 'Well, what are you goin' to do? Standin' there like stuffed dummies!' She tried to pull herself from Jimmy's hold, but he held her fast and shook his head at her. 'Leave go, will you!' She was lifting her other hand, the fist doubled at him, when Broderick spoke to her, calmly, deadly. 'Enough woman, enough,' he said. 'I think whatever Hughie did he's had to pay for.'

'My God!' The words were deep and guttural, as if they were issuing from the throat of a bass singer. At the moment she was seeing no-one but her husband. 'You would turn against me in this. I've carried the load for years, on me own shoulders I've carried this load and you would –'

'I've said be quiet. For your own good, be quiet!' Broderick now turned to Hughie, and his voice still low, he said, 'We want none of your money, Hughie. . . .'

'I know that, Broderick, at least I know you don't. And I wouldn't see you short, only I know you'd never keep it for yourself.'

'What about her? He owes her something.' Hannah was spitting the words out like grit as she pointed to Karen, and Karen snapped her fascinated gaze from Hughie's face, the man who had become her father, and looked at her grannie. A moment ago she had wanted nothing from Hughie because then she thought she stood no chance, but now things were different, she had a claim on him. And when she looked back at him her expression showed this claim and he read it. And he answered it, but looking again at Hannah. 'Not a farthing, not a brass farthing,' he said. 'I paid you for her keep from the day she was born until she started to work. Many's the time I could only meet me board, but you wanted that two pounds for her or else. . . . Yes' – he nodded towards the staring faces that surrounded him – 'two pounds a week I had to pay. Do you wonder now that she had me brought back twice? My wage was four pounds five.' He glanced at Broderick. 'And as the years went on, many a time you had a job to find that, hadn't you, Broderick? But it all went back into the kitty, two pounds for me keep and two pounds for Karen. . . . And you took it, didn't you, Hannah?' His eyes were on her furious face again. 'And let me go around with hardly a rag on me back; and this too' – he nodded at her – 'whilst these last few years the lads were being decked out like lords. Nor did you spare me when Karen started work either. No, I had to pay for the goodwill of the shop then, if I wanted to keep it on, you said. So you had four pounds a week from me.'

'Then why the hell did you put up with it? It's your own fault and it's no use yarping on now.' It was Arthur speaking, and Hughie turned towards him and nodded at him before he said, 'I'm not yarping, Arthur, I'm opening me mouth for the first time in me life in this house. And why did I put up with it? Well, as I said, I hadn't any guts. Time and time again she threatened to tell you all and set you on to me. And' – his lips went into a twisted smile – 'you were all big lads, the lot of you, and somehow I didn't fancy seeing meself battered to death. But there was another reason, a reason none of you would understand because you had what I wanted, what I needed, a family, somebody belonging to you. . . . Well now, I think everything's been said that need be said, so I'll be leaving you . . . I'll . . . I'll just get me things and then . . .'

'Begod! you won't. You won't take a stick out of this house; that's somethin' I can stop you doin'.'

'Oh, very well.' He smiled at her. 'You're welcome to what there is.'

Except for Rosie and Karen, they were all on their feet. Rosie had her hands joined together on the table. The knuckles were showing white and she had her eyes fixed on them.

But now Karen rose from her chair and her movement stopped Hughie from turning about. She was going to speak to him, and he waited, looking at her quietly, even gently, waiting to hear what she had to say. And what she said was, 'I never liked you afore, and I like you less now, and you can keep your money and stick it. I hope it does you some good. You said you had no gumption and you're right, you're gutless. I've often wondered who me father was. But you! You'd be the last man in the world I'd pick for a father. So now you have it.'

'Thank you.' He moved his head as he spoke. 'Over the years I've been glad there was little of me in you, but on the other hand, I was sorry there was so much of your grannie in you.'

On this last shaft, Hughie turned, and amid a moment's silence walked across the room towards the kitchen door, but as he opened it a glass dish, accompanied by the concerted cries of protest from behind him, caught him on the back of the head and sent him flying, covering him at the same time with sliced peaches.

Hannah, with all the power of her big body concentrated in her right hand, had grabbed the thing nearest to her, a heavy glass fruit dish, and she had flung it like

158

a disc, and it had held most of its contents until it reached its object.

Rosie was the first one to reach Hughie. He hadn't fallen but had staggered back against the door. Then her father and Arthur were on either side of him. 'Are you all right, lad?' shouted Broderick above the screaming voice of Hannah and the cries of Jimmy, Shane and Barny, as they restrained her from sending the other articles on the table in the same direction as the glass dish.

Hughie looked dazed. Slowly he flicked a peach from off the lapel of his coat; then pushing his hand out in an assuring gesture towards Broderick, he nodded before going into the kitchen.

'Are you fit enough to go?' Broderick closed the kitchen door behind him as he asked the question.

And Hughie said, 'Yes, I'm all right.'

'Go with him, Arthur,' said Broderick.

Arthur did not speak and Hughie said, 'No. No, thanks, Arthur. I'm all right. I'd rather be on my own. It's nothing.'

'You're bleeding behind the ear, Hughie.' Rosie's voice was full of sympathy.

'Am I?' He still seemed dazed, and when he put his fingers to his neck, then looked at the blood on them, he said, 'Oh, it isn't much.'

She took a tea-towel and wiped the syrup from his jacket, then she held his top coat and he got into it, and as he buttoned it slowly he said, 'Thanks, Rosie, thanks.' And looking at Broderick, he added, 'I'm sorry, Broderick. I shouldn't have done it like this. I'm sorry.'

'I'm sorry too, lad, but it's done. An' you wouldn't

159

have been human not to have hit back. I understand, I understand. But go now, if you're able to.'

Hughie lowered his head, then pulled on his cap and, turning about, went out of the back door.

When he was gone Broderick looked from Arthur to Rosie and said, 'Who'd have believed it? God Almighty, who'd have believed it? Him, Karen's father an' I never knew! All these years livin' with her and I never knew.' He shook his head.

He looked at Rosie now. 'Your mother's a strange woman, lass, a strange woman. She's got power in her that's too big for her body.' Still shaking his head, he turned from her and went towards the room door, and as he opened it the sound of her mother's crying came to Rosie.

Arthur, standing near her, waited until his father had closed the door, then turning to her, he said under his breath, 'This has been an eye-opener for all of us, I'd say. But it's learnt me one thing; she's not going to keep me fastened the same way she did him. You don't blame me, do you?'

Rosie didn't answer his question but whispered back, her voice shaking, 'I think you'd better go after him, he looked dazed, he might collapse in the street, and there'll be few people about tonight.'

Arthur shook his head. 'He won't take it that way, not kindly, he'll think I'm sucking up, an' I don't want any of his bloody money. Not that I don't think he's a mean swine to go off like that. He could have given us all a night at the club to show there was no ill-feeling, that wouldn't have hurt him. No, I'm not goin' after him.' On this, he too went into the living-room, leaving Rosie alone in the kitchen. For a moment or two she stood nipping rapidly at the ends of her fingers, then she pulled her coat off the peg and got quickly into it, and wrapping one of the men's mufflers round her head, she opened the back door quietly and ran, slithering, down the garden path and into the back lane, then along its length and round the corner and into the street. The knowledge that Hughie would likely make for the shop took her in that direction, and she came upon him walking like someone slightly drunk as he crossed the road towards the school.

Gasping for breath from running and the cold snow-filled air, she caught at his arm, saying, 'Hughie, Hughie, are you all right?'

He stopped for a moment in the middle of the road. Then as the headlights of a car approached he moved forward to the opposite pavement, and there he stopped again, peering at her through the dim light. 'You shouldn't have come out a night like this,' he said. 'Go on back, I'm all right.'

'You're neck's all blood.'

'I'll . . . I'll soon see to that . . . there'll only be trouble for you. I've caused enough the night.'

'Are you going to the shop?' she said.

'Yes.'

'Why don't you go to Dennis's. Florence will see to you; you're all shaken up.'

'I'll be all right when I get to the shop. Go on now. . . . ' He went to push her away but his hand didn't touch her, it groped at the air as he swayed; and she caught at his arm and steadied him, then said firmly, 'Come on.'

161

'No, no, Rosie.' He still protested weakly, until she moved him forward. Then he became quiet and they spoke no more during the journey, except once as they were going up the hill towards the shop, when he said to her, 'Can you stop a moment, Rosie, I'm out of breath?'

When they reached the shop he gave her the key and she opened the door; in the back room he dropped down into a chair and, putting his head on his folded arms on the desk, muttered, 'There's some whisky in the cupboard beneath here, Rosie.'

She had to move his legs before she could get at the bottle. She poured him out a good measure, but had to hold the cup while he drank it. Then she lit the oil stove and put the kettle on the gas-ring; and when she turned to him again he was attempting to lift the seat of the chair.

'The foot comes out and makes a sort of bed,' he said; 'I'd feel better if I could lie back.'

'Let me do it.' When she had fixed the chair and he was lying on it he smiled at her faintly and said, 'That's better. It'll pass in a minute, I just feel dizzy.'

As she stood looking down into his grey face she murmured, 'She could have killed you.'

'I'll take a lot of killing.' Again he smiled, but kept his eyes closed.

When the water was hot she bathed his neck. The cut was just behind his ear and about half an inch long.

'You should have a doctor, Hughie it's quite open.'

'Just put a bit of sticking plaster on, there's some in that drawer.' He pointed.

When she had done so, he said, 'Thanks . . . thanks,

Rosie. . . . I'm all right now; you'd better get home. She'll only go for you if she –'

'I don't care.' She had her back to him now, speaking from the sink. 'I don't care what she says. . . . I'm getting out as quick as possible. I'll know tomorrow if I'm to have this job and then I'll get myself a room. I couldn't stay there, not after tonight I couldn't.'

'Rosie.'

When she came to his side, he had his eyes closed again, but his face was turned up to her as he said, 'I can think what I like and say what I like about her because she's not my mother, but she's yours and she's been good to you; she . . . she thinks the sun shines out of you.'

'I know, I know.' She turned quickly about and walked the short distance to the oil stove and back before she continued, 'That's what nearly drives me mad. She steals from the others . . . because that's what it amounts to, and then gives it to me with both hands. It frightens me. It always has, but more so since I came back this time. I've got to get away from her. I was in a hole . . . I was near my wits' end or I wouldn't have come back this time, but now I know I must get away and stay away.'

'Yes, I know, I know, you've got to get away or she'll eat you alive. People like her can. All their emotions have power, their hate equally as much as their love. Were you . . . were you shocked at what you learned the night, Rosie?'

'Shocked?' She gave a 'Huh!' of a laugh, as she looked down at him. 'Shocked at that? No, Hughie. Surprised, yes, because she's not like you; Karen, I

163

mean, not any part of her. We've never got on as you know, and if there'd been anything of you in her we would have.' She smiled weakly at him; then bit on her lip before she ended, 'She must have put you through the mill all these years . . . me mother.'

'It was my own fault entirely. I should have up and gone. When I got older I mean, but in the beginning she scared me to death, she seemed to melt the spine in me. I suppose before I die I'll forgive her many things, all, I think, with the exception of one.' He opened his eyes with an effort and said, 'She made me afraid of women, Rosie.'

'Aw, Hughie.' She was gazing down at him with pity and compassion in her face and her voice fell on him softly as she said, 'There plenty of time. What are you, thirty-five? You'll meet some nice woman, and she'll be lucky, very lucky. I could tell her that. Because you know' – she shook her head at him – 'you're quite attractive. Oh, you don't need looks to be attractive, you've got something in your make-up. And then . . . then you're kind, Hughie, besides.'

He opened his eyes wide now as he stared into her face, then his lids drooping once more, he said, 'You're a great comfort, Rosie.' He remained quiet after this for a few minutes, and when he next spoke his voice was a faint whisper. 'Rosie,' he said, 'I feel I'm going to pass out,' and before she could touch him he had fainted.

Two hours later Hughie was comfortably at rest on the studio couch in Dennis's sitting-room. The doctor had been and proclaimed that he had slight concussion, nothing serious, nothing that a couple of days' rest wouldn't cure. He had given him some tablets that made him drowsy, so he did not notice Rosie's departure.

She stood in the little cramped kitchen of the flat, opposite to Florence and Dennis. They were waiting for the sound of the taxi, and looking at his watch, Dennis said, 'He's late, but he'll come. If he got here once he'll come again.' He smiled at Rosie. 'It's a good job you made the arrangements without asking him' – and he nodded towards the main room – 'else he would have slept there all night and you never know what the result might have been.'

'He scared me. I thought he was dead . . . I thought all kinds of things.'

'It isn't her fault that he isn't dead, is it? By!' – Dennis moved his head from shoulder to shoulder – 'that woman will do something one of these days that'll put paid to her. I know it, I've always felt it.'

'What will you say when you get back, Rosie?' Florence spoke in a clear, precise way.

'If she asks I'll tell her.'

'You can be sure she'll ask all right.'

'Yes, she'll ask all right.'

'Do you want me to come back with you?' Dennis was bending towards her, but Rosie shook her head. 'No. After tonight I'll tell her what I think . . . I mean if she goes too far. But I want to get away without any trouble.'

'I wish we had another room,' said Florence.

'Thanks, Florence, but . . . well, you know what would happen if I were to come here.'

'We won't go into it,' said Dennis, pursing his mouth and looking down at his lips. 'We just won't go into that.'

165

'There's the car now,' said Florence. And as she opened the door she turned to Rosie and added, 'Come over tomorrow, you'll want to see how Hughie is anyway.'

'I'll try, but if I don't come you'll understand.'

'Goodbye, Rosie.'

'Goodbye, Florence.'

Before Dennis closed the taxi door on her he said under his breath, 'I would have given a month's pay to have heard Hughie drop his bombshell.'

'It was worth hearing.'

'I bet it was. Goodbye, Rosie. Keep your pecker up.'

But the taxi hadn't been moving for a matter of seconds before she thought, 'It's unnatural, we're both glorying in her humiliation. In Dennis's case it's understandable, but not in mine. I was glad to have her to come home to last Friday. Yet I can't help feeling against her, I can't.'

She got out of the taxi at the top end of the street and went down the back lane and up the garden and let herself quietly into the kitchen, but quiet as she was Broderick came hurrying out of the living-room before she had her coat off. 'Where've you been?' he said.

'I went after Hughie. And it's as well I did, he passed out. He had to have a doctor, he's got concussion.'

Her father moved nearer to her. 'Bad?' he asked anxiously.

The self-condemnation that she had felt in the taxi had vanished on entering the house and the nearer proximity to her mother. She wished at the moment that the news of Hughie was such as would worry her mother – that is if she was capable of feeling remorse for anything she did – and she had the desire to pile it on, but she could not distress her father. 'He just needs a few days' rest, the doctor says. But it could have been serious. He had to stitch it.'

'Where is he now?'

'At Dennis's.'

'Oh, dear God, that'll cause more trouble.' He turned his head towards the living-room, adding in a low voice, 'Your ma's gone up to bed.'

Rosie drew in a long breath. The words were like a reprieve, and her relief was not lost on Broderick. His voice muttering now, he said, 'In the mornin', when she's more herself, she'll want to talk. Be kind to her, gentle, for she's suffered a bad blow this night. No matter how things look to you or anybody else she's suffered a bad blow.'

There were many replies that Rosie could have given to this, such as: She's asked for it. She's treated him like a dog for years. The blow she's suffering from is the awful truth that the despised Hughie could have lifted her wholesale into number eight Brampton Hill. But she said none of these things for she did not want to hurt him.

'Will I make you a hot drink?' he said.

'No, Da, thanks; I had something at Dennis's. I'll go to bed now if you don't mind.'

'Away with you then, lass, and get a good night's rest. The morrow, things'll look different. It's a new day, the morrow. . . . Forget and forgive. And what you never had, you never miss. That's what I say.'

Her father's philosophy held no comfort; he was just using platitudes that had been stuffed into his ears from birth, and which he selected to fit certain situations. He didn't believe in anything he said, but he had to say something.

Rosie went quietly up the stairs, but as she crossed the landing her eyes were drawn to her mother's bedroom door. It was half open and Hannah's voice came clearly to her. It was as if she was talking to herself, but Rosie knew that her mother never wasted words on herself. She was saying, 'Them that aren't with me are against me. You can cut your heart out and serve it on a plate and still some folks wouldn't be satisfied.' There were more words in the same vein but fainter now, and the reproaches followed her up to the attic. Even when she closed the door and she could no longer hear her mother's voice, Hannah's power weighed on her, seeming to press her shoulders forward, making her want to double her body up.

There was no bottle in her bed tonight, nor the oil stove warming the room. As she stood shivering inside and out, she said to herself, 'You've got to get away; you mustn't wait till next week, for if she goes too far with you, you might even tell her the truth, and then what will happen? If she thinks what Hughie's done is bad, then what you've done will bring her to murder.'

Wednesday

In the morning Rosie escaped from the house early, leaving Hannah surly and beetle-browed. Not a single word had passed between them. Hannah needed time to come round after the shock of last night, on top of which there was the open defection of her daughter.

Rosie had no idea what she was going to do with herself until the afternoon when she would go for interview at the factory, and it was more to occupy her time that she called at another agency in Newcastle and was given the name of a firm of wholesalers who had just phoned in, requesting a shorthand-typist.

Within half an hour she was in an office above a warehouse demonstrating her skill to a fatherly man who smelt of bacon and nutmeg. He seemed very pleased with the letter that she had taken down from his dictation, and then he went on to explain why they needed someone in a hurry. It appeared that his secretary, whose name was Miss Pointer and whose age was forty-five, had run off with the storekeeper, a man with a wife and three grown-up daughters. 'The older they are the dafter they get,' he said to Rosie; and ended, 'The silly old trout!'

In spite of his bald description of his late secretary, Rosie felt she would like working for this man. What was more, she would be working on her own, with no-one to boss her except the boss. When he asked her how soon she could start and she replied, 'Now if you like,' he slapped her on the back, saying, 'You're a lass after me own heart. Get at it. There's three days' work piled up there.' He pointed to the desk. 'I gave her three days to find out her mistake, but apparently it's not long enough, and the work can't wait. Our business depends on letters.'

'You'll want my reference,' said Rosie.

'Aye, I suppose I will,' he said.

'I'll give you the address of the London firm.' As she wrote the address he laughed as he asked, 'Will they give you a good one, do you think?' and she laughed back at him as she replied, 'I've no fear of that.' And she hadn't.

So Rosie started her new job at eleven o'clock on Wednesday morning, and when she left at quarter-past five in the evening her new boss, looking at the pile of letters ready for the post, nodded his head and said, 'You'll do.'

She felt better, not happy or elated, just a little better.

When she arrived home the tea was over and there was no place set for her. Her mother must have cleared away almost before the men were finished, and she imagined she could hear her saying, 'Well, I'm the kind of woman who, if met halfway across the river will carry you over the other half on me shoulders.'

Hannah, bustling about the living-room, neither spoke nor looked at her, but kept her broad back turned towards her all the time.

It was Broderick, whose face wore a troubled look

170

tonight, who tried to put things on a normal footing. 'Well, lass, had a nice day?' he asked her.

Rosie went to the fire and held out her hands. 'In a way, Da,' she said.

'What you been doin' with yourself?'

'Working. I've got a job.' She smiled down at him.

'Begod, you have?' He screwed himself to the edge of his chair.

'Where? In that factory? What doin'?'

Rosie was conscious that her mother had stopped her bustling and had turned towards her as she answered, 'My own kind of work. Shorthand-typist, but not in the factory. It's in a wholesale firm, just a small place. I'm the only one.'

'I'm glad for you.' Her mother's voice, coming soft and controlled from behind her, forced her about. Hannah was smiling at her, the old apologetic look on her face. 'I'll get you some tea, lass,' she said. 'I didn't know.'

When Hannah walked quietly from the room to the kitchen, Broderick put his arm around Rosie's waist and shook his head as he whispered, 'She's been through hell the day. She . . . she had the idea you were along of Hughie. . . . You haven't seen him?'

'I've been wondering how he is all day. It frightened me last night, that concussion business.'

'I'll slip over to Dennis's after tea and find out.' She was whispering, and he whispered back, 'No, no, I wouldn't do that if I was you. Things are quietenin' down; let them simmer, there's a good girl, let them simmer.'

'Tell me about it. Where is it? I mean, where in

171

Newcastle is it?' Hannah was coming into the room, talking now as if there had been no interlude between yesterday morning and tea-time tonight.

And Rosie told her where the warehouse was, what it was like inside and the type of work she was expected to do. And all the while Hannah fussed around the table, handing bread, pouring tea, pushing a tart to her hand; cutting a pie and placing a fish slice under a portion of it ready to be lifted.

Then, 'What's his name?' she asked.

'Bunting,' said Rosie.

'Oh, Bunting. It's a plain name. Is it young or old he is?'

'About sixty I should say, and he's got a slight cast in his eye.'

At this Broderick let out a bellow of a laugh and cried at Hannah, 'Are you satisfied, eh? Are you satisfied?'

'I just wanted to get a picture of him in me mind,' said Hannah, 'that's all.'

'That's all,' said Broderick. 'That's all.' And he laughed again.

When Rosie had finished her tea she sat by the fire for a few minutes before she remarked in an off-hand manner, 'I think I'll go to the pictures, I haven't been for ages.'

Hannah looked sharply at her averted face, and her eyes narrowed for an instant before she exclaimed, 'Why! Those are the very words Arthur said, just afore he went upstairs. He said he thought he'd go to the pictures. I'll call him an' you can go along together.' She was out of the room before Rosie could protest, calling, 'Arthur! Arthur! Are you up there still?' And

172

when Arthur's voice came to her, she called back, 'Rosie's goin' to the pictures an' all; you can go along with her.'

She came back into the room, saying, 'Go an' get yourself ready, go on now, a night out'll do you good.'

As Rosie went out of the room she knew that her father had grown quiet and was looking into the fire, and she knew also that Arthur would be cursing her upstairs. She met him on the landing coming along the little passage from the end room, his face glum, the corners of his mouth drooping, and she said to him aloud, 'I won't be a minute. Well, not more than five,' but she accompanied this with a wagging of her head and a shaking of her finger, and the action drew the lines from his mouth and brought his head nodding at her.

Upstairs she powdered her face and combed her hair and put on an extra jumper beneath her coat. Altogether it didn't take her five minutes, and then she was down in the living-room and her mother was spreading her smile over her and Arthur. It was like a blessing. 'Where you goin'?' she asked them.

'Oh, likely the Plaza, Alec Guinness is on there. He's always good for a laugh. What about it?' He looked at Rosie.

'Suit me. Yes, I'd like that. I like him.'

As she let them out Hannah said, 'I'll likely be in bed when you get back, but enjoy yourselves.'

Yes, yes, they said, they would enjoy themselves.

When they reached the street they walked in an embarrassed silence for some minutes, before Rosie asked, 'You weren't going to the pictures, were you, Arthur?'

'No. Were you?'

'No. I was going to see how Hughie was.'

Arthur didn't say where he was bound for, he didn't have to, but he did say, 'Well, it isn't much out of my way, I'll look in on Hughie with you. But afore we get that far we'd better call at the Plaza and see the times of the pictures. You never know, she might start cross-examinin' us the morrow night. We'll get a good idea from the stills what it's all about.'

They examined the stills at the Plaza, and in the bus ride towards the outskirts of the town Arthur brought laughter to Rosie in giving her his version of the sequence of the story. Later, as they neared Dennis's flat, he suddenly exclaimed, 'Look, Rosie, I won't come in now; if I do I'll likely get stuck. You know what it is when we start talkin' and especially if last night comes up. So I'll go straight on, but I'll come and pick you up, say . . . about ten?'

'All right,' she said. 'About ten.'

'So long then.'

'So long, Arthur.'

Dennis's flat, Rosie had always considered, was bare when compared with her own home, and she never visited it, or her brother and his wife, without a sense of embarrassment. Her mother had at one time made her believe that Dennis was estranged from his family solely because of his wife, who was nothing but an upstart and a nagger. But the opposite was the truth, for on her previous visits, embarrassed as she was, she had sensed an odd something between them that she wasn't able to define. It wasn't until her return home last year that she realised that what had puzzled her between this husband

and wife was a sort of friendship. She had never thought of friendship between a married couple. Girls of her acquaintance had married and for the first few months the husband and wife were seen about together, then the pattern changed. The man went back to his nights at the local club, and his Saturday afternoons at the football match, and if they were fortunate enough to possess a car they went out on a Sunday, very often accompanied by one set of parents. But that wasn't Dennis's or Florence's pattern. They had always gone everywhere together, even to the football match. And Dennis didn't belong to any club. Yet they argued, even violently at times. One ordinary word would start a discussion between them which often led to an argument but it nearly always finished with them laughing at each other and saying, 'Well, we'll work this out later.' Before she had first left Fellburn for London, Rosie considered that Dennis and Florence were a funny couple. But now, as she entered their uncluttered sitting-room, she knew that she envied her brother and his wife their way of life, and that she was jealous of Florence, not because she was the wife of her brother, or that she was happy, but because what had happened to herself would never, or could never have happened, to Florence. Florence would have used her mind and it would have guided her heart, whereas the power of her own mind became non-existent where her feelings were concerned.

'Oh, I'm glad you've come, Rosie.' Florence was leading the way into the room. 'Hughie wondered if you would make it.'

'Is he any better?'

'Yes. Here's Rosie, Hughie.'

She went slowly towards him. 'Hello, Hughie.'

'Hello, Rosie.'

'How are you feeling?' She was standing over him, where he lay propped up on the couch.

'I've never felt so good before. This is the life.' He patted the back of the couch. 'Talk about being pampered. I'm going to make something out of this, I'm going to make it last as long as I can.' He nodded up at her, then turned his smile towards Florence.

'Look, take your things off and settle down.' Florence pushed a chair forward towards the couch, and as she did so Hughie said to Rosie, 'How long can you stay?'

'How long?' She glanced quickly back at Florence. 'All the evening if you don't mind. Arthur's picking me up about ten.' She looked back at Hughie; then down at her hands as she admitted, 'We're supposed to be at the pictures guarding one another.'

A ripple of laughter passed between the three of them, then Hughie said, 'Good. Now get yourself away, Florence. There's a do on at the school' – he looked at Rosie, explaining, 'Florence's got the idea in her head that I mustn't be left alone, and I don't want to be.' He smiled over Rosie's shoulder. 'But now you can go in peace, go on.'

'All right, then, I will.' Florence protested no further. 'We'll be back before you go, Rosie.'

Dennis's voice now came from the hall, calling, 'Is that you, Rosie?' The next moment he appeared in the doorway, naked to the waist, rubbing his head with a towel.

'Hello, Dennis.'

'You made it?'

'Yes, I made it.'

'I'm coming with you; Rosie's going to stay until we get back,' said Florence.

'Good.' Dennis flicked the towel towards his wife. Then turning to Rosie again, added, 'This problem of baby-sitting is difficult . . . and if you do well tonight we'll book you for later on.'

'Go on, get yourself ready.' Florence was pushing him into the hall.

When the door closed behind them Hughie looked at Rosie and asked quietly, 'How's things?'

'Oh, very subdued, Hughie.'

'How about last night when you got back? I was worried. . . . At least I was worried today, last night seems very hazy to me now. There's a blank between when I left the kitchen and when I woke up here on the couch. The only thing I seem to remember is that you were with me all the time, and then this morning when my head cleared . . . well, I wondered what happened when you got back.'

'It was all right, she was in bed.'

'And she didn't say anything to you at all?' He seemed surprised.

'Well, just a parable.' She smiled faintly at him. 'The bedroom door was open and it was thrown at me as I passed.'

'Just a parable?' he shook his head as if in disbelief.

Dennis came into the room now, putting on his tie, and looking at Rosie, asked, 'Well, what have you been doing with yourself all day?'

'Working.'

'Working!'

177

'I've got a job.'

'What, already? Where?'

'At a little wholesale place called Bunting's in Newcastle. I think I'm going to like it.'

'Well, well, you haven't lost much time. . . . What do you think of that, Hughie?'

Hughie jerked his head to the side but he said nothing.

Florence now came into the room fastening up her dress at the back. 'Do this top button for me, Dennis, will you?' She turned her back to him.

'What do you think? Rosie's got a job already.'

'You have?' Florence screwed her head round.

'In her own line too.'

'Oh, I'm glad. Where is it, Rosie?'

'In Newcastle.'

'Are you going to travel or get digs?'

'I'm going to get a room.'

'Have you told her?' asked Dennis.

'About the job, not about getting a room.'

'Coo!' Dennis closed his eyes. 'I would get yourself built up before you spring that one. . . . Well' – he put his hand on Florence's arm – 'if we want to get there in time we'll have to be off. Be seeing you.' He nodded towards Hughie and Rosie.

As Florence was hustled towards the door she called over her shoulder, 'Make some coffee, Rosie. And there's plenty to eat in the pantry.'

For some minutes after the front door closed they sat without speaking, until the silence made itself felt and Rosie said, 'Do you think you'll be able to go on Monday, Hughie?'

'Oh, aye. Yes, I'll be quite fit by then. I should be all

right by Saturday. The doctor said two or three days.'

'Did he . . . the doctor ask how it happened?'

'Yes, an' I told him some bairns threw a snowball with a brick in it.' He laughed weakly.

'Oh, Hughie.'

'Well I couldn't say I was walloped with a dish of peaches, could I?' He was aiming now to make her laugh, but didn't succeed.

She said quietly, 'I'm going to miss you when you're gone. I . . . I seem to have got to know you more these last few days than during all the years we lived together. . . . Funny, isn't it?'

'Aye, it's funny, but it wasn't my fault that we didn't know each other better.' He lay back against the head of the couch and stared towards the low ceiling as he said, 'I once bought you a birthday present. You were sixteen. It was a bunch of anemones. They were all colours and very bonny, and I had them in me hand when she came into the kitchen. She didn't ask who they were for, she knew, an' she took a big gully and sliced the heads off them as clean as a whistle, there in me hands.'

'Oh, Hughie.' She lowered her head.

'Oh, I suppose she was right. I suppose in her way she was right. To her mind I had raped her eldest daughter and she was making sure it wasn't going to happen with her youngest.'

'Oh, don't say that.' She screwed up her face at him. 'It sounds awful . . . you would never have . . .'

'How do you know, Rosie, what I would have done?' They were looking fixedly at each other, and it was some seconds before he went on, 'She had made me almost petrified of girls; but not you, you were easy to talk to; you were the only girl I could talk to, although you always appeared like a child to me, and even from a baby you were extraordinary beautiful . . . and good . . . the goodness shone out of you. I saw you the day you were born, and it was evident then. I had just turned thirteen the day you were born.

She looked for a moment longer at the warm, tender expression on his face. He was looking at her as she had seen people look at the statue of the Virgin Mary in church, almost in rapt contemplation; it was unbearable. She sprang up from the chair and walked towards the gas-fire in the far wall, where his voice came to her, contrite, saying, 'I'm sorry, Rosie, if I've upset you.'

'Hughie' – she paused and cleared her throat – 'I'm . . . I'm not a child any longer, or even a girl. I'm a woman. And . . . and I'm not good.' She had her head back on her shoulders as she spoke, staring at the picture above the gas-fire. It was the only picture in the room and it showed a scene of sea and sky with no dividing line between them.

'It all depends on what you mean, Rosie.' His voice was low and his words slurred as if he were thinking hard, but about something else. 'Nothing you could do in the world would ever make me think of you as bad.'

'No?' She was still looking upwards.

'No, Rosie.'

Her eyes were moving over the picture as if she was searching for the horizon line as she said, 'When I left home, Hughie, I thought I knew all about men, good men and bad men. I was Rosie Massey, brought up among a horde of men and with a mother to whom the word delicacy was unknown. I grew up with the feeling that every conception of hers had been a public affair.'

'Don't, Rosie.'

'Am I shocking you, Hughie?'

'No.' He paused. 'You couldn't shock me, but still I don't like to hear you, above all people, talking like that.'

'Not if I think like that? Have always thought like that?'

'You don't think like that, you're upset inside.'

There followed a stillness, and it was broken by him saying tentatively, 'You said the other night that if you could tell anybody what was troubling you it would be me.'

She turned from the fire and looked towards him; then coming slowly across the room again and sat down by the couch facing him, and crossing her feet she joined her hands around her knees and began to rock herself. Leaning forward he put his hand across hers and stilled the motion. 'Try me,' he said.

She looked into his face, close to hers, now. Hughie was nice, kind. That's what you needed in a man, kindness. But that's what had trapped her, hadn't it . . . kindness? When she shuddered he straightened himself and lifted his hand quickly from hers and as quickly she grasped at it, saying, 'If I tell you and . . . and you think I'm dreadful, don't show it, will you, Hughie? Don't show it, I couldn't bear it.'

He looked at her solemnly, 'I tell you nothing you could do could alter my opinion of you, so go ahead.'

'Hold my hand,' she said; and when he gripped her hand and rested it on his knees she began.

It was quarter to eight when with her eyes cast down she had started talking. It was half-past eight when she finished and she hadn't raised her head once. When she ended and slowly and stiffly straightened her neck it was she who spoke again. Her green eyes looking almost black in her white face, she stared at him as she said, 'You're shocked, aren't you? Shocked to the core?'

'No.' His voice sounded husky as if he hadn't used it for a long time, then clearing his throat he repeated, 'No, only . . . well – he wetted his lips – 'hurt to the heart for you. . . . Oh, Rosie!' He looked down at their joined hands.

'You won't tell Dennis or anyone?'

'No.' They remained quiet for some moments. Then letting go her hand, he said, 'Whatever happens you'll have to keep this from . . . from your mother. Don't ever feel there'll be a time when you could confide in her.'

'I know that,' she said. She moved from the couch and began to walk about the room, round and round. Then stopping quite suddenly, she asked, 'Would you like some coffee?'

'Yes . . . yes, I think I would.' He did not look at her as he spoke, and when she reached the kitchen she stood near the table with her two hands cupping her face. It had been a mistake – she shouldn't have told him; she shouldn't have told anyone. It came to her now that Hughie was the last person she should have told. She liked Hughie and she knew he liked her. She wanted him to think well of her. She had imagined that in telling him what had happened to her he would have seen that she wasn't to blame, well not altogether, and the burden of guilt would have been lightened. But somehow he hadn't. He said he wasn't shocked, but he was shocked as much, or even more, than any of the lads would have been if she had told them.

She became overwhelmed by a feeling of emptiness, as if she had lost something she valued. But she had never valued Hughie, not until this moment. How much she valued his good opinion came to her now almost in the form of a revelation. And she whimpered to herself: No, no, not that. Why couldn't I have known before I told him?

Thursday

When her mother opened the back door to let her out the air cut their breath from them and Hannah exclaimed, 'My God! Every place is like glass; all that slush frozen hard. Now mind how you go, lass; it's far too early to make a start to my mind.'

'I can go later tomorrow but the buses mightn't be running to time and I don't want to be late the first mornin'.'

'No, that's understandable the first mornin', but keep that coat buttoned up.' She put her hand towards the top button of Rosie's coat and went on, 'And mind, go and get a good dinner into you, no sandwiches and tea mind, and I'll have somethin' hot and tasty ready for you the minute you enter the door. About six, you say?'

'Yes, if I can get a bus. But you never can tell.'

'Goodbye now, lass; mind how you go.'

'Goodbye, Ma.' As Rosie stepped carefully on to the icy path Hannah, turning into the room, exclaimed, 'Are you off an' all now, Jimmy? Well you can go some of the way with Rosie, here. See her to the bus or she'll be flat on her back afore she gets to the end of the street.'

'Aye, Ma, aye. So long.'

'So long, boy.'

When they had let themselves out of the garden gate Jimmy took Rosie's arm up the lane, saying, 'It'll be all

184

right when we get on the road, the lorries will've been out with the gravel. You won't want me to come with you to the bus, Rosie, will you?'

'No, of course not.'

'I would but I'm a bit late, an' if you're not on the job afore the whistle they cut your time, crafty bastards.'

'It's all right,' she said. 'I'm going up Tangier Road, anyway; it'll bring me to the bus depot and I'll have more chance of getting a seat from there.'

'Aye, aye, you will.'

Just before they neared Tangier Road Jimmy asked in an assumed off-hand way, 'You and Arthur went to the pictures last night?'

'Yes.'

'No kiddin'?'

'Of course we went; where else do you think we would go?'

'Well' – he laughed – 'I know where Arthur would go if he got the chance, an' I thought he might have given you the slip or somethin'. I can't see him sitting in the pictures all night when he could be with her.'

'Well he did . . . he was.'

Rosie didn't ask herself why it was necessary to lie to Jimmy. Instinctively she knew she didn't trust Jimmy; of all her brothers she trusted him the least, he was too close to her mother.

'Well, I'm turning off here,' she said. 'Goodbye.'

'Goodbye, Rosie, an' mind how you go. An' see you work for your pay.' He laughed as he turned from her.

It was not yet fully light, and as she hurried as fast as she could down Tangier Road, the scurrying figures of the men making their way to the factories, and to buses to take them into Newcastle, and as far away as the docks on the Tyne, all looked like black huddled phantoms. Collars up, cap peaks down, their breath fanning out from scarves, they went their particular ways. Some had travelled the same road at the same time each day since they were lads, and would go on until they retired or died, or, fearful thought, were stood off. But Rosie, although she had not been a part of this scene at this time before, was unconscious of any strangeness, for it was almost the same scene as was enacted at the other end of the day. She had been familiar enough with that.

She did not go straight to the bus terminus, but she cut down a side street, and this brought her to the bottom of the hill where Hughie's shop was. When she reached the shop she passed by with just a glance towards the window and knocked on the door next to it, thinking as she did so that if this was a door to a shop it gave no indication of it because there was no window in the wall to the side of it, just a board hanging there with the faded letters on it, reading, JAMES CULLEN – Furniture Repairer.

After knocking three times on the door and receiving no answer, she looked at the key and the paper she had taken out of her bag. Hughie had asked her last night if she would take the key of the shop and the written notice to Mr Cullen. He, Hughie said, was always in his shop around seven. Rain, hail or snow, he'd be there, whether he had work to do or not, and he would see to any customers who called for their shoes.

Now, after knocking yet once again, she was left wondering what to do. Hughie had added that if for some reason Mr Cullen shouldn't be there, she should put the key at the back of the hopper head on the top of the drain pipe. She would have to give herself a boost up from the step, he had said. And she could push the notice through the letter-box. But that he knew she wouldn't have to do, for there had never been a morning in years that old Jim hadn't been in his shop before him.

Hughie had not asked her to do this service for him until Florence and Dennis had returned, and it had created the impression that everything was normal. But she knew that it wasn't.

But this was the one morning when Mr Cullen wasn't here before Hughie, so she pushed the piece of paper which said, 'Closed for a few days. Please apply next door,' through the letter-box, and standing on the step and putting one foot on the coping of the wall, she gripped the drain pipe and hoisted herself up. She just managed to place the key on the ledge of the hopper where it joined the wall. This done, she made her way carefully down the hill again and to the bus station.

Although her new job, which she found very pleasant and knew she was going to like, kept her on her toes as it were, on this first day there still remained a section of her mind that was not touched by it. All day long, from the moment she had got up, she had not been able to get the thought of Hughie out of her mind. She wished now, oh she wished from the bottom of her heart that she hadn't talked last night. She had felt sure that telling him would ease her, and that he would comfort her. That's what she had thought, he would comfort her, saying, 'It wasn't your fault, Rosie, you're not that kind of girl. You would never have got into that scrape on your own.' She had thought he would tell her the things she tried to tell herself, and coming from him she could believe them, then she would again be able to like herself . . . just a little. But Hughie's reaction had taken the form of silence. Except for an odd word now and again, he had said nothing until Dennis and Florence had returned. It was as if he had again been hit on the head, and this time the blow had knocked him stupid.

Just before she left the office Mr Bunting again expressed his pleasure at her work. 'I see you're going to do fine,' he said. 'And as Joe down below said, it's a change to have something good to look at, for there's no getting away from the fact that although Miss Pointer was good at her job she had the kind of face that put you off, if you know what I mean. Joe always said it was like a battered pluck. He meant no offence, but that's how she appeared to him.' He had hunched his rounded shoulders at her as he ended, 'An' to me an' all.'

As Rosie left the office she smiled ruefully to herself. A face like a battered pluck . . . no offence meant! It was funny. People were funny, the things they said. But Miss Pointer with her face like a battered pluck had run off with a married man. Love was another funny thing. . . . Love! She found her lip curling backwards from the word.

A thaw had set in and the market place was a river of slush when she alighted from the Newcastle bus. As she went to cross the square Shane's voice came from behind her, calling, 'Rosie! Rosie there! . . . Gettin' the bus?' he said as he came up to her.

'Oh, hello, Shane. Yes.'

'Isn't this hellish? It's never going to end. We'll all be in the workhouse if it keeps on; we're not goin' in the morrow.'

'You haven't been working on the building today, have you?'

'No, they've kept us busy inside the last few days, but that's finished. It means the Exchange the morrow. The bloody dole. An' what's that?'

Shane talked about the work on the building, and the uncertainty of it; the rotten gaffer; the way they were throwing the houses up on the estate; the money the speculators were making out of them; the Labour Party; the Bosses; and the scapegoats in the Union until they got off the bus at the top of the road. Shane never needed answers. But as they were making their way down the back lane to the garden gate he said something that did need an answer. 'What really brought you home, Rosie?' he asked.

'Eh?' The question, apropos of nothing he had been talking about, startled her, and he went on, 'Well, I mean to say. Well, we got talkin', the others and me, and we wondered . . . well, if you'd had a row with a fellow up there. . . . Had you a fellow?'

'No, no, I hadn't a fellow.'

'All right, Rosie, all right, don't snap me head off.'

They were going up the garden path now between the mounds of snow and he put his hand out and touched her shoulder, saying, 'Don't be ratty, Rosie; I don't want to know anything; it was just . . .'

She hurried from him, and opened the kitchen door, and the warmth flooded at her. And so did her mother's voice, crying, 'Three lots today there's been. Two lads at dinner time sayin' they wanted their boots. Where would they find them, they wanted to know. An' . . . an' I told them to to to hell and he'd likely be there.'

Shane, looking at Rosie, pushed his brows up and wagged his forefinger under his nose. He was about to lean forward to whisper something when Hannah heralded her approach to the kitchen and came in, saying, 'Oh, there you are. Did you meet up? You go out with one and you come home with another.' Hannah was nodding at Rosie, her face one large beam. 'Well it's been a day and a half, hasn't it? Come here and let me have your coat. Oh, look at you! you are clarts up to the eyes. I'll let it dry and then give it a sponge down. Away into the room and get warm. Your da's just in. I've been baking, that Swedish cake with the apples that you liked, and steak and chips it is, afore that, with mushrooms.'

'Pass it along! Pass it along!' Shane went into the kitchen sniffing the air, and Rosie followed him. She hadn't opened her mouth; it wasn't necessary when her mother was in this happy mood. . . .

The meal over, the boys upstairs getting ready for their nightly visit to the club, she sat for a while telling her father about the work at the office and Mr Bunting, while her mother, her ears wide, busied herself about the room. It wasn't until Karen came in that she went upstairs and changed; and when she came down dressed for outdoors once more Hannah exclaimed tersely, 'Where you off to? You're not going out again? I thought you were telling your da you were goin' to look at the telly.'

'Yes I am, but later on. It's Thursday. I'm . . . I'm going to church.'

'Ooh! Aye.' The ooh brought Hannah's chin up and

the bun of hair at the back of her head nodding loosely from its pins. 'Oh, aye, I forgot it was Thursday. That's a good lass. Are you going to confession?'

'Yes, Ma.' Rosie did not look at her mother as she spoke.

'You won't be long then,' said Hannah loudly. 'There's not many that'll turn out the night.'

'No, I don't suppose so. Bye-bye, Da.'

'Bye-bye, lass.'

'Bye-bye, Ma.'

'Bye-bye, lass.' Hannah followed her into the hall. 'If it wasn't so treacherous underfoot I'd come along with you.'

Rosie made no remark to this but went hurriedly through the door that Hannah held ajar, and she walked up the street because that was the way to the church, and she knew her mother would be at the front room window, and the street was well lit.

When she got out of sight around the corner she doubled back down the next road and made her way to the shop.

The long cul-de-sac at the top of the hill was not well lit but she could make out by the light from a distant lamp that there was no notice in the window.

With her foot on the coping and gripping the drain pipe once again, she found the key where she had left it that morning. She opened the shop door and, switching on the light, picked up the folded piece of paper that she had dropped through the letter-box. On the shop counter there was a reel of sticky paper used for sealing the parcels; she tore off a few strips and with them pressed the notice on to the window.

She should now go to Dennis's and tell Hughie that Mr Cullen hadn't been at his shop today. Hadn't she come here to give herself some excuse for going to see Hughie? All day long she had felt she must go and see him tonight. But she wanted an excuse; it wasn't enough to say she had come to see how he was. He had money now, and then Dennis and Florence might think. . . . Well, you never knew what people thought. Relations were the worst. She stood looking about her for a moment sniffing at the dry, musty air. She was uncertain what to do. She had the excuse but she was afraid to use it, afraid, not really of what Florence and Dennis might think but of the silence with which Hughie would greet her, the awful silence that had come between them after she had finished talking last night. And his opinion of her would likely be no better tonight than it had been last night; with time to think it might even have got worse.

She went into the back shop and switched on the light, then putting out the shop light she closed the door to the back room and pulled the blind down over the glass half of it. And as if she had been used to doing it every day she put a match to the oil stove, lit the gas and put the kettle on; then sat down near the stove and waited for the kettle to boil. She didn't really want any tea but she wanted something warm, and she wanted to do something, occupy herself in some way. After she had made the tea she remembered the whisky that Hughie kept in the cupboard underneath the desk, and as she took out the bottle she thought, Hughie won't mind. Then she poured a good measure into the cup of tea. She didn't like whisky, or brandy, or gin. She knew she had no real taste for liquor of any kind, but she needed something; as her hands needed to be busy to check the unrest in her mind so her body needed warmth. The fact that Hughie had offered her no warmth last night was affecting her strangely. She had never imagined she would lay such stock by his good opinion.

After she had drunk the laced tea she pulled the chair nearer the desk, and more because her hands were restless than out of curiosity she opened the drawer. It was filled with neatly stacked sheets of paper, and she sat looking down at them for some time. If she read them she would be prying she thought. Perhaps Hughie wouldn't like her to read what he had written. Well Hughie wasn't there, was he? She moved her head as if asking the question of the desk, and she wanted to pry, to pry into his affairs, into his mind. She lifted a few sheets from one pile and put them on the desk; then closing the drawer, leant over them and began to read. There was no title to the first page, it just began:

'What is more important than education today? What will get you in, what will give you preference is . . . an accent, just an accent. Accent still has the power to give one person an advantage over another, and strangely enough it has nothing to do with intelligence or learning but everything to do with background. So the solution for success would seem to be get yourself born with a background; then automatically you'll have an accent. . . .'

Underneath this piece of writing were the words 'Strip and extend. Could be made amusing.'

Yes, it could at that, she thought. Fancy Hughie being funny.

193

On the next page, headed 'Return to the soil after imprisonment' were the words:

'I walk on you, my soles tight pressed; I lie on you, and my body wallows in your lushness; I weep my tears of love and see them soak into your groins; my sweat lies on you in glossy globules. In ecstasy I rise and take up the blade and in your rich black blood my soul is reflected. I am one with eternal life.'

After reading this three times, Rosie looked at the wall opposite. Her eyes were narrowed and her mouth hung slack. She couldn't associate the writing with Hughie, not any part of the Hughie she knew. When she had poured out her troubles last night she had been seeing the man who sat in the corner of the kitchen, but the man she had been talking to and who had fallen silent was the man who wrote stuff like this. She didn't know anything about this man.

She brought her eyes down to the papers again and began to read the next page. It had no heading.

'From the bed I rise and fly, my body draped in skin alone. The air, the width of the universe, the length of eternity, is my raiment and enfolds me but does not hide me, and I care not. I pass over nations all peopled with faces of my neighbours, and they look at me and I laugh and cry down to them: "Why be afraid of your body? Look at me, look at me." And they look and I laugh. And on I float, and glide, and soar, and whirl in wind pockets, and I grip a tall spire and dance round it and my feet bounce off the air as off a trampoline, and I shout at the life that I know is within me: "You're there! You're there! This is you . . . jumping, jumping." And my shouting cleaves the clouds as it always does. And

194

then I fall and fall and land in a field full of men, with one woman in the midst, and she is standing up to her waist in filth, and I awake in the blackness and wonder if I'll ever drop into a field of flowers. . . .'

'Oh! Hughie . . . Hughie.' The name came out of her mouth like an expression of pain, and again she said, 'Oh! Hughie, Hughie.' As fantastic as this piece of writing was she could understand it . . . oh yes, she could understand it. Dreaming of a field full of men with a woman in their midst . . . her mother. Dreaming that he was afraid of his body except in the night. . . . And last night she had told him what had happened to her and her body. No wonder he was silent. Gently she pushed the papers aside, and leaning her head on the desk she began to cry.

It wasn't long after this that she returned home, and as she mounted the steps the front door opened to let out Councillor Bishop. Her mother stood behind him, the door in her hand, her face bright, her manner at its best. 'Oh, there you are, me dear,' she greeted her. 'You've met me daughter, Councillor?' She inclined her head towards the plump, bespectacled man.

'Indeed, yes, I've had that honour. But many years ago. How are you?' He held out his hand.

'Very well, thank you.'

He was holding her hand, pumping it up and down as he went on, 'Your mother tells me that you've come home to stay. Now this is good news.' He spoke as if he knew all about her, as if her going or staying was of some importance to him. 'Now you must come round one evening and meet Mrs Bishop. I know she would love to meet you.' Still holding her hand in a grasp which did not allow her to extricate her fingers without tugging them from him, he turned to Hannah and ended, 'When you've moved we'll do an exchange of evenings, eh?'

'That'll be grand, that'll be grand indeed.'

'It's settled then.' Mr Bishop patted the hand within his own before finally releasing it, and as Rosie turned away, her face unsmiling, he said to Hannah, 'We'll be meeting again on Saturday then, Mrs Massey. I'll have all the papers ready. There's nothing to be gained by hanging about in matters like this. It could be snapped up.'

'I'll see that it's snapped up, Mr Bishop, but by the right one.'

Hannah's laugh followed Rosie into the living-room. She took off her coat and hat and, leaving them on the chair, went to the fire and stood waiting.

A few minutes later Hannah entered the room. She did not speak immediately, but engaged in her usual technique, that of preceding anything of importance she had to say with a silence, a telling silence. But on this occasion Rosie did not allow her mother to play her little game; instead, turning to her, she asked, 'You're not really going to take the place, are you, Ma?'

'Not really going to take it!' Hannah's voice was high but quiet; it held a surprised note as if it was unbelievable to her that anyone should imagine that she wasn't going to take number eight Brampton Hill. 'Of course I'm going to take it, child. . . . We're going to take it, an' it'll all be settled on Saturday.'

'But me da . . . and the lads?'

'Your da has always left things of this nature to me.

196

As for the lads, if they don't like it there's the wide world before them and the door is open.'

Rosie gazed at her mother. You really had to admire her effrontery and the game of pretence that she played. . . . There was the wide world for the lads and the door was open! Without the lads she could never hope to make Brampton Hill, and yet she could talk like this with apparent sincerity.

'But if you don't sell this . . . ?'

'This house will be sold, never fear. Mr Bishop put it on his books three weeks ago. He's had several enquiries. He's not in the smallest doubt that it'll go like wild fire once the fine weather comes. He's so sure of it, me dear, that he says he'll take it off me hands himself if it isn't sold.'

Mr Bishop, Rosie thought, was an astute man, a crafty, astute man. A councillor, a speculator and a chairman of a building society. He had, since the day he rented Hannah her first house after Bog's End, taken her measure. For all her cunning, her mother was so naïve in some things. . . . Exchange of visits for instance. She could see Mrs Bishop entertaining her mother. Mrs Bishop who in her young days had graced the Ladies' Circle, who had, as her husband alternately clawed and sucked himself up through the business élite of the town, made the right friendships, the right connections. Her mother and Mrs Bishop exchanging visits! If it wasn't pathetic it would be laughable.

As if Hannah were reading her thoughts she said, 'What you don't seem to understand, lass, is that times are changin'. I'll grant you that at one time it would have been out of place, the very thought of us moving to Brampton Hill, but not now. There's been a levelling, and not afore time. It's the front you put on the day that you're judged by. Half of them in this town are living on an overdraft. Now I know that for truth.' She wagged her finger in Rosie's face. 'It was Mr Bishop himself who told me that. He's opened me eyes about lots of things. "Mrs Massey," he said, "anybody who can put two thousand pounds down in cash for a house the day needn't have any worries for the future." '

'You're putting the two thousand down?'

'I am. But mind you' – she lifted both her hands towards Rosie now – 'this is atween you and me, for the present moment at any rate. Now don't you let on; mind, I'm tellin' you. Anyway, putting the two thousand down will bring the mortgage to practically half; we'll be paying no more than what we're paying off the house at the present moment, it's all been worked out. And when we sell this there'll be three thousand in the bank to set us up with.'

'It's all cut and dried then?'

'It's all cut and dried as you say, lass,' Hannah nodded at her.

'Barry'll be on the dole next week. He won't feel like giving the Hill as his address at the exchange.'

'Now, are you trying to be nasty, lass. What's come over you?' Hannah scrutinised her daughter through narrowed lids. 'Fancy sayin' a think like that, aiming to put a damper on the whole enterprise. It isn't like you; you never used to have a barb to your tongue. And as for Barny not wantin' to give the Hill address to the exchange, there'll be no need, for if I know Barny he'll be in work afore he's out of it.'

198

'I hope so.'

As Rosie turned away and picked up her coat and hat, Hannah said to her, 'I'm the one for speakin' me mind an' I'm goin' to say now that I feel there's something wrong with you. From the minute you stepped in at the door I felt it. You've hardened, lass, all the gentleness has gone out of you. As I remember you, you never contradicted me in your life, nor yet raised your voice in opposition to me, yet you've never stopped battling since you've been home. An' what's cut me to the quick is to know that you took the sod that's gone's part. Him that wronged me. You know, I've the feelin' that if the devil was to appear in the kitchen this minute yes, begod, I've the feelin' that you'd even take his side against me, I have.'

There was so much truth in what her mother said, and so much hurt in the tone in which she said it, that Rosie was forced to turn round before she left the room and say quietly, 'I'm sorry, Ma; it's because I'm not feeling well, I suppose.'

'All right, all right, we'll leave it at that, lass.' Hannah hurried forward. 'Go and get yourself up to bed, it's rest you want. Good feeding and rest. I've put your bottle in and the heater's on, and by the time you're in I'll have somethin' hot up to you.'

She patted Rosie's arm as she pushed her towards the stairs.

What could you say in the face of such tenderness and concern? You could say nothing, but you could do something, you could run . . . run before you reached Brampton Hill.

PART THREE

HANNAH

Friday

It was the events of this day, Friday, which were to point the way to Rosie's future life.

The routine of the day was the same as yesterday, except that during her dinner hour she went looking for a room, and by chance found one only five minutes' walk from the office. It was clean and comfortable and in a respectable neighbourhood. She liked the woman, a widow, who owned the house and made her living by letting. She paid her a small deposit in advance and told her that she would come on Monday next.

During the afternoon she hadn't much time to worry about how she would break the news of her going to her mother, but as she neared home in the evening she became agitated.

When she went into the house she still hadn't decided whether she would tell her mother straightaway or leave it until tomorrow, after she had signed the lease on eight Brampton Hill, for by that time she would be in a much better frame of mind.

But Hannah herself decided, for she greeted her with such heartiness that it would have been impossible to say to her, 'I'm leaving, Ma.'

They were all in except Barny and Karen. Jimmy had come home early because a severe gale had held up the work on the bridge. Arthur, too, was on short time from the quarries because they couldn't get the lorries to move. Shane had apparently returned home first thing this morning after signing on at the labour exchange. Yet in spite of all this, which meant lighter pay packets, Hannah was gaiety itself.

Being Friday, there was naturally fish, and the men had finished a large side-dish full of fried cod and chips.

'I didn't do yours, me dear,' said Hannah, 'I wanted you to have it fresh.' And when she went scurrying into the kitchen, Broderick, pulling at Rosie's hand, drew to his side of the table, saying, 'Sit yourself down and have some tea and this new bread to be getting on with. There's nobody bakes flat cake like your mother. In fact,' he widened his eyes at her, 'I'd like to bet you she's the only woman in this town who still bakes her own bread.'

As Rosie sat down Shane passed her the plate of bread, saying, 'How's it going?' But before she could answer him Arthur put in, 'Don't ask daft questions, man, the boss has asked her to marry him, didn't you know?'

'No!' said Shane, his hand still extended with the plate but looking at his brother now, his whole face portraying an idiotic expression of wonder.

'It's a fact, I'm tellin' you.' Arthur raised his hand. 'As true as God and Hannah Massey's my judge. He asked her this very day; an' he's got a title an' all.'

'No!' Shane's hand was still extended, holding the bread plate, and now he moved it upwards until it was above his head.

'Aye.'

Broderick and Jimmy were laughing now and Rosie was forced to join in.

'Give over, you couple of clowns,' said their father.

'Clowns! He's calling us clowns. Do you hear that, Arthur? Roll your sleeves up, go on, get at him.' Shane dropped the plate on the table.

'No, no, I never raise me hand to little chaps.' At this Arthur put his forearm up as if warding off a blow, and, his eyes laughing, he peered over his fist at his father. And Broderick said, 'Little chap is it? I'll have you turning a somersault and you won't know but 'twas a cuddy that'd kicked you.'

And so the chaff went on; it was almost a repeat of the same time the previous week. When Rosie had longed for home it was this part of it she remembered, the lads pulling each other's legs, and their father's, while her mother bustled about feeding them all. And by their attitudes now Rosie knew that as yet they were unaware of what was going to happen tomorrow. Had they known they were really booked for Brampton Hill the scene in the kitchen tonight would have been quite different.

Hannah, coming to Rosie's side now and putting her arm around her shoulder and her face down to hers, said, 'Look, what about comin' along of us the night to the club an' seein' a bit of life? It's all very nice and refined. Now isn't it?' she appealed to her sons. 'Since this new manager's been in she wouldn't know the place, would she? What about it?' She brought her eyes back to Rosie, adding, 'You can have a bit of a dance, or a quiet drink, just as you like. There's a room been opened just across the passage, select it is. . . .'

'An . . . an' a penny a pint on the beer for the selectness.' Broderick opened his eyes wide and threw his head back as if he had just voiced something extremely funny.

205

'Aye, come along, Rosie,' Shane said over the table. 'It's a long while since we had a dance together.'

'I used to love to see you two dancin' together,' said Hannah, nodding from one to the other. 'You were so smooth it was like running water. What do you say, lass?'

What could she say without appearing churlish or ungrateful. She could say nothing but 'All right, Ma. Yes, I'd like to.' She nodded towards Shane now.

'That's settled then. Good, good. Aw, we'll make a night of it. It's about time we had a bit of jollification. We've all been acting like frozen corpses for long enough . . . Come on now, finish up the lot of you and let's get cleared and away. I'll leave the others' set for them; they can see to themselves for once.'

The next few minutes was all bustle, and as Rosie went to leave the room Shane called after her, 'By the way, what you wearin'? Put on something dandy, I want to show you off . . . that suit you came home with, that'll do.'

Hannah's voice followed Rosie up the stairs, crying at Shane, 'Did you ever! Wantin' to show his sister off! Now I ask you.' There was laughter in her tone, but it died away as she ended, 'And that suit she came back with, I'm not struck on it a bit. It's as plain as a pikestaff, there's nothing to it. . . .'

When, sometime later, Rosie came down the stairs with her coat on they were all gathered in the living-room. Hannah was wearing a heavy blue coat with a high collar, the whole tending to emphasize her large-ness. She wore a blue velour hat set straight on top of her grey hair, and although there wasn't any sign of taste

206

in her clothes she looked an imposing figure – regal, one would say. As she pulled on her gloves she turned to Rosie and said, 'Ah, there you are, let's have a look at you. Open your coat.'

'But you've seen it before, Ma.'

'Yes, I know, but I want to see it again.'

When Rosie opened her coat Hannah, looking at her from head to foot as if she were appraising a model, remarked, 'I maintain what I said, it's too dull.'

'You don't know class when you see it. Come, let's away,' said Shane, taking hold of Rosie and pushing her forward.

'And come along all of you, else it will be closin' time afore we get there. We should have had a taxi, anyway,' said Hannah as she went down the front steps.

'Taxi! Listen to her,' called Broderick. 'You'd think she'd come up by way of the landed gentry. Taxis to go to the club!'

Between them Broderick and Jimmy helped Hannah along the slushy street to the bus stop while Shane and Arthur took Rosie by an arm, and, all the way, there was laughing and chaffing. And like this they entered the club.

The Workmen's Centre, or The Club as it was usually called, was the most modern of its kind. The main room was well over fifty feet long with an added L piece half that length. The bar counter took up the curve on the corner of the L; in this way it protruded into the dance section while dominating the main portion of the room which was filled with small tables. Adjacent to the end of the bar was a raised platform on which stood a piano, and as Hannah and her party entered the room there were two men on the platform giving an imitation of famous mimers, as was indicated by their small gingham skirts and bibs.

The Fellburn Club was very proud of its standards of entertainers; hadn't two of their local talent been snatched up by telly? That the two men had only appeared once on television made no odds, they had been . . . snatched up by talent spotters. And so everyone who went on the stage at the club acted as if for an audition.

The room was already packed, and Hannah and Rosie alone found seats in a corner against the wall, while the men stood about them making signs with their hands and heads to acknowledge greetings from the occupants at other tables.

When the turn was finished, amid great applause, the men made their way to the bar counter while Hannah, with restrained conviviality, acknowledged the greetings from those around her. To their 'Hello there, Hannah,' 'How goes it the night, Hannah?' she made suitable replies accompanied by dignified movements of her head; and when a woman from close by rose and came towards her, saying, 'Don't tell me it's Rosie you have here,' Hannah replied, 'Who else, Mary?'

'Why, hello, Rosie!' The woman bent forward 'By! I wouldn't have known you . . . you've grown so.'

Rosie didn't bother to answer that, but smiled her greetings. What the woman really meant to say was, 'I wouldn't have known you, you look so changed.'

'How long are you here for?' the woman asked.

'Oh, for some time.'

'She's home for good, Mary.' Hannah nodded

solemnly. 'She's already fallen into a fine job in Newcastle.'

'Ah, there's no place like home, is there? It's always the same; they go off to London but they're glad to come scurrying back to their ma's.' She pushed her hand towards Hannah's.

'Yes, yes, you're right there, Mary.' But Hannah did not enlarge on her friend's remark. Perhaps it was something in Rosie's face that deterred her, a certain tightness.

The men returned with the drinks, a double whisky for Hannah and a glass of Guinness, pints of beer each for themselves and a gin and ginger for Rosie.

As they drank, talked and chaffed, Rosie looked about her. The atmosphere was one of jollity and good fellowship. When the master of ceremonies announced they were going to have community singing, this was acclaimed by loud clapping. And when everybody sang she, too, sang, and she wondered why she was singing. She wondered why she was here at all, for she had never liked the club and she didn't like it now. If she'd only been strong enough to say no; if she'd only had the gumption now she would finish her drink and say to her mother, 'I'm going home.'

But why didn't she like this kind of thing? These were her people. She had been brought up amongst them. In the main they were good solid people, working hard and playing hard, like now, the way that suited them. She had found from experience that you couldn't judge by accents, smooth tongues, or by clothes, yet this noise and bustle from table to lip, depressed her. She remembered Florence once saying to Dennis during one of their . . . queer arguments, 'The working classes need stimulating today more than they ever did, for there's very little natural gaiety left in them. And is it to be wondered at? What in their lives stimulates gaiety? They had to have the gin shops in the last century, and just as badly they need the clubs in this.'

So what was the difference between the working man being stimulated in a working-man's club or other men in a smart restaurant or a night club in London. As Florence had said, natural gaiety was like inborn holiness, it was very rare. At one time people had said that she herself was naturally gay, but she would never be naturally gay again, and she didn't want to be stimulated into being gay. What did she want? Some hole, perhaps, or quiet place into which she could crawl, and stay there until she died. She understood why animals sought solitude when they were wounded, there to die, if not in peace, alone with their agony. Yet if she felt like this why had she come back at all? Certainly her home was no hole in which to hide, more like a market place, or, more appropriate, a stage where all the emotions were up for viewing.

She was brought back to the present by Shane saying, 'That's over. Now we'll have a dance. Come on.' He pulled at her arm.

'But they haven't started yet.' She was reluctant to leave her seat.

'They will in a minute. Let's go to the other side.'

'Go on,' said Hannah, 'an' take the floor.' She was desirous of seeing her daughter being viewed, not as one of the crowd, but as one standing out from the crowd.

And this would be achieved only if they were first on the floor.

And so for the next two hours the entertainment went on; dancing, ballad singers, community singing and comic turns, one following hard on the other. And during this time they were joined by Barny. Also during this time, Hannah had consumed three double whiskies and three glasses of Guinness, and now she was mellow. Her eyes dancing, her lips ever parted, there had flowed from them joke after joke. Most of them against herself as a Catholic, and the Church as a whole. For was it not known that the best Catholics always told jokes against their creed? It was a way of proving that they were thick with God who also had a sense of humour. Above all, it proved that nobody could entertain like Hannah Massey when she got going.

Rosie had just started on her second gin when Jimmy asked her to dance.

She looked up at him, saying, 'But it's a twist they're playing.'

'Well, who says I can't do the twist. Listen to her!' He looked around the group at the table. 'She thinks it's only in London they can do the twist. Come on with you.' He tugged her out of the chair as if she were a child and pulled her through the crowd of tables to the dance floor, where already there were couples wriggling and contorting amid jeers and calls from those seated at the tables.

'Come on, let's make for the far corner and I'll show you who can do the twist.' Jimmy was at an amiable point of fullness and in high fettle, and he went into the dance like a big lumbering cart-horse, and at the sight

211

of his efforts Rosie, in spite of herself, began to laugh. When her body began to shake, she put her arm round her waist and cried, 'Oh, Jimmy! Jimmy, stop it.' But Jimmy, like his mother, knew when he was being amusing and her laughter only encouraged him to redouble his efforts, and not only because of Rosie but because now he was attracting attention from the tables in the far corner of the room.

Rosie was standing with her back to the wall as Jimmy contorted himself before her, and it was as she turned her face sideways that she looked towards the end of the bar counter and to where a woman was standing talking to a man. The woman was wearing a fur coat which was open, showing beneath a tight-fitting yellow wool dress. But it was not the dress that Rosie was looking at, but the woman's face, a long, narrow face with thin, red lips. She was hatless and her hair was dyed a pale mauve and dressed in a youthful style with a fringe which made her appear rather ludicrous.

As quickly as water rushed from a burst pipe the laughter rushed out of Rosie's body. Her mouth fell agape and she closed her eyes, but only for a second. When she opened them again it was to see that the woman, following her companion's gaze, was looking at Jimmy. Rosie remained still, fixed against the wall as if she were nailed there: If she made no movement the woman wouldn't see her and she would be able to get out. Her heart-beats pumping against her ribs vibrated through her head and seemed to cut out the blaring sound of the band. Without moving her eyes, she saw that the woman wasn't amused at Jimmy's antics. She wouldn't be, she wouldn't be. She prayed that Jimmy wouldn't

212

call to her but would be satisfied with his own exhibition. But Jimmy did call to her. He held out his hands and cried, 'Come on, Rosie, girl. Shake a leg.'

As the woman came slowly forward, Rosie kept her eyes fixed on Jimmy.

'Well, hello there. Fancy running into you.'

Rosie turned her head slowly and looked at the face before her, and as she looked she wished she had the power to strike the woman dead; yet it was to this woman she owed the fact that she was in Fellburn at this moment.

'Well, if this isn't a bit of luck. . . . Come on, say something, don't look so surprised.'

The band stopped amid loud applause, and a special kind of applause from the people sitting near for Jimmy, who, puffing and blowing, came towards Rosie now, saying, 'You're a fine partner.' As he finished speaking he stopped and looked at the woman. He looked her up and down before turning to Rosie, saying curtly, 'Come on . . . come on, girl.'

'Aren't you going to introduce us?'

Rosie's chin made a wobbling movement. 'This . . . this is my brother, Jimmy. Miss . . . Miss Lang,' she was stammering.

'Please to meet you.' The woman inclined her head towards Jimmy, and he inclined his, too, but he did not speak.

Definitely Jimmy was puzzled. He might have more brawn than brain but he was no fool where women were concerned, and he was asking himself how in the name of God their Rosie had come to know a Flossie like this one, and an old worn one into the bargain, not one of the smart new types that you couldn't tell from respectable lasses.

'Well, it looks as if I'm on me own. Can I join up? I was with a fellow, but I can't see him about.' She looked around. 'He's scarpered.'

Rosie, half turning away and speaking to Jimmy in an undertone, said, 'Tell me ma I won't be a moment and . . . and bring me bag, will you, Jimmy? . . . I'll be in the saloon.' She lifted her hand in a despairing motion and pointed to the door just to the right of her.

Jimmy made no reply, but he cast another glance at the woman before turning away, and he had gone some distance across the floor when Rosie running after him caught hold of his arm and whispered urgently, 'Don't . . . don't say anything to me ma, will you not?'

'Where's she from?' His face looked dark, no vestige of laughter on it now. 'How in the hell did you get to . . . ?'

'Jimmy . . . Jimmy, go on, I'll try to explain later, but . . . but don't say anything to me ma about her, will you?'

'I'm not a bloody fool altogether.'

He turned away and Rosie went back towards the woman. Passing her without speaking, she walked towards the door, then into the passage, and through another door and into the saloon.

There were only three couples in the room, which made it almost empty, and going to the corner farthest from the door she sat down, and the woman, following after her, took a seat opposite to her. She took a packet of cigarettes from her bag and she lit one before asking in a flat, sulky tone, 'Who's that?'

214

'I told you. My brother.'

'Huh! Your brother. Honest . . . ? Well, he's some beef, isn't he?'

Rosie looked down at the polished table. She picked up a drip pad and bent it back and forward between her hands, and as she did so the woman leant forward quickly and said under her breath, 'Aw come off it, you don't have to be afraid of me; at least you should know that. 'Cos remember if it wasn't for me you'd likely be getting dressed up . . . or the reverse, for your first night among the dusties this very minute . . . an' I'm not kiddin'.'

Rosie closed her eyes and swallowed, then asked, 'Why are you here, Ada?'

'All right, straight answer to a straight question. I came along to find out what you did with the ring. That's all.'

'The ring?' There was surprise, yet relief, in Rosie's tone.

'Yes, the ring.'

'I . . . I pawned it.'

'I guessed you would, not having anything on you. Well . . .' She drew on her cigarette, then blew out a thin stream of smoke before she said, 'I would like the ticket. That's all, so you needn't look so damned scared, you needn't be afraid of me.'

Slowly Rosie slumped against the back of the seat. 'How . . . how did you know where to find me?'

'Well, you'd told him you lived in Newcastle, but that time I was out with you – the time I tipped you off, remember? – I saw you posting a letter. It had the name Fellburn on it; so . . . well, I took a chance and came down yesterday and my God I can understand you saying

215

you lived in Newcastle, because this is a dump if ever there was one . . . Talk about the last place God made. And the customers! Good God! Customers! They can't make up their minds. Anyway, I found out where you lived this afternoon and I was going to look you up . . . but here we are. Well now, that's my story so what about the ticket, Rosie?'

'I haven't got it.'

'Aw, now, fair's fair. Don't come that line with me. Look, I mean you no harm. I've proved it, haven't I? I risked something when I put you wise, I'm telling you. Now come on, all I want is the ticket. . . . By the way, how much did you get on it?'

'Ten pounds.'

'Christ! What? You telling me the truth?'

'Yes.'

'The bugger only gave you . . . ?'

'That's all I asked.'

'Are you barmy?' The woman screwed her face up at Rosie, 'Well, I suppose you are, that's why I was sorry for you. I could see right away you hadn't any sense, not for this game, you hadn't. But God almighty! Ten pounds! Do you know what that ring's worth . . . ? Five hundred to say the least.'

Rosie's eyes stretched wide and her jaw sagged, and the words came out in awe. 'Five hundred? But why did he give it to me if it was worth all that?'

The woman shook her head slowly. 'Have you asked yourself why he gave you all the grand furniture and clothes, eh? Why a mink stole, eh? Why? Because they were all part of his stock in trade, and that ring was the biggest draw. I've lost count of the times he's had it altered to fit different fingers. It's part of his bank, that ring, and the centre diamond is worth God knows what. Do you know where that stone came from?' She pulled a face in enquiry at Rosie. 'A tiara. The dame that lost that tiara has sleepless nights even now. There's one thing I'll say for you, you had some nerve to go to his pocket and take it.'

'He'd given it to me. When we first met he gave it to me. It was a sort of . . .'

'A wedding ring. Yes, I know. Oh, God almighty! You know, Rosie, you make me want to vomit just to listen to you. Still, I suppose,' she spread out her hands on the table, palms upwards, 'if it wasn't for the innocents he'd be out of work. But it's hard to believe the likes of you are still born in this day and age. But now,' she leant her body halfway across the table, 'about the ticket.'

'I haven't got it, Ada. I'm telling you the truth, I tore it up.'

The woman remained still for a time as she stared into Rosie's face, then slowly moved back until only her hands were resting on the edge of the table. 'No kidding?' she said.

'It's the truth.'

'Well, you didn't think you'd get away with that, did you? What if he had found you? You might have smoothed things over by giving him the ticket.'

'I didn't know the ring was so valuable. Honest . . . honest.' Rosie rubbed her hand across her mouth where the beads of perspiration had gathered, then whispered, 'Did he send somebody down?'

'Yes, he did; he sent Scottie to Newcastle on Saturday

night. He came back on Tuesday saying he'd drawn a blank. It was when I heard this that I thought I'd take a trip meself and see if I'd have any better luck . . . in Fellburn. I had to get out of his way, anyway, because he threatened to put Dolan on to me. He guessed I'd tipped you off in the first place. He's no fool, is Dickie, and I didn't fancy meeting up with Dolan. I saw the last girl Dolan handled. She was out of business for a long, long time, so I said to myself, "Ada, you're due for a trip. You find Rosie and she'll tell you, out of gratitude like, where she pawned the ring". Because I knew, as he did, that was the only way you'd get the money. Lord! If you could have seen him when you didn't come out of that shop. He was watching out of the window all the time. I must say you put on a good show. If you had sauntered on the beat like you did that morning you'd have been made, and him and you would have lived happy ever after. You had got a good ten minutes start before he thought of looking in his pocket. The ring was the last thing he took off you, wasn't it?'

Rosie bowed her head.

The woman laughed, a thin confined laugh. 'Same old pattern,' she said; 'but none of them had the nerve to go to his jacket. You must have done it like lightning, you weren't in the bedroom a couple of seconds.'

'Well, what did you expect me to do?' Rosie glanced fiercely upwards as she asked the question.

'Oh, I just expected you to make a run for it once you got in the street, then go to the Salvation Army or something, anywhere that would get you home. Except the Police Station; I didn't expect you to go there after I warned you.'

218

'I nearly did.'

'It's as well you didn't, kid, for he would have got you. If he had done time he would still have got you. Dickie's vindictive, I've seen it. An' he's scared of jail. . . .'

'Be quiet!' Rosie was looking towards the door through which were coming Jimmy and Shane, their faces set. She knew what had happened. Jimmy had brought Shane with him to confirm his opinion of the woman their Rosie knew.

Ada, following Rosie's gaze, turned her head slowly towards the approaching men. Her look was lazy, confident. 'Another brother?' she mumbled through her teeth.

'Yes.'

'I don't believe it.' She pulled herself up straight, and looked at Shane as he came to the table, and as Shane stared down at her, she said, 'Rosie's brother?'

'Yes, I'm Rosie's brother.'

The woman laughed. 'Any more at home like you two?' She moved her head in Jimmy's direction, then looked back at Shane.

'Two more,' said Shane; 'and me mother's a nig woman an' all.'

'No kidding?'

'No kidding.'

'I'd like a drink,' she said.

'Come on, Rosie.' Jimmy lifted his head in a beckoning movement to Rosie, but looking pleadingly at him she said, 'I'd like a drink an' all, Jimmy. Would you bring two gins?'

Jimmy hesitated for quite some time, then sucking in

219

his lips he went to the bar counter at the end of the room for the drinks. Shane remained standing gazing down at the woman, taking in the nipples of her breasts imprinted sharply through the dress, the length of uncovered knee crossing the other and the tightness of the dress where it pulled in under her stomach. He said to her, 'Staying long?'

'It all depends.'

'How did you get in here?' her asked her. 'It's members only.'

'A gentleman friend brought me.' Her eyes narrowed and her face became grim. 'And don't you be so snotty.'

'Shane . . . look, Shane. Go on, please. I'll come along in a minute.'

'I've plenty of time. I'll go when you do.' Shane was now carrying a good few drinks and he looked and sounded stubborn.

When Jimmy came back to the table bringing the two gins and no drink for himself or Shane, Rosie said to him, 'I won't be five minutes, Jimmy, I'll join you in five minutes.'

'I've told her we'll go when she goes, not until.' Shane nodded at Jimmy.

At this Rosie bounced to her feet saying under her breath, 'Look, Shane, leave me alone. I'm not a child. Now get yourself away. And you an' all, Jimmy. You don't want me mother to come in here looking for me, do you?'

At this pointed question the men exchanged quick glances, and Shane said, 'All right, all right, but if you're not back in five minutes, ten at the outside, we'll come for you.' He nodded significantly at her. And Jimmy repeated like a parrot, 'Aye, we'll come for you.' He, too, nodded at her before turning away.'

'Who do they think they are, anyway?' The woman pulled the glass of gin towards her and gulped at it.

'They didn't mean anything,' said Rosie.

'Oh, don't start to consider my feelings or I'll cry.' She knocked the bottom of her glass twice on the table. 'And look, you're not getting rid of me until I know where I can lay my hands on that ring.'

'I can tell you the name of the shop; it was Gomex's.'

The woman's eyes stretched wide, and there came into them a gleam that looked like a smile. 'Gomex's?' she said. 'Well, fancy! How did you know about him?'

'What do you mean? I didn't know anything. I . . . I used to pass the shop coming from the office, that's all. It was quite near the office.'

'Well, for your information you hit on one of the biggest transferers . . . that's a nice term, isn't it, transferer, one of the biggest in the business. I bet he put two and two together and hoped you would die before you got that ring out again.' She paused. 'Did you put your own name and address on it?'

'I put my own name but not my address.'

'What address?'

'Eight Brampton Hill.'

'Rosie Massey, eight Brampton Hill, eh?'

'Yes.'

'Well, things seem to be going my way after all. From what I know of Mr Gomex, he's not partial to our dear Dickie. Here.' She pulled open her bag and pulled out an address book. 'Write along there: I authorise Miss Ada Lang to redeem the ring I pledged under the name

221

of Rosie Massey, of 8 Brampton Hill, on February twenty-second. I have lost the ticket . . . and sign it at the bottom. It mightn't carry any legal weight but it will help to convince him that I know you, and when I tell him the whole story he'll likely see it my way and we can come to some monetary arrangement.' She smiled now with her lips only. 'That's after I point out to him that if he doesn't produce it after twelve months and you fail to turn up there could be some enquiries. . . . Now what about another drink, just for old times' sake, eh?' As she turned her face towards the bar, the room door opened again, and as a man entered she exclaimed, 'Oh, I know this bloke, I was talking to him last night. He could be easy. Ooh-ooh, there,' she called down the room.

Rosie made no protest, but just stared like a fascinated rabbit as Ronnie MacFarlane came walking towards them.

When she had hailed him Ronnie had looked at Ada Lang, but only for a second before his gaze had jumped to Rosie, and he kept his eyes on her until he reached the table; and not until Ada Lang asked, 'You looking for me?' did he blink and turn towards the woman, saying, 'Yes. . . . No . . . no, I wasn't, I was looking for a pal.'

'Well, make up your mind. . . . Anyway, sit down now you're here.' She flicked out a chair with the point of her long shoe, and he looked at it for a moment before he sat down. Then he stared at the table for another moment before, his glance slipping between them, he said, 'You two know each other?'

'Of course we know each other. This is,' the woman

222

jerked her thumb across the table, 'this is Rosie, Rosie Massey.'

'I know it's Rosie Massey.' Ronnie was staring at the woman now, then slowly turning his head and addressing Rosie's averted face he said in an odd tone, 'Hello there, Rosie.'

Slowly Rosie pulled herself to her feet. She had felt sick before but it was nothing to the feeling she was experiencing now.

'What's your hurry? Sit down.' As Ronnie put out his hand to touch her she curved her body from it as if it was a reptile. At this he laughed, a deep laugh, a man's laugh, yet it sounded like laughter preceding madness.

'Look, sit down . . . sit down. What's your hurry?' The woman was looking up at her. 'Anyway wait till those pieces of beef come for you.' She put out her hand, and Rosie, knocking it aside, snapped, 'You've got what you want, now leave me alone.'

As she walked down the room she was conscious that they were both looking at her and she had the desire to run. She was almost on the point of it when she reached the door, there to be confronted by Jimmy and Shane again. She walked between them and into the passage before turning and facing them.

Jimmy's brows were down, his lower lip was moving as though it were an independent feature from side to side, as it always did when he was beginning to carry a heavy load.

She was surpised at the steadiness in her voice as she said, 'It's a long story, and you wouldn't believe me if I told you.'

'We'll take a chance on that.' It was Shane speaking.

'She's a tart. You know that, don't you? And an old one at that.'

'How do you know?' Her voice was snapping now.

'Ah, come off it, Rosie, it's sticking out all over her. An' what's more, she was here last night and tried it on with one or two of the lads.'

'If me mother knew you knew anybody like her she'd go clean up in the lum,' said Jimmy now, 'an' if I catch you with her again I'll clout your lug, as old as you are.'

'Steady on, steady on,' said Shane, pushing his brother with the flat of his hand. 'Those dames are clever; they make friends with people an' not everybody can spot 'em. Come on, come on.' He took hold of Rosie's arm. 'Me mother's been asking for you. An' for God's sake, an' your own,' he nodded solemnly towards her, 'don't let her and that piece meet up.'

'I'm going home.' She pulled her arm from Shane's.

'Oh no, you're not, you're coming back to me ma and we'll all go home together. Come on.' Jimmy's grip was not as gentle as Shane's, and Rosie found herself being hustled through the door into the main room. Someone had just stopped singing and everybody was clapping. When they reached the table Hannah greeted her with a broad, oily smile. 'Where've you been, me dear?' she asked. Her voice was thick and lazy sounding.

'Talking,' said Rosie.

'Talking? Who to? Was it young Graham Benson? He was at me a while ago enquiring after you. "How long is she staying?" he asked. "She's a smasher," he said. He's a nice fellow is young Benson, and doing well.'

'I think I'll go home, Ma, I'm feeling a bit tired.'

'Aw, home hell!' Jimmy looked warningly at Rosie. 'We'll all go shortly. Let's have another round first. An' it's your turn, Shane, me boy.' He turned to his brother. 'An' I'll have a double meself this time, I'm sick of beer.'

There was a babble of talk now and it went over Rosie's head. She watched Shane go for the drinks and return with them, and as he placed them on the table someone began to play the piano and a voice broke into song, and soon almost everybody in the room was singing.

It was when the community singing ended that Rosie saw Ada Lang and Ronnie standing by the bar. Ada had one elbow on the counter and was looking at Ronnie, but Ronnie, with his broad back tight against the counter, was looking directly at her.

Hannah had seen him too, and leaning heavily towards Broderick, she whispered thickly, 'Who's that piece with Ronnie MacFarlane over there? I've never seen her here afore. She doesn't fit in . . . cheap she is. What's things comin' to? She can't be a member, I've never seen her here afore,' she repeated. 'He should have his wife with him; aye, he should. She looks loose, that one. . . .'

'I'm going home, Ma.' Rosie was on her feet and she glanced at Jimmy defiantly as she made this statement, and Hannah looking up at her and still smiling said, 'Oh, it's early. What time is it?'

'It's after ten.'

'Aye, it's after ten,' put in Broderick, 'an' not far off shutting-up time.'

'Is it, begod! Well then, just a minute, just a minute.' As Hannah looked back at Rosie she appeared to be the essence of amenity. 'Let me drink this an' I'll come along. Always go when you're feeling happy I say, never overdo a good thing. It's been a grand evenin'. What say you?' She looked round the table but did not wait for their affirmation, and emptying her glass she rose unsteadily to her feet, crying, 'Ups-a-daisy,' and as she staggered slightly she grabbed at Broderick and they both laughed.

'Where's Barny and Arthur?' she asked.

'Over at yon side,' said Shane. 'You get goin' an I'll collect them. You go along with them, Jimmy.' Shane nodded at his brother, and Jimmy said thickly, 'Aye, I'll go along with them.' What his tone implied was that he would go along with Rosie.

And he did go along with her. He preceded his mother and father out of the room, pressing Rosie before him as he waved goodbye to right and left, and swaying and lunging on the crusting slush, he hung on to her until they reached home. Yet he didn't speak a word to her. Although he was talking all the time all his remarks were thrown over his shoulder to his mother and father, who, arm in arm, came slithering and laughing behind them.

Rosie made no protest whatever against Jimmy's possessive hold on her. Outwardly, she appeared docile, but inwardly she was in a turmoil. She must get her things together and get out of the house as soon as possible. It wasn't Jimmy or Shane's questioning she was afraid of as much as Ronnie MacFarlane's. Whereas Jimmy and Shane could not believe that she was more than lightly acquainted with a woman like Ada Lang, Ronnie seemed to have gauged the truth from the moment he saw them together. And Ada's form of introduction had clinched it. When she had left them she hadn't considered whether or not Ada would give her away, and when she had seen Ronnie looking so pointedly at her she had come to the conclusion that Ada hadn't said anything. But the fact remained that Ronnie guessed at what the lads didn't want to believe, and she must get away. When they were all in bed sleeping their drink-drugged sleep, she would bring downstairs just what she could carry, and she would go to Dennis's until the morning, and from there she would go to her new digs in Newcastle.

Flopping into the big chair near the banked-down fire, Hannah shouted at Broderick, 'Oh, take me shoes off, lad, they're killing me.' Then flinging her arms out towards Rosie, she cried, 'Have you had a good night? Have you enjoyed yourself, lass? You still dance like a fairy. I came and watched you once or twice. You didn't know I did but I did. Oh, you were a sight, with the finest pair of legs in the land. I've always had the faculty of enjoying a pair of legs, like a man.' At this she let her head flop back and the laughter gushed from her. And Broderick roared with her, but not Jimmy. Jimmy was looking really surly now. He was sitting by the table, his elbow on it, his head resting on the palm of his hand, his brow puckered and his lip working as if his fuddled mind was trying to puzzle something out.

'Let's have a bite to eat.' Hannah was shouting now as if they were all in another room. 'I'm as hungry as a hunter. Oh God, oh God, I wish it wasn't Friday so I could have a shive of meat. But there's cheese and pickles and cold fish in the pantry. Go on, fetch them out, Broderick; you're steadier on your pins than me, man.'

'That I am, that I am. You can't carry it, girl, that's your trouble,' said Broderick. 'Come on, Rosie. Let's see what we can rake up.' He held out his arms to her.

In the quiet of the kitchen, his arm still about her, Broderick attempted to focus his wavering gaze on his daughter, and he asked gently, 'Are you all right, me girl, are you all right? It's quiet you are.'

'Yes, I'm all right, Da. Yes, come on.' She turned from him. 'Let's get the things.'

As they went back to the living-room with the food on a tray, Broderick waving a jar of pickles in each hand, the others came in the front way. They were headed by Shane, and as soon as Rosie looked at them and found their gaze directed pointedly towards her she knew that she had been under discussion.

But if the lads were not their usual rowdy Friday night selves, it went unnoticed, because Hannah and Broderick kept up an exchange of quips that evoked their own laughter, and all the while Broderick hung on to Rosie, protesting against her wanting to break up the party and go to bed.

It was nearly an hour later, when Jimmy and Shane were making for upstairs, that the front bell rang. It silenced them all for a moment, and Hannah looking about her said, 'Who can it be at this time of night? You did say Karen was in, didn't you, Arthur?'

'Aye, I saw her coming out of the bathroom.'

'See who it is, Jimmy. See who it is.' Hannah made the request while Jimmy was already on his way to the door.

'Perhaps old Watson's bad next door.' Shane jerked his head to the wall.

'Aw, she would have knocked through if that had been the case,' said Hannah.

'Perhaps old Ma Parkman can't get to sleep for us laughin', an' she's come to complain again.'

'Begod! If she has it'll be the last time, for I'll spit in her eye and christen her Paddy. . . . But whist! Whist! What's that?'

When they all became silent a voice came from the hall, crying, 'I want to see her.'

'It's MacFarlane!' All eyes in the room said it, and Hannah looked quickly towards Rosie where she was standing at the end of the table one hand holding her throat. Then as Jimmy's voice came to them, shouting, 'Look, get yourself to hell out of here unless you're askin' for trouble!' They all, with the exception of Rosie, moved towards the hall, and there wasn't a steady gait among them.

Now Ronnie's voice, thick and fuddled, rose above all the exclamations, crying, 'I'll . . . I'll take you on . . . but one at a time, if you're men enough to do one at a time. An' after I've finished with you all I'll see her. But see her I will.'

'Is it mad you are, Ronnie MacFarlane, disturbing a respectable household at this hour of the night?' Hannah was bawling. 'Get yourself home and to your wife. Aye, to your wife who at this minute might be bringin' a soul into the world. It's ashamed of yourself you should be.'

'Ashamed? Me? Huh!'

The huh! was cut short by Shane. 'Are you goin' to

229

get out,' he cried, 'or do you want your bloody teeth knocked in?'

'Knock me teeth in, will you? Let me tell you, lad, it won't be like last time. I've come prepared.'

There was a pause; and then Broderick's voice, saying, 'Knuckledusters, begod! That's a low trick, Ronnie. Now look, we want no trouble; get yourself away, man.'

'You dirty sod!' It was Hannah again; and quick as lightning Ronnie answered her. 'Dirty sod, am I? You call me a dirty sod, Hannah Massey? With a daughter like you've got, you call me a dirty sod?'

'Shut your bloody mouth and get out!'

As Jimmy's voice came to Rosie she groped blindly at a chair and sat down. And she held her face in her hands as Ronnie cried, 'Come a step nearer an' I'll let you hev it right atween the eyes. You all know, don't you? You all know what she is. That's why you're scared bloody stiff. But perhaps your dear ma doesn't know. No, perhaps she doesn't. You'd be frightened to tell your ma, lads, wouldn't you? But I'll tell her. . . .'

'Get him out!' It was Shane yelling.

'Hold your hand . . . I'm warning you!' The voice was like thunder. 'Mind it! Mind it! Afore this fist splits your face open. No, the lot of you big sods'll not shut me mouth. I wasn't good enough for your Rosie, was I, Hannah Massey? I mustn't touch her. An' begod! I wouldn't now if you paid me, for she's a whore! An' she's been workin' under a whore master for the last three months with that tart in the bl . . .'

As the house vibrated to the screams and shouts and the thuds of blows, Rosie put her hands over her ears, and, dropping her face down to the table, she moved it back and forward in agony. Then her head was brought up to see Karen by the table shouting 'What's the matter? What's it all about?' When she looked at her for a moment before dropping her head again, Karen ran back towards the hall but it was empty now.

Outside Jimmy and Shane and Ronnie were tangled up on the icy road, while Arthur and Barny, trying to separate them, were involved in the blows. And as Hannah, at the bottom of the steps hanging on to Broderick, screamed unintelligibly, light after light appeared in the windows of the houses up and down the street.

The Parkmans and the Watsons were at their open doors, and now Bob MacFarlane came rushing down his steps buttoning up his trousers and shouting, while Jessie followed him, hugging her fur coat over her nightdress.

The light from the Batemans' front door across the road streamed on to the huddle of men. The Batemans had never been on speaking terms with the Masseys, they considered that the whole family was out of its element living in Grosvenor Road, and now Mr Bateman did what he had wanted to do for a long time, he phoned the police.

When the patrol car, which must have been in the vicinity, came whisking down the street and two policemen joined the mêlée, Hannah's loud voice was stilled for a moment and she staggered back against the stone pillar of the gate, exclaiming in a whisper, 'No! No! Jesus, Mary and Joseph.'

Mr MacFarlane was now aiding the police, as was Mr Bateman, and when the combatants were separated it was hard to tell which was Ronnie or Jimmy or Shane. The only difference between them was that one of them lay still on the ground, and Mr MacFarlane, recognising his own, lifted the blood-stained head, shouting, 'Ronnie! Ronnie!'

The policeman now spoke to Mr Bateman, and once again Mr Bateman was pleased to go to his phone.

At this point Jimmy went to tug himself from the policeman's hold. He didn't like policemen. 'Leave go of me!' He felt fighting mad now, and when he found he was still being held he lashed out with his other arm, and the policeman, losing his balance on the slippery road, fell on his back. He wasn't down for more than a second, and when he got to his feet again his companion came to his aid and they advanced on Jimmy. Shane, standing swaying on the kerb, was in a bad way, but not so bad that he was going to let the 'bloody polis' get at their Jimmy.

Once again there was a mêlée in the road, and now Hannah was only restrained by Broderick from joining in, but her voice soared above all the sound, screaming at her brood to give over, to give over. She did not recognize the police van as such until it stopped almost at her feet, and when she did the disgrace cut off her voice and there was nothing left in her but a whimper which said, 'The Black Maria! The Black Maria!' The Black Maria had come for her sons.

The road seemed full of policemen now, and they were bundling her lads into the van. Barny went in protesting, 'I've done nowt, I've done nowt. Me an' Arthur's done nowt.'

He gripped at the side of the van door and, putting

232

his head back on his shoulders, he strained to look at Hannah, where she was being held in his father's arms, and he cried to her, 'Ma! Ma!' before being pushed forward.

They did not put Ronnie MacFarlane into the van, but into an ambulance. His father was allowed to go with him, but his mother stood on the pavement hugging the coat around her shivering body, and as the police van and the ambulance drove away, one after the other, she turned and looked towards Hannah. And Hannah looked back at her, and neither of them spoke.

Broderick, his face wearing an utterly stricken look now, turned Hannah about and led her up the steps and into the hall; and of a sudden Hannah's legs gave way beneath her and she would have fallen to the floor had not Karen pushed the hall chair forward. 'Almighty God! Almighty God!' Hannah moved her head in a slow wide sweep. 'Me sons, every one of them, taken to jail. Me lads.' She looked up at Broderick. 'What's happened to us? What's happened, I ask you, that me sons . . . What's to be done?' She stared at him wildly.

'They . . . they can get bail, I think, sort . . . sort of,' Broderick stammered. 'I . . . I better go and get D . . . Dennis.'

'Dennis? No! No! Begod, no!' The name seemed to rouse her back to normality.

'I'll have to, woman. He's got a head on his shoulders, he'll know what to do better than me or any of us. You'd rather have that than they'd be kept in jail, wouldn't you now?' He bent towards her. 'I'll put on me coat and get a car and I'll be there in a few minutes. Now stay quiet.' He turned to Karen. 'See to your grannie, that's a good girl, see to your grannie.' He did not go into the living-room or mention Rosie's name, but lifting his coat from the hall-stand and not bothering about his muffler or cap, he slunk out of his front door like a thief in the night, and Hannah was left sitting looking at Karen. She looked at her for some minutes before she said, 'Go on up to your bed.'

'No, I'll stay with you. Me grandda . . .'

'I've told you . . . go to bed. I'm all right.'

'But . . .'

'Did you hear me?' It was the old Hannah speaking, and hearing her, Karen saw no need to worry, at least about her grannie's condition. Shrugging her shoulders, she crossed the hall, glancing into the living-room before she mounted the stairs.

Hannah continued to sit on in the cold hall, and as she sat she looked about her. She looked towards the door of her front room, and through the heavy panels she could see every article of the fine furniture that adorned the room. She looked at the bright red-and-green-patterned stair carpet. She looked down at the rug on the hall floor; it had a two-inch fringe on it. She could have got the same rug without the fringe for four pounds less, but she liked the fringe, it gave an air of quality to the rug. And lastly, she turned her eyes towards the open door of the living-room, and she kept them there until she pulled herself to her feet and advanced slowly towards it.

When she entered the room she saw Rosie sitting at the top end of the table, her face as white as a corpse, her eyes staring out of her head; and as she went towards her she saw her rise to her feet and then back towards the wall. And she followed her until she could touch her with her outstretched arm. But she didn't touch her, she just stood looking at her. And then she began to speak, her voice quiet. She said, 'It's true, isn't it? It's true what he said, that you're a whore?'

'No, no.' Rosie moved her head – it was tight back against the wall, her chin up – not in defiance, but in fear.

'He said you were a whore, and you lived with a whore master for three months.'

'I wasn't, I wasn't. I lived with him . . . I didn't know. . . .' Her head was moving in a tormented, desperate fashion.

Hannah made a movement with her hand that said, 'Say no more', and she went on, 'I wondered who you reminded me of when you stepped into the house a week ago this night with your skin-fit skirt and your short waist jumper that pushed out your breasts like balloons. I wondered then. But who, I ask you, but somebody with the mind of the devil would have put the tab on you. An' that piece that Ronnie was talkin' to standin' at the bar, that was her he meant . . . your pal! It was her you were with, wasn't it, when you disappeared during the evening? And then the story you told me the night you came back. There wasn't a word of truth in it, was there?'

'Ma . . . Ma.' Rosie's head was still moving, and now her eyes were closed and the tears raining from beneath her lids. 'I didn't know, I didn't know.'

'You didn't know you were a prostitute?'

'I wasn't, I never was.'

'Did you live with a whore master?'

'I didn't know he was, I didn't know, I swear by our Lady. . . .'

'Quiet! Quiet!' Now Hannah's voice had changed and it came as a deep growl from her throat. 'Don't dare soil her name with your lips. . . . You tell me òut of your own mouth that you lived with this man, and for your companions you had pieces like that one the night, an' you tell me you know nothin' about whoring? I wasn't born yesterday, girl, at least not all of me.' She shook her head until her coiled hair became loose and a strand fell down on to her shoulder. 'Only the part that believed in you; you the shining light of me life, me daughter Rosie. I always held me head high when I mentioned me daughter Rosie. They used to laugh behind me back . . . the neighbours. . . . Oh, I knew. I knew. But when they saw you with their own eyes they thought, She's right. She's right. Her Rosie's a lady if ever there was one. An' those that didn't think along those lines I sensed it, and plugged you at them until they did. Until they knew that Hannah Massey's daughter, Rosie, was a somebody. . . . Aye, begod!' Her voice dropped now and her mouth fell agape before she went on, 'A somebody! A London street whore, a strumpet. Can you hear them? Can you hear them laughin', Rosie?' It was a question. 'Answer me, girl.' Her voice was as terrible as her face now. 'Can you hear them laughin'? They're splitting their sides. They're sick with their laughin'. They're spewing with their laughin'. "The higher they climb," they're sayin', "the longer the fall", and begod! Hannah Massey's fallen hard. Her an' her beautiful daughter, Rosie! Can't you hear them? Can't you hear them laughin', Rosie?'

'Oh, Ma. Oh. Ma, stop it, stop it.'

Hannah stepped back, making a wide sweep of her arm as she did so, crying, 'Don't Ma me, I'm no relation to you. From this minute onward I'm no relation to you, do you hear?' Bending her body forward now she said, 'Do you know what you've done to me this night? Do you?' The words were once again coming deep and guttural, but now they were coated with a terrible anger. 'You've destroyed me. If you'd taken a razor and cut me throat it would've been kind, but no. No . . . you had to disgrace me. Me sons are in jail, me four sons are in jail because of you, do you hear? As for me . . . me life's over. The morrow I was goin' to sign the contract that would take me to Brampton Hill . . . and now what have I?' She wagged her head slowly. 'I haven't even got this home, I'm finished.' Again she wagged her head. 'I've put a face on things, all me life I've put a face on things, but I couldn't put put a face on this, I couldn't look the street in the eye after this. Nor the town. I'm crawling in the muck . . . in the muck. From this moment on I'm dead and I'll have you remember it's you that's done it. You'll take it to the grave with you. Oh dear God, when I think.' She dropped her head back and looked at the ceiling now, her big body sagging as she went on, 'Puttin' you afore everythin' and everybody. Worshipping you. . . . Aw God has strange ways. Indeed, indeed. Ye shall not have false gods afore me, He says, an' if ever a woman has been paid out for havin' a false god it's me this night.' She brought her head forward again, and her lips curling widely from her large square chin, she allowed her eyes to range slowly from Rosie's hair over her terrified face

237

and down to her feet, then up again. And her nose pushing upwards from the force of her curling lips, she ground out, 'You smell! You stink! You're not fit to touch. Me own flesh has gone putrid on me.' As she spoke her body drooped forward into a crouch. Her arms lifting, she shuffled a half-step nearer to Rosie, muttering thickly as she did so, 'You're not fit to touch but I'm goin' to touch you, an' for the last time, I'm goin' to give you somethin' you'll remember for destroying me an' me house.'

At this, Rosie, who had been spread-eagled against the wall, brought her arm in front of her face, crying, 'Don't hit me, Ma! Don't hit me.'

For answer, Hannah's fist shot out, and as the blow caught Rosie between the eyes her scream seemed to rend the house. And when again the fist landed full on her mouth and then on her nose, Rosie's screams turned to a moaning whine.

Hannah, her face distorted, her fist ready to strike again, paused as she watched her daughter slide down the wall to the floor. Her thick arms dropping to her side, she stepped back and looked at the huddled, shaking, moaning form, and she cried, 'Get up!' Then again, 'Do you hear me? Get up!'

After a long moment Rosie got up, raising herself like a cowed animal from the floor, and when she was on her feet she covered her face with her hands as she stumbled forward intending to go towards the table to sit down. But Hannah's voice checked her, screaming at her now, 'Get out! Get out! You trollop you!'

Dazed, moaning and swaying, Rosie stood, until Hannah's single finger dug in her back, thrusting her towards the kitchen, through it and out of the back door, which Hannah almost lifted off its hinges, so fierce was the pull with which she opened it. Then not pausing a moment she closed the door with a bang and bolted it. Following this she moved towards the table and stood leaning against it, blinking down at the conglomeration of dirty plates and cutlery on it. Then lifting her head with a jerk she went out of the kitchen, through the sitting-room and up the stairs, pulling herself up by the banister, and into the bathroom, and there, after taking a bottle of tablets from the cupboard and filling a glass with water she went into her own room and put the bottle and glass on a little table near the bed.

Now inserting her hand into the front of her dress and vest she took out the key of the bottom drawer of the chest, and when she had opened the drawer she carried it to the round table in the middle of the room, after which she went to the altar in the corner near the bed and took from the shelf a box of matches. Following this she went back to the table, and, without even pausing to consider, she lit a match and applied it to the end roll of notes in the drawer. When it was well alight she went to the bed and, sitting down, emptied the tablets from the bottle into the glass of water; still without a pause she swilled them round once or twice then gulped at them, choking and spluttering on the half-dissolved mass. And now she did pause; her movements became less controlled. Slowly she drew the pad of her thumb across each corner of her mouth, then she took in a deep breath and sat watching the smoke rising from the drawer for a moment or two, waiting for the flame to come over the top, but when a whirling movement in her head told her she was going to fall forward she lifted one heavy leg after the other on to the bed and lay down and waited. There was no panic in her waiting, only thoughts of the impress her death would make on her family, and on one member in particular until the day she too died.

She was dead before the breath left her body, and she knew this. She knew she had died when Ronnie MacFarlane knocked on the door.

The Aftermath

It was 5 a.m. when Dennis returned home for the second time that morning. Florence had heard the taxi and was standing at the open door. She put out her hand to him but didn't speak. His face looked white and pinched and his eyes wide. She helped him off with his coat, and still she didn't speak. It was Hughie, standing between the kitchen and the room door, who asked, 'How did you find her?'

'She's dead.'

As Dennis came towards him, Hughie turned and walked back into the room, and together they sat down side by side on the studio couch that was still made up as a bed.

'Give me a drink of something?' Dennis looked up at Florence, who was standing in front of him now.

'Coffee?' she asked quietly. 'It's all ready.'

'No.' Dennis shook his head. 'Have you got a drop of whisky left?'

When she brought him the drink he just sipped at it. Then he looked at the carpet as he said, 'I can't take it in. She was so full blooded you would have thought her aggressiveness would have defied death itself.' Then raising his eyes, he looked at Florence, and it was as if he had forgotten Hughie's presence when he spoke to his wife, saying, 'When I looked at her lying there, so quiet, so peaceful, shouting no more, never again to be unreasonable, or irrational, I felt a flood of tears rising in me; and then I thought of what you've always said about death, and it being the plastic surgery that turns a renegade into a saint, and it checked the flood.'

'Oh don't let it, Dennis, don't let it.' She dropped on to her knees before him and took hold of his hand. 'It's all right talking about these things and being clever when they don't affect you, but . . . but she was your mother.'

Dennis had his eyes closed now and his head was moving in small jerks as he said, 'Don't recant, Florence. Please don't recant, because I'm not going to. She killed herself; out of spite she killed herself; just because her idea of respectability had been shattered, she killed herself. Yet all her life she's been her own stumbling block in her efforts to reach her goal, and by her very last act any glory that her family might have bestowed on her will be tarnished in their own minds by what she did. And I don't mean just her taking her life. Do you know how much money she had stacked away?' He looked from Florence to Hughie.

Hughie, inclining his head, said softly, 'I could give a pretty good guess.'

'I never dreamed she had that much. Nearly three thousand.'

'Three thousand!' repeated Florence in awe. 'Where?'

'In the bottom drawer of the old chest in the bedroom. And she set fire to the lot before she took the pills.'

Florence moved back slowly on her heels, and her buttocks slipped to the floor and she rested there staring at Dennis; and he nodded at her, and then to Hughie, saying, 'When I dropped me da off at the door from the

242

taxi after coming from the station, apparently he went straight upstairs to find the place full of smoke and Karen nearly demented. She had smelt the smoke and gone into me mother's room. The drawer, full of notes, was smouldering, some apparently had been alight but had died down, but the whole could have burst into flames at any minute. She didn't know what was in the drawer at first, she just threw water over the lot then tried to wake me mother up. It was then me da came in. He tried to get her on to her feet and make her sick, but she was too far gone. It would have been all right but she'd had a number of chasers in her before she took the tablets. Karen ran out and phoned the hospital, and then . . . well, you know the rest, she came on here for me.'

'Have they let the lads out, knowing this?' asked Hughie.

'No. I haven't been back to the station yet, and I don't know how I'm going to tell them. Anyway, their case won't come up until the first Court. If our Jimmy and Shane hadn't hit the polis they might have stretched a point, but they weren't too easy with them when they got them down there I understand.'

Dennis finished off the whisky; then looking at the glass, said, 'They'll mourn her. Each in his own way they'll mourn her, but on the quiet they'll be thinking she meant to burn every penny of that money . . . their money. Yet being very much her sons they'll remember what she used to say, "Speak nicely about the dead", she used to say, "for where they've gone they've got power and can bring good or bad to. you." '

'Rosie will get the blame for this.' Hughie was speaking almost to himself, and Florence answered, saying, 'Yes, from all sides it'll be levelled at her.' She turned her head towards Dennis. 'You didn't hear any more, where she went I mean?'

'No, only Karen heard me mother at her. But I found Karen a bit cagey about what went on. Of course she's upset. She said she heard me mother put her out and bang the door. You know I . . . I just can't take it in about her. If it hadn't been me da who told me . . .' He shook his head. 'Rosie on the streets. . . .'

'No, no!' Hughie's tone brought Dennis's head round, and also Florence's eyes towards him, and he said again, and emphatically, 'No, no! She wasn't on the street, Dennis. I . . . I didn't say anything afore, because . . . well I was shaken about it all coming out and wondering where she had got to in the dark, and on a night like this, but I can tell you now the mess she got into wasn't her fault. She told me about it the other night when she was here, the night you went out.'

'Aye?' Dennis moved slowly round to face Hughie, saying, 'Well, go on. What's her side of it?'

Hughie pursed his lips. 'Well, as she told me it was like this. As you know, for the first year or more she was up there she shared a flat with two other girls at the office. Well, she said it was an expensive place and very nice. Then one of the girls goes back home to Gloucester and the other gets married, and it was impossible for her to keep it on. She then pals up with another girl and shares her flat. But this place is real slummy and dirty. And she doesn't like the girl either, and she's lonely. She was on the point of packing the job up, she said, and coming home, when one Sunday night, coming out of Benediction, she sees a fellow standing on the kerb

244

right opposite the church. She had seen him there two or three times before when she came out of church and had thought naturally that he'd just come out too. Well this night he speaks to her, and that was the beginning. He's very smartly dressed, he speaks well, he's courteous and extremely kind and . . .' Hughie looked down at his hands. 'To use her own words, she went down before him like warmed snow off a roof. Apparently he was quite open about himself. He was married but his divorce was going through. He was in the property business which fluctuated from time to time. Sometimes he was in the money, he said, and sometimes he was broke. At this particular time, apparently, he was in the money. He asked her to go to his flat, but it was six weeks before she finally paid her first visit. It was a beautiful place, she said, furnished with the kind of things you see in expensive magazines. A month later she gives up her job and moves in.' Hughie pulled the knuckle of his first finger, and there was a sharp cracking sound; then he went on, 'He had to be away a lot on business, she said, but when they were together everything was marvellous. The only thing she didn't like was that he had to go to clubs to meet business associates and he always insisted she went with him. She didn't like his business friends, and apparently neither did he, and he apologised for them. All this time he is piling on her furs, jewellery and expensive clothes. Then one night he comes home worried. He's in a bit of a jam, he says, he's got to meet a client who can make or break him. Will she be nice to the man? They meet this client in a private room in a hotel, and after dinner this fellow of hers is called away and she is left alone with this man, who begins to paw

245

her. But . . . but she manages to push him off and get out of the room. She can't find the other fellow and she goes home. When he turns up he's terribly upset for her. Later in the week he tells her that the client has been spiteful and has put him in a real fix, in fact he's broke; at least for a time and won't be able to keep up the expensive apartment. Rosie said it didn't matter a jot when it came to pawning her clothes and furs and all the expensive presents he had given her. But now she was uneasy, yet she really wouldn't face up to why she was uneasy.'

'It's . . . it's fantastic,' put in Florence. 'Like . . . like a novelette. Fancy her being taken in by it . . . Rosie . . . she seems so all there.'

'Be quiet a minute,' said Dennis. 'Go on, Hughie.'

'Well, she tells him she would take up a job again, but he won't hear of it. Then they moved to another flat . . . one of three in an old house, towards the outskirts of London, and it's in sharp contrast to the luxurious place they have left. The fellow gives Rosie to understand that she has the power to put him back on . . . on his business feet if she'll only be nice to the fellows he introduces her to. Even when she knows what these supposedly business associates want she doesn't really connect it with him until she realizes the girl in the flat above and the one in the flat below are call girls; and not until it's brought home to her that they are both known to this fellow does she face the truth. And then she is terrified. The fellow now hardly ever goes out, hardly ever leaves her alone. The only time she goes out alone is when she goes to the shops along the street, and then he doles her out the money for food. She has no clothes, only those she stands up in, and he had bought her these. And by now she is so frightened she does everything without protest. When the other girl upstairs – her name was Ada – hadn't customers she came down and talked to Rosie, and apparently she felt a bit sorry for her. Rosie even heard her telling the man that he was wasting his time and that she, Rosie, hadn't . . . hadn't what it took for the game. Eventually, the fellow seemed to realize this himself but he wasn't going to lose anything on her. Apparently he did a side line in shipping girls abroad, and that's what he intended to do with Rosie. It was this girl Ada who gave her the tip that she was to be moved on that Saturday night.'

'God in Heaven!' Dennis looked at Florence's stretched face. 'Can you believe it?' he asked now, and when she just moved her head, he said to Hughie again, 'I'm sorry, go on.'

'Well, Rosie said when she first met him he had given her a ring, it was an ornate affair and he called it their wedding ring. She thought it was worth about twenty pounds, and he had let her keep it when he took all her other things. As long as we have the ring, he had said, we'll be able to eat. But on the Friday morning, he took it off her hand, seemingly full of regret, and said, "It's the last lap." And then he asked her would she like to go home because he couldn't see himself ever getting on to his feet again. It was then that she used all the resources in her and played his game and said yes, she would like to go home.

' "We'll see about it the night, the sooner the better," he said, and having, he thought, allayed her fears, he had no hesitation in giving her the money to go and get

247

some shopping. Yet she knew that every move she made was watched by him through the man who sold papers on the other side of the street. When she went into the bedroom for her coat she whipped the ring from his pocket. It was the only way she could think of to get the money to come home. It was either that or go to the police, and she couldn't bear the thought of coming into the open about her position in case the news was transferred to the police here, and the thought of . . . of her mother hearing of what had happened terrified her even more than the man. . . . Well, she pawned the ring for ten pounds. That was last Friday.'

They were all silent for some time; then Florence, rising to her feet, murmured, 'It's unbelievable, yet it's happening every day. But you wouldn't think girls would be so gullible now. . . . And . . . and Rosie. I say again, she looked so all-there, so self-assured.'

'What we've got to remember, Florence,' said Hughie, 'is that Rosie didn't fall in love with a pimp, she fell in love with a polished, soft-spoken, kind man. She went to live with him because she was fascinated by him and thought she loved him, and she stayed with him because she really believed he was going downhill and in trouble. The pattern was so simple, it was almost diabolical. And you know what influenced her in the first place?' He looked directly at Dennis. 'She had met him outside a Catholic church. It was a sort of symbol to her.'

'Shades of Hannah Massey,' said Dennis pitifully, as he rose to his feet. Then covering the lower half of his face with his hand, he went out of the room.

Florence gazed after him but did not follow him; she got up from the floor and sat down beside Hughie, and pressing her hands between her knees, she said, 'All our philosophizing and theorizing doesn't mean much when it comes to the push, Hughie, does it? The plastic surgery takes effect whether you like it or not, at least with most of us. I only hope it does with Dennis, I do. I never liked his mother and she always hated me, but then there was no blood between us; but no matter what he says or thinks he still remains part of her, and you can't get away from yourself, can you? That's the one thing no theory can do for you, remove you from yourself. But,' she straightened herself, 'the one I'm worrying about at the present moment is Rosie. Where do you think she got to in the night? She couldn't wander the streets, she would freeze, or the police would pick her up. Do you think she would go into any of the neighbours?'

'No, I don't think so, Florence.' Hughie was staring across the room. 'And she wasn't at the station; I thought this was the likely place.'

'You went to the station?'

'Yes. When I found Dennis and Broderick had left the police station I called on me way back. But it was closed. I never knew they closed it at night. They don't open until the first train at five o'clock.'

'It's so hard to take in all at once.' Florence looked at Hughie. 'Her dead, and the four lads in jail, and Rosie God knows where. It doesn't seem as if it could have happened in such a short time . . . and all because a well-dressed man with a smooth tongue spoke to Rosie outside a Catholic church. . . . Fantastic, isn't it, that everything began at that point?'

'Oh, I think you can trace it back earlier than that, Florence.' Hughie moved his closed fist over his mouth.

249

'In fact, you could start at the moment Rosie was born when Hannah determined to make her into a lady, her kind of lady. Or the day Hannah stopped in the middle of her washing and took her to the typing school. Oh, there are many points where you could start. You could even go back to the day when Hannah was born, or the day when she landed with her mother from Ireland . . . or perhaps the real point from where all this started was the day when she went to work on Brampton Hill. The grandeur of number eight fascinated her and it was her life's aim to imitate it. But she was a poor mimic was Hannah, she was always a poor mimic.' He began to rub one shoulder with his hand as if to smooth away a pain.

Florence stood up now, saying, 'Lie down for a couple of hours, Hughie; I'll try to get him to do the same. There's going to be a busy day ahead.'

Hughie nodded to her. 'Yes, yes,' he said, but when he had the room to himself he began pacing the floor, still rubbing his shoulder. Then as he was about to pass the couch he sat down suddenly on it and, swinging his feet up, he turned his face into the pillow. It was many a long day since he had wanted to cry, but he wanted to cry now. Not for Hannah. No, no, he was no hypocrite. He could say he was glad she was dead. But he wanted to cry for Rosie who would have to carry her death. All her life till she died she would have to bear the weight of her mother's death. For they would saddle her with it, every one of them. 'If it hadn't been for our Rosie,' they would say, 'me Ma would've been alive the day.' Yet their blame would be nothing to the weight of her own conscience.

And where was she now? Perhaps sitting in some

all-night lorry driver's café, or getting a lift south. But wherever she was he had the feeling she was far away and that he would never see her in his life again.

It was about half past six when Dennis put his head tentatively round the door to ascertain whether Hughie was asleep, and seeing him sitting up on the couch he whispered, 'I'm just off to catch the first bus.'

Hughie, getting to his feet, said, 'Tell your da I'm sorry, and if there's anything I can do later on in the morning, standing bail or anything, he's just got to say, because if the money in the drawer is half burnt it'll have to go through the Bank before it's valid again, you know.'

Dennis nodded dully. 'I'll tell him,' he said. 'Florence is asleep, I'm letting her lie.'

'Yes, let her lie. So long, Dennis.'

'So long. . . .'

Florence was still asleep when, at half past eight, a knock came on the door, which, opened by Hughie, revealed two small boys.

'Are you the cobbler, mister?' said the taller of the two.

'Yes, sonny,' Hughie nodded at them.

'Well we want wor boots. We've been to the shop umpteen times an' it's shut, an' we went to t'other house and it's shut an' all. An' we went t'other day to the house where you live, an' the wife chased us, but me ma sent us back this mornin' an' the man there told us to come here and tell you.'

'Didn't you see a notice in the window telling you to go next door?' asked Hughie.

'Aye, we did. Aa told ya. We pummelled that door an' all, but there's nebody their neither.'

'Come in, out of the cold,' said Hughie, 'and wait till I get me things on.'

'What is it, Hughie?' Florence came to the bedroom door, blinking the sleep from her eyes as she looked at the boys, and when he explained their visit, she said, 'Oh! You'll have to go then. Sure you feel up to it?'

'Yes, I feel perfectly all right.'

'What time did Dennis go? I didn't hear him.'

'He caught the first bus. . . . Come on,' he said to the two boys as he tucked his scarf inside his coat and pulled on his cap, and together they went out.

'Did you go round the back lane at all?' he asked them. 'Mr Cullen's got a big yard there, that's where he works. Perhaps that's why he didn't hear you.'

'We didn't know there was a back-way,' answered the elder boy, 'an' the man from farther up said that the joiner was in bed anyway with rheumatics. But that was just this mornin' when we was knockin' again.'

In the bus the smaller boy turned up the bottom of his shoe and said, 'Me sole's been lettin' in all week.'

'I'm sorry,' said Hughie, and he was sorry. He knew he should have written to Lance Briggs, who would have been along like a shot after he had finished at the factory and seen to things, but Lance wouldn't have come on his own, not before this afternoon when it had been arranged he should take over, because he would be too afraid of appearing pushing.

When they reached the shop he stretched up and felt for the key on the back of the hopper. It surprised him when it wasn't there, and the thought did flash through his mind that perhaps Rosie hadn't been able to reach it. He didn't ask where else she would have put it but thrust his hand into his jacket pocket and took out a key ring. He had always kept a spare. When he opened the door the boys followed him into the shop and the small one said immediately, 'There they are,' as he pointed to one of the shelves.

'Oh, your name's Ratcliffe,' said Hughie, looking at the ticket on the boots. 'You're Mr Ratcliffe's boys?'

They nodded, and then the younger one put in again, 'Me ma's always sayin' to me da it's too far to bring mendin', but me da says you're cheaper and better than the Co-op.'

Hughie was forced to smile. 'That'll be fifteen shillings,' he said.

When the boys counted the money out to him he looked down at them and asked, 'What would you do with fifteen shillings, eh?'

They screwed up their faces at him.

'I'm leaving the shop,' he said, 'there's a new man taking over on Monday, but tell your da the work'll be as good and as cheap as ever. Now here . . .' He took the ten shilling note and handed it to the older boy, saying, 'Give that ten shillings to your ma and tell her to get something nice for your teas, and split this atween you.' He then handed him the two shilling bits and a shilling.

'Ee, mister! You sure it's all right?'

'Of course it's all right.'

'Me ma mightn't believe us.'

'That's true.' He nodded at them. 'Wait a minute.' He pulled a loose pad towards him and wrote on it, 'I've given your boys the boot money back.' Then he signed his name.

'You won the pools, Mister? Is that why you're givin' up?'

'Well something like that.' He nodded at them, and with a hand on each of their shoulders he turned them about and pushed them towards the door.

'Thanks, mister.'

'Aye, thanks, mister.'

'Mind how you go.'

'Aye, mister.'

They didn't mind how they went, they went running and skipping down the icy hill, and Hughie watched them for a moment with a sort of envy before turning into the shop and closing the door. As he did so he noticed the paper lying in front of the window, and, picking it up, he saw it was the notice he had given Rosie. So she had been here, or Jim Cullen had. Well, anyway, he'd have to stay this morning, until Lance turned up in case anybody came for their boots. There were about fifteen pairs of shoes and boots to be collected and about the same number to be repaired. He should have got in touch with Lance before now; he didn't know what he had been thinking about.

He went round the counter and entered the back shop, and what he saw transfixed him for a moment in horror.

Rosie was lying on the bed chair. He knew it was her by her hair and her figure; he would never have been able to recognize her by her face.

'Ooh! Ooh! Ro-sie.' He groaned out the words as he moved slowly towards her, and, dropping down by the

254

side of the chair, he put out a trembling hand to her face. As he did so she opened as much of her eyes as she could. The whole expanse of the upper part of her face was black, swollen and distorted, while her mouth, that tender once laughing mouth, was now a shapeless bloody mass. Her lips were fixed apart and showed a gap where two or three teeth were missing.

'Oh! Rosie, Rosie.' He lifted up her hand, which too was bloody and dead cold.

When he saw her lips trying to move and the narrow slits of her eyes close in pain with the effort, he gabbled, 'Don't don't. Don't move, don't say anything; lie still.' He got to his feet and looked about him as if not sure what to do. The room was like death and she was wearing nothing but the dress he had seen her in the night she first came home.

'You'll be all right, you'll be all right.' He was still gabbling. 'Just lie still.' He rushed to the stove and lit it and put on the kettle; then back to the oil stove and, lighting that turned it to its full extent. Coming to her again, he bent over her. Then saying to himself, 'What am I thinking about?' He tore off his coat and covered her with it. Dashing into the shop, where hung an old coat and an overall on a peg, he snatched these down and came back to her. Gently he raised her feet and folded the coats about them. Then kneeling by her side again he brought his face down to hers and asked very quietly but urgently, 'Who did this to you? Tell me, Rosie. Who did this to you?'

When for an answer the slits of her eyes closed again, he said, 'When I find out who's done this I'll kill them. I swear to God I'll kill them. . . . Aw, Rosie.' He put out his hand to her hair, but so light was his touch that she didn't feel it.

When the kettle whistled he jumped to his feet and mashed a pot of tea, but before he poured the rest of the hot water into a basin he had to take the towel and wipe his face. Last night . . . or this morning it was, he'd had to stop himself from crying, but now he had been crying and hadn't known he was. It was many, many years since he had really cried. It was the day Hannah had cornered him up in the attic and told him that he had fathered Moira's child. She had beaten him black and blue where it didn't show, and nobody knew except him, and her, and Moira. It was from that time he'd had a room to himself . . . the box room, in which you could turn round and that was all.

When he brought the bowl and flannel to her side he was afraid to touch her face, until her lips making a stiff motion she spoke his name, 'Hughie.'

'Yes, Rosie, what is it?'

'I'm . . . I'm v-very cold, Hughie.' He could just make out the words . . . 'Me hands.'

'Put them in the water.' He lifted one hand and put it in the dish that stood on the chair, and taking the hot, wet flannel, he wrapped it around the other hand.

He left her for a moment, to pour out a cup of tea, which he brought to her, saying, 'Try to drink this.' But when he put the hot cup to her lips she started and gave the first real movement since he had come into the room.

'Oh, I'm sorry, I'm sorry.' He was all clumsy contrition. 'I should have thought, I should have put more milk in it. Look, I'll pour it in the saucer.' But when he put the tea in the saucer she couldn't swallow it and it

256

ran down the side of her mouth and over the dried blood and on to her dress.

'Rosie.' He hovered above her. 'Look, you're in a bad way. 'I'll . . . I'll have to get a doctor. There's one just lives two streets away. If I slip out now I'll catch him afore he finishes his surgery. Look, I'll go now, I won't be five minutes. Lie quiet now. All right?'

When she made no move he turned from her and hurried through the shop, just as he was, without cap, coat or muffler, and, locking the door, he pelted down the hill, across the road, and didn't stop until he reached the doctor's surgery. . . .

'A young girl been beaten up?' said the doctor. 'By whom?'

'I don't know.'

'Funny.' The doctor didn't say this but his look said it for him. 'I'll be with you in a minute.' He left Hughie, and when he returned carrying a bag, he said, 'We'll go now,' and led the way to his car. A few minutes later he was looking down at Rosie.

'How did this happen?' he asked her gently.

She made no effort to answer, just an almost imperceptible movement with her head. His hands were tender as he touched her face, and his voice was equally so as he said, 'I'm afraid you'll have to go to hospital, my dear.'

She made another movement, and now her eyes turned in Hughie's direction.

Hughie, too, thought with the doctor that she should go to hospital; that was, until he remembered that Hannah was in hospital . . . in the mortuary. There was only one hospital in the town. It wasn't possible that

257

Rosie would be long there before she found out about her mother.

He found himself stammering, 'I don't think she wants to go to hos . . . hospital, doctor. She'll be all right at her brother's. If you would just tell me . . . tell me what to do.'

The doctor moved slowly away from Rosie. He moved into the shop as though he was still walking in the same room, and Hughie followed him.

'Her lip will have to be stitched inside.' The doctor looked at Hughie. 'There's nothing much can be done to her face only apply an ointment. That will take time. But she's suffering from shock, and she should go to hospital.'

Hughie looked down at his own twisting hands, and then he said, 'Her mother committed suicide this morning, doctor. She was taken to hospital. She,' he motioned towards the room, 'she doesn't know. There was a fight, a . . . a family row. If she knows what has happened to her mother she'll blame herself . . . because, well' – it was difficult for him to say what he had to say – 'well, in a way she was the cause of the . . . the row . . . you see?'

'Yes, yes.' The doctor's brows moved upwards. 'Yes, I see what you mean. She'll be all right at this brother's?'

'Oh, yes, yes. And I'll be there.'

'Are you a relation?'

Hughie's eyes flicked downwards again. 'No, but I've lived in the same house with her since she was born.'

'Have you any idea how she really came by this?' The doctor touched his own face. 'As you said earlier, it looks as if she's been beaten up. Can you throw any light on it?'

'No, no.' Hughie shook his head. 'Except . . . well, there's a man she's been connected with. He could have done it, but . . . well, it's the time factor. I understand she left home after twelve last night. He could have been waiting for her, but I just don't know. And then there was a woman . . . she was with her at the club earlier on. . . .'

'Oh, that isn't a woman's work.' The doctor paused before moving back into the room and said under his breath, 'If she'll name who did it, he's in for a nice quiet stretch.' He flicked his eyes towards Hughie and his words were scarcely audible as he asked, 'Was . . . was she a good girl?'

Hughie returned the doctor's glance without blinking. 'Yes,' he said definitely. 'Yes.'

The doctor's brows moved upwards again and then he asked briefly, 'Good looking?'

'Beautiful.'

'Hmm! Well, let's hope that this will leave no mark outside or in. But only time will tell that.'

Yes, thought Hughie, as he followed him back in the room, only time would tell that. And then he found himself replying, as it were, to an inner voice, saying, 'Well, she is a good girl, she is.'

It was odd how the mind worked.

Dennis came slowly out of the bedroom and into the hallway where Florence and Hughie were waiting for him. He looked more shaken now than when he had returned in the early hours of the morning from the hospital. He glanced from Florence to Hughie, then swung his head sideways, and with it held at an angle he passed them and went into the room.

'Terrible, isn't it?' Florence went to his side.

He did not answer her but drew his hand around the back of his neck; then looking up at Hughie who had come to stand in front of him, he said. 'You know who did it?'

Hughie shook his head. 'She didn't say.'

Now Dennis looked from one to the other of them again, and his lips moved, but he didn't speak until he turned his head towards the window. Then he said, 'Me mother.'

No exclamation came from either Florence or Hughie, and Dennis said no more. The situation had gone beyond discussion for the moment. . . .

Nor did they bring the topic up during the hours that followed. Dennis related in a somewhat desultory fashion that the lads had been allowed bail and their case adjourned until a week come Monday because of the circumstances of their mother's death; that Ronnie MacFarlane was still in hospital but would likely be out in a day or two; also that there were a few lines of Stop Press in the *Fellburn Observer*, which Dennis said, would keep the appetites whetted until the full account came out next week. And all the while Rosie lay sleeping in the bedroom. She would sleep, the doctor said, for around twenty-four hours, and this would be the best medicine for her.

It was on Sunday afternoon just as the light was fading that Dennis made a statement which startled Hughie. It was a bold statement, and apropos of nothing that had ever been discussed between them. 'You're in love with our Rosie, aren't you?' Dennis said.

The question actually brought Hughie out of his chair, and he stood looking down at Dennis while the bones of his jaws moved backwards and forwards; then, he said, 'What makes you think that?'

'Look, come off it, Hughie. Don't stall. If I'm wrong, well I'm wrong, but it isn't the day or yesterday that I've known how you felt about her; at least,' he jerked his head, 'I felt sure I was right. Anyway if I'm wrong about that, well I must be wrong about lots of other things too. . . . But it's true, isn't it?'

Hughie turned his back towards Dennis and walked to the window and looked out on to the slush-strewn road.

'How many other people think they know how I feel?' he asked in a tight voice.

'Florence.'

'And all the lads I suppose?'

'No. No, it never entered their heads, I'm sure of that. . . . But . . . but she did.' Dennis did not say, 'Me mother.'

'Yes, she did.' Hughie inhaled deeply; then turning and coming back towards Dennis he asked, still in a tight, stiff fashion, 'Well what difference does it make? Why had you to bring it up, Dennis . . . ? It's no good.'

'Sit down, man. The trouble with you . . .' Dennis nodded rapidly up at Hughie, 'the trouble with you is you don't know your own worth, you never have. Sit down.' He jerked his hand towards the chair, and when Hughie sat down he leant towards him, saying earnestly, 'Take her away with you, Hughie, take her out of this.'

'Aw, Dennis, talk sense. Do you think for a moment she'd come with me?' His voice ended on a high derogatory note.

'Yes I do, and so does Florence. Women sense these things quicker than men. Florence feels that you'll have little persuading to do, specially now.'

Hughie beat his knuckles together as he repeated, 'Especially now when she's at a disadvantage, eh? If she did say she would come I'd always know she took it as a last line of escape.'

'Well you want to help her, don't you?'

'Yes, I want to help her.'

'Then do it just because of that.'

Hughie got to his feet again. 'She'd never come.'

'Well, you won't know until you ask her, will you? And you'll be in no worse position if she refuses; you were going away on your own, anyway, weren't you? Don't you think it's worth a try . . . ? Think about it, there's plenty of time.'

'Do you think so?' Hughie turned and looked at Dennis over his shoulder. 'I mean about time, an' I don't mean in my case but in hers. I think the quicker she gets away from this town the better, because if she hears about her mother God knows what effect it will have on her.'

'Well then, there you are.' Dennis was also on his feet now, but Hughie brushed the conclusion aside with, 'I'm thinking about arranging for a holiday for her so that she can get away as soon as she gets on her feet. She needn't know about a thing. It isn't likely that the lads will come here, is it?'

'No, it isn't likely; but don't you be such a blasted

fool, man. And what will happen to her on her own at some guest house or hotel? She wants someone near her who knows all about her. There's a strong sense of home in Rosie, it's in all of us; that's why she came back. I would have done the same in her case; in fact I've been doing it for years. Even when I knew there'd be a row as soon as I put my nose in the door, I had to go home every now and again. Rosie will never survive on her own . . . and I don't like to think what she will come to if she's left on her own . . . you know what I mean, don't you?'

Hughie made no answer but started to walk about the room again, until Dennis asked, 'Is there much more to do to the caravan?'

'I don't know.' Hughie paused in his walk. 'Old Jim's in bed, I hear . . . I . . . I think I'll take a dander over now and see how far he's got.'

Dennis nodded at him. 'Do that,' he said. 'And if he's not up to it I would get somebody else to finish it. The funeral's on Wednesday . . . I'd get away before then if you can.'

'Aw, but . . .' Hughie turned, his hand out, protesting, towards Dennis, and Dennis making the same gesture back said, 'No aw buts. Go on, man and get that bit settled; and who knows but the rest will fall into place.'

Rosie became fully awake by seven o'clock on the Sunday evening. She was shuddered into awareness by a voice echoing down a long corridor. It was her mother's voice and she was running away from it. Her shuddering moved the muscles of her face, and the pain brought her hand up sharply to her head. She opened her eyes as wide as she could and saw Hughie sitting by her side.

'I've . . . I've had . . . an awful dream, Hughie.'

'You're awake now; you're all right, Rosie.' He took hold of her hand and smoothed it gently.

'I thought . . . I thought for a moment she . . . she was dead.' Like Dennis, she hadn't said 'me ma'. The words came through the misshaped mouth in a whisper. 'It . . . it was a terrible dream.'

Hughie's hand had become still, and with it his whole body, while his pores opened and he began to sweat; and now he said, his voice shaking just the slightest, 'Don't let it worry you, it . . . it was just a dream. . . . How are you feeling?'

She looked at him, then made a small movement with her head. 'Awful, Hughie,' she said. 'Awful. My mouth's so sore.'

'That's the stitches,' he said. 'You'll feel better soon.'

'Will you stay with me, Hughie?'

'As long as you want, Rosie.'

And he stayed with her until an hour later when, after another dose of tablets, she went to sleep again. . . .

On the Monday when Florence asked her if she would like to get up for a while she seemed a little taken aback, for she felt she hadn't the power to move, but with an effort she sat up in a chair.

But on the Tuesday morning she got up and dressed, putting on once again her blood-stained suit. But she did not leave the bedroom. Now she could move her lips a little but the whole of her face felt more painful than ever, and when she caught sight of it in the mirror it was impossible for her to believe that she was looking at herself. She stared at the black, blue and yellow contorted mass, at the shapeless lips and the black gap where her teeth had been, and she said, 'Oh God! Oh God! How could she.' Yet hadn't she always known that her mother was capable of all kinds of cruelty? That was why her lavish generosity towards her had always frightened her. Her mother's giving had been a kind of insurance which one day she expected to pay off in such a way that the name of Hannah Massey would be enhanced.

If she had come home and told her she was going to have a baby she would have gone mad, but it would have been a controlled madness, for she would have arranged for her to go away until . . . the disgrace was over. And she would have comforted herself with the thought that 'her poor innocent child was took down'. Looking back now, Rosie knew that if she had told her mother the real truth Hannah might have wanted to kill her; and she would, without doubt, have told her to get out, but still she would have kept everything under control. The men would have known nothing about it. And when she didn't come home again Hannah would have declared to her family, 'Well, that's daughters for you. You bring them up on the best and then they do well for themselves and don't want to know you.'

But the unforgivable thing in her mother's eyes was that her sin had been made public. She had destroyed her, she had said, meaning that she had blown up the ivory tower of eight Brampton Hill.

Florence came into the room now and Rosie, looking

at her through the mirror, asked pitifully, 'What am I going to do, Florence?'

Florence put her arms about her, saying, 'In a few weeks it'll be back to normal. The doctor says there won't be any marks, the split was inside your lip. Don't cry, my dear, don't cry. You're more than welcome to stay with us, you know you are. . . . But . . . but . . .'

As she floundered, the sound of a door opening caused her to exclaim, 'If that's Hughie I'll just slip out for a bit of shopping and get back before Dennis comes in. Will you be all right, dear?' She bent over her.

'Yes, Florence, thanks.'

'Now don't cry, everything will be all right, you'll see.'

When Florence reached the kitchen Hughie was standing warming his hands over the boiler. He turned at her approach and asked quickly, 'How is she?'

'She's up.' Florence shook her head. 'She was at the mirror and I thought she was going to pass out; she's upset. And who wouldn't be? How did you find things?'

'Oh fine; the fellow will be finished the night. Everything's ready, I can start anytime.'

'I, Hughie?' Florence repeated. 'Not we?'

Hughie rubbed his hands over the top of the boiler. 'I haven't got the nerve, Florence, and that's the truth.'

'But you want to help her, Hughie, don't you?'

'Of course; but there's other ways than asking her to come with me, when . . . when she's at this low ebb.'

'It's the best thing that could happen to you both, Hughie.' Florence was standing close to him. 'You could make her happy, I know you could. And she could make a different man of you. Not' – she put out her hand and touched him – 'not that I want you any different, but you know what I mean, Hughie. Inside, you'd feel different, self-assured. . . . No more timidity.'

'Oh, I know fine well all about that part of it, Florence.' He drew his breath in. 'But it seems like taking advantage of her. . . .'

'Aw!' Florence gripped his arm and shook him. 'You make me wild, Hughie . . . Well anyway, go on in with her now. I'm going out to do a bit of shopping.'

'Oh, I'll run you there . . . Look.' He drew her to the kitchen window and pointed. 'I called at the garage and picked it up. Everything's in shape.' He pointed towards the Land-Rover out on the road, and Florence said, 'Good, good. But the shop isn't ten minutes away.'

'But you might slip, it's all slushy.'

'I never slip. Have I slipped yet? Go on,' she pushed him and hissed at him, 'and do something.'

A few minutes later Hughie nervously knocked on the bedroom door, but when he entered the room and saw Rosie sitting by the bed his face brightened, and he said cheerily, 'Well, that's more like it . . . how do you feel?' Then without waiting for her answer he went on, 'You're bound to feel mouldy for some time but you're up, that's something.'

When he sat down opposite her she looked at him for a moment before saying, 'It's Tuesday today, isn't it, and you were going yesterday.'

'Oh, things weren't quite ready. Old Jim Cullen had rheumatism and couldn't finish the caravan.' He smiled.

'You won't be going then . . . not yet awhile?'

'Well' – he dropped his head to one side and looked towards the floor – 'everything's ready now. There

267

wasn't really much to do, and Jim didn't mind me getting another fellow to finish it. The roads are still a bit slushy but I've just got to drive the lot to the airport. I've decided to have it taken to the other side by air ferry. Amazing to be able to do that, isn't it?' He lifted his head and glanced at her as if to confirm that she agreed with him on the wonders of aviation.

She was staring fixedly at him through the swollen narrow slits of her eyes. 'When are you going?' she asked.

'Well . . . well . . .' He had his hands joined and was rubbing the palms together. 'Well I could leave to-morrow, but you've got to give a little notice for the plane and things, you know.' He nodded at her. 'I'm going to phone the night; I just may be lucky and get a booking.'

'I'm . . . I'm going to miss you, Hughie.'

He did not say, 'I'll miss you, too,' but said in a small voice, 'Will you Rosie?'

She remained very still, just looking at him. And he returned her gaze as he said, 'Well . . . well you know, there's . . . there's an alternative, Rosie. You needn't miss me.' Now his head jerked and his voice had a nervous gabbling sound as he rushed on, 'I'm no good at this, I'll put it all wrong. The whole thing is, I . . . I don't want to take advantage of you, but it isn't the day or yesterday that I've wanted . . . well . . . Oh, Rosie. . . .' He closed his eyes, then shading them with his hand he murmured, 'I want you to come with me . . . but only for a time, until you're better and on your feet again. I . . . I won't make any claim on you, don't think that, or . . . or think you will marry me or anything like that.

You can be just as free as you are now, but if you came with me you would . . .' He stopped when he felt her hands on his, and as he gripped them he rose to his feet, saying, 'You would, Rosie?' There was awe in his tone.

For answer she moved her head in the direction of his arm as if searching for some place to rest it.

He had held her for only a second when the front door bell rang, and his body stiffened before he whispered, 'Let them ring.' As he pressed her gently to him the bell rang again, and he looked down into her face now and said, 'It couldn't be Dennis has forgotten his key, it's too early for him. Anyway, the back door's open.' When the bell rang for the third time he smiled at her, saying, 'I'd better see.' But before he moved away he brought his eyes on a level with her hers, and looking into them, he said softly, 'Aw, Rosie,' and the words were like a passionate endearment.

He didn't hurry out of the room, but walked as he felt, in a relaxed fashion. He was warm inside, glowing as with joy. He had never experienced joy before. Then as he crossed the hall to the front door the kitchen door opened and he was confronted by Broderick.

If the devil had risen up out of the floor he couldn't have been more startled, not only because of the unexpectedness of Broderick's presence at this particular moment in the house, but also at his changed appearance, for he was not looking at the spritely, virile man of sixty-two but at an old, stooped, haggard man, with pain-filled eyes.

'Anybody in?'

'No. Well, I mean Florence has gone out shopping, Broderick, and . . . and Dennis isn't back yet from

269

school.' He pushed past the older man, drawing him back into the kitchen, saying, 'I'll make you a cup of tea, you look cold. Sit down, Broderick. I won't be a minute.'

Broderick came and stood by the table. 'Don't make any tea for me,' he said; and then he asked, 'Is Rosie here, Hughie?'

Hughie had been half-turned towards the sink, and now he swung round and asked, 'What makes you think that, Broderick?'

'Oh, just somethin' that Dennis let slip last night when him and Jimmy were going at it. Jimmy was blaming her for Hannah's . . . mishap,' he did not say death, 'and Dennis then told him the rights of the case. An' when it was told, well, it wasn't like Ronnie MacFarlane had made out; and we . . . the others saw that, but Jimmy kept on and then Dennis . . . well, Dennis said that Hannah had done her best to take Rosie along of her by . . . by beatin' her up . . . I couldn't, I wouldn't believe it, not at first, 'cos, well, she loved her . . . she . . . she thought the sun shone out of her.' His head was moving slowly from side to side now and he muttered something to himself that was inaudible to Hughie. Then looking at him again, he said, 'Dennis says she's gone back to London.'

'Aye, yes, that's right, Broderick, she . . . she went back to London.'

'She went back knowing her mother was dead and to be buried the morrow.'

'She didn't know, Broderick, she was in a bad way. The doctor said it was best not to tell her, it might affect her.'

270

'But she'll have to know sometime, better sooner than later.'

'The doctor didn't see it like that, Broderick.' Hughie's voice was soft. 'He . . . he agreed . . . I mean said, it might affect her mentally if she was to know . . . all her life. And . . . and . . .'

'Then she might never know because she'll never come back.' Broderick pulled in his lower lip between his teeth. 'She was more sinned against than sinning as I see now. I'm not one of those that is blamin' her for Hannah's going; there's many things that helped towards Hannah's going. She was a strange woman was Hannah.' He nodded his head. 'A strange woman, but a fine woman; a strong woman, but strange. Me life's finished without her, the pin's gone.'

'It's early days yet, Broderick.'

As Hughie finished speaking the sound of soft footsteps in the hall made him start towards the door, but before he reached it Rosie pushed it slowly open and Broderick gaped at the figure for a full minute before realization came to him, and then he lifted his hand and covered his face.

'I . . . I thought I heard your voice, Da.' The words were uneven and thick as if they had their shape coming over her lips. 'I thought you might go without . . . without . . .' She didn't finish because Hughie's voice cut in, saying, 'I'm sorry, Broderick, I . . . I thought it best.'

Broderick took his hand from his face but kept his head lowered as he moved forward, and as his hands groped for hers, he muttered brokenly, 'Aw, lass. Aw, lass.'

'Oh, Da.'

'Your face . . . you poor face. Aw, my God, lass.'

'Don't worry, Da, it's all right, it'll . . . it'll get better.' But even as she said this she didn't believe it ever would get better. At least not so that she would be able to recognize herself as she once was. But through the trembling hand that held hers she realized that her father was in need of comfort much more than herself at this moment. And as his shoulders began to shake with the compressed weeping within, she whispered, 'Aw, don't, Da, don't. It's all right: I tell you it's all right.'

He drew away from her and rubbed his face with his hand, and as he looked at her again his eyes focused on her mouth and he muttered, as if he could almost feel the agony of the moment they had been knocked out, 'Your teeth, lass. Oh, your teeth.'

She said brokenly, 'Don't worry, Da, please.' Then, 'Come and sit down for a minute, Florence'll be back soon.'

'No, lass, no, I've got to go. I've . . . I've business to see to. . . .'

As he said this his eyes were drawn to Hughie and he answered the message in them by omitting to state the type of business that called him away; instead, he said to Rosie, 'What are you thinkin' of doin' with yourself, lass?'

It was Rosie who now looked towards Hughie, and when she turned to her father again she did not lower her eyes as she answered his question, in a minimum of words, 'I'm going with Hughie, Da.'

The effect was to startle Broderick, bringing his mouth agape, and his back straight as if the words had injected him with aggressive life. As he turned towards Hughie it was as if Hannah herself had entered into him, and for a moment Hughie thought he was going to be attacked, at least by a spate of words, accusing, derogatory, spiteful words. Then as Broderick, drawing in a deep breath, turned from him and looked at Rosie again the spirit of Hannah seeped out of him and he asked, quietly, but tersely, 'You know what you're doin'?'

'Yes, Da.' She cast a glance in Hughie's direction, not towards his face but to him as a whole.

Broderick, turning towards the sink, gripped its edge and let his body fall towards it, as if to rest for a moment; then straightening himself, he said in a hopeless tone. 'I'd better be off.'

'Da!' The appeal brought him round to her, and after looking at the face that had filled the last twenty-three years of his life with pride and on which now there was left not one recognizable feature, he clamped his teeth down on his lip and, thrusting out his arms, drew her to him.

'Oh, Da! Da!'

'There now, there now.' They stood close for some moments, then, after passing his hand over her hair, he pressed her gently from him, saying thickly, 'Wherever you go, lass, I pray that you have peace . . . and . . . and happiness. Goodbye now.' He lifted her hand and held it to his face for a moment before pushing her away.

Silently, and with her head deep on her chest, she turned from him and went out of the kitchen; and when she was gone Broderick moved towards the back door, and he stood facing its blankness as he spoke to Hughie. 'I've got nothing against you, Hughie,' he said. 'I never have had, but I'll say straight to you now, I wish from

273

the bottom of my soul this wasn't happenin'. But as it is, it's thankful to God I am she's where she is at this minute, for if she'd known of this there'd have been more than one burial the morrow. Rightly or wrongly she would never have suffered it. Her first daughter an' her last. No, she'd never have suffered it in this world.'

When no word came from Hughie, Broderick raised his head and looked back at him, saying, 'I'm not blamin' you, I'm not blamin' you. As a man I understand. Nevertheless, you must grant it's an odd situation.'

'I do grant it, Broderick, but in me own defence I'll say what I've said before. Karen wasn't really my doing; if ever there was a rape that was it. But with Rosie, well . . . I'll admit to you now, I've sat in the corner of your kitchen for the last few years just so that I could look at her, or be there when she came, and that's the truth. I've always said to meself that I didn't make the break because I hadn't any guts; the other excuse was that I wanted a family, to be a member of a family; but what I really wanted was to be near Rosie. . . . But' – he lifted his hand towards Broderick – 'I never had any hope, don't think that. Not in my wildest dreams did I have any hope of one day having Rosie, that would have been too fantastic, and she wouldn't be coming with me now but she's in a jam, at least that's how I see it. I'm not going to hold her to anything, Broderick.'

'You're not marrying her then?' The question was sharp.

'Not unless she wants it. When she gets on her feet again it'll be up to her.'

'You're a strange fellow, Hughie, a strange fellow. Are you staying in the country?'

'No, Broderick, I'm going abroad as I planned.'

'To stay there?'

'Aye, to stay there.'

'Then I don't suppose we'll meet again, and I'll never see her again.'

'You never know, I can't tell you that, Broderick. Anyway, you might decide to take a trip.'

'Not this side of the grave. . . . One last thing . . . what if she finds out her mother's dead and how she died? The world's a small place; a chance word and she'll know it.'

'I'll meet that emergency when it comes, Broderick. In any case, she'll be in a better state of mind to face up to it than she is now; but if I can help it she'll never find out.'

Broderick opened the door, and pausing before he stepped into the street, he said, 'It's a queer business. . . . Well, there's nothing more to say then. I wish you goodbye, Hughie.'

'Goodbye, Broderick.' Hughie waited for the old man to extend his hand, his own was half wavering forward, but when Broderick made no move in this direction Hughie said, 'I'd like to say thank you, Broderick, for the kindness you've shown me over all the years.'

Broderick now looked straight into Hughie's face and he kept his concentration on him for fully a minute before he said, 'I could say that you've shown your thanks in an odd way, Hughie, but when I've time to reflect I might be thinkin' it's the best thing that could have happened to her, for God knows when a lass takes one step down the ladder there's plenty of willing hands to help her to the bottom. Goodbye, Hughie.'

'Goodbye, Broderick.'

Not until Broderick had disappeared round the corner of the street did Hughie go in and close the door, and then he stood with his back to it, his eyes tight shut and one hand inside his collar gripping it hard. He felt exhausted, as if he had been struggling physically with an opponent; and he had, and not only during the past ten minutes, but for years past. But now he had won. No, no, not quite. Perhaps it would be months ahead before he would know for sure, but he'd be content to wait. He was used to waiting, he'd had a lot of practice. But this period of waiting would be different. He'd be waiting as a man waits, not as a mouse in the corner of a kitchen. The thought brought him from the door straight upright on his feet. He squared his shoulders and lifted his head and went out of the room.

It was ten o'clcok the following morning and they were ready to go. Everything that had to be said had been said. Now, with brotherly awkwardness, Dennis held Rosie to him, saying, 'Forget everything as I said and enjoy your life, Rosie.' He bent his head forward under the deep fur hood which covered her face, and gently he put his lips against her discoloured cheek.

'Thanks, Dennis, thanks for everything.' Her voice was unsteady.

Now Florence was standing before her. Her hands adjusting the hood, she said, 'This is the very thing, you can hardly see your face at all. But if anyone gets curious, just do as I said, tell them you were in a car accident.'

'It's so good of you, Florence, I'll send it back.'

'You'll do no such thing. But when you can get about yourself get another coat; this' – she touched Rosie's sleeve – 'would fit three of you. I was mad to let him go shopping on his own.' She cast a tender glance towards Hughie. Then putting her arms about Rosie, she pressed her close as she whispered, 'God bless you.' They were strange words coming from Florence, who didn't believe in God, only in man.

And now Florence was enfolding Hughie in her embrace and was crying unashamedly; then pushing him abruptly from her she said, 'Go on, get yourselves off this could go on all day. We won't come to the car, the less attention drawn to your going the better.'

Hughie and Dennis were now gripping hands in the open doorway. Both were evidently deeply disturbed and Hughie had difficulty in speaking. 'We'll all be together again and before very long, I know. Anyway,' he moved his neck upwards out of his collar, 'you'll be hearing from me later in the day.'

'Aye, aye,' said Dennis, 'phone us from the airport.'

'Oh, may be afore that. So long, Dennis.'

'So long Hughie. You know what I wish you.' The hands gripped for the last time, and then Hughie, holding Rosie's arm, led her to the waiting car, and before they reached it the door of the flat closed behind them.

Hughie hoped that Rosie hadn't noticed this for it might set her wondering at the peremptoriness of it. It might appear as if they couldn't get rid of her quickly enough. But Dennis and Florence were now, he knew, scurrying into their clothes to be ready when the taxi called to take them to the house for the funeral.

But apparently Rosie hadn't noticed anything unusual.

Getting into the car, she settled herself down, and as it began to move cautiously forward she did not turn and take one last look at the flat, but from the depth of her hood kept her eyes directly ahead. She was so full now of a mixture of emotions that she felt the slightest move would cause her to break down. There was on her mind an oppressive weight. Oddly enough the weight did not seem to be connected with what had happened to her in London. Strangely she found she wasn't thinking of that any more. Somehow it had been wiped out by the blows her mother had showered on her; it was, she knew, the thoughts of her mother that were weighing on her, encasing her. And she felt sad, so terribly sad with the knowledge that when she left this town she would never see her father again. She had no regrets about never seeing her mother again.

Hughie was talking now, rapidly, nervously. 'It'll be better when we get on the main road, it'll be clearer. We should be at the airport in two hours, but I'm giving meself four just in case. It was lucky about the booking, wasn't it? That's because there's not so many travelling across this time of the year. I've got to make a call before we leave the town, Rosie. I've got to go to the bank. I might be five or ten minutes. You won't mind?'

'No, no, Hughie.'

'Look,' he was nodding to the road ahead, 'how would you like to sit in the caravan time I'm in there? You could lie down, the curtains are drawn. How about it? You're supposed not to ride in the caravan, but what odds.'

'I . . . yes, I think I'd prefer that, Hughie.'

'We'll stop at yon side of the road. You know,' he

made an effort to laugh, 'I only want an excuse for you to see inside. You've never seen it yet.' He glanced towards her and saw the movement of the hood. She did not turn her face towards him.

They stopped on a quiet road at the top of the park and Hughie unlocked the caravan door, and when Rosie entered, her surprise brought the first touch of lightness to her voice. 'It's wonderful, wonderful, Hughie. I never thought it would be like this, it's . . . it's like a house.' She turned to him now, saying, 'Oh, Hughie,' but he did not look at her. Instead, going to the settee opposite an actual fireplace in the middle of the caravan, he said, 'Lie on this one, will you, it'll make the balance better. The end one there,' he inclined his head, 'might tip it up at the back a bit and . . . and I'm not yet used to the feel of her.'

When she sat down saying, 'I'll just slip me boots off,' Hughie said, 'Oh, don't bother about that.'

'Oh, but I must, they're dirty.'

As she took her boots off and laid them aside he smiled at her. It was an appreciative smile. She would look after nice things, would Rosie. When she was lying down he put a rug over her; then squatting on his hunkers and bringing his face level with hers he said, 'Do you know what I'm going to do?' He sounded excited, like a young boy. She made a small movement with her head. 'I'm going to see the bank manager. I'd arranged with him to send the cheque to Dennis the morrow but I think now it's too long to wait, so I'm going to have him send it by special messenger. He'll do that for me. I've never given them anything, in kind I mean, not a thing, and being human they might just wonder, so I'd like to do

279

this afore we go!' He raised his brows at her. 'There's one thing I'm sorry for, an' that is I won't see their faces when they get it. Anyway it'll be nice to think of the bairn being born in a nice little house, their own house.'

'Oh, Hughie.' She put out her hand with the intention of touching his cheek, but before it reached him he had risen to his feet. 'Better be making a move,' he said; 'I'll need all the time I've got to get to that airport, not being Stirling Moss.' He turned away laughing. Then from the door he nodded to her. 'All right?'

'Yes, Hughie, I'm all right.'

Starting up the car once more he gulped in great draughts of air. It had all been easier that he expected. For he had a horror on him of someone stopping them and saying to her, I'm sorry to hear about your ma, Rosie. It would be just like the thing, he thought, if it happened almost at the last minute. He felt easier now she was in the caraven.

He was in the bank less than ten minutes and he was smiling wryly to himself as he emerged. How smoothly the wheels of life ran when you had a little oil to grease them with. A special messenger would be at Dennis's at one o'clock. Dennis had only the morning off from school so he would be home by then, but if he wasn't home the messenger would return again at half-past four; the letter had to be delivered personally.

As he stepped briskly across the pavement to the car and caravan he knew that he wouldn't be able to relax or get rid of this jittery feeling until they were out of the town, because he knew that his future life, and that of Rosie's, depended on her not knowing that Hannah was dead.

He had gone some distance when he stopped the car again, and getting out and opening the caravan door, he looked towards her, where half-risen, she was leaning on her elbow. 'We're nearly out of the town,' he said, 'but there will be Craig Hill to go up and that's pretty steep; it might be a bit frightening for you if you found yourself up on end. Would you like to come in the car again?'

'Yes, yes.' Hastily she pulled on her boots and he helped her out of the caravan and into the car.

'All right now?' he asked as he started up. 'Comfortable?'

'Yes, very comfortable.'

'You warm enough?'

'Yes, it's lovely, I can feel the hot air around my feet.'

'Yes, the heating's good. By! The cars these days have everything.' He spoke as if he had owned cars that hadn't quite everything. 'Would you like the wireless on?'

'Not unless you want it, Hughie.'

'No, I don't want it. Well now, there's only one more set of traffic lights and we'll be away.'

The traffic lights were against them. In front of them was a small van. It was somewhat to the left of Hughie's bonnet, obscuring the view and the traffic coming from Dean Road. But he wasn't concerned with the passing traffic, he looked to where his route lay straight across the road and up the hill. That was, until he saw Rosie lift her right hand reverently to her brow and a chill passed over him that brought with it a sickening dread as he watched her making the sign of the cross. The hood turned towards him and from the folds of it she whispered, 'It's a funeral.' He stared back almost

281

mesmerised into her sad distorted face; he knew the words she would be saying to herself: 'May the souls of the faithful departed, through the mercy of God, rest in peace. Amen.' He remembered vividly scenes, right back down the years, of Hannah stopping whenever she saw a funeral and blessing herself and repeating the words, and the children with her following suit.

A fear born of premonition paralysed him until he found himself leaning forward and fiddling with a switch on the dashboard of the car. And now his voice almost croaked as he said, 'Rosie, I wonder if you'd mind getting down and looking just under your seat – there's a tool tray there. Would you pull it out and get me a screwdriver?'

'Yes, Hughie, yes.'

The motor-drawn hearse passed slowly before the van and came into view, and as he looked at the coffin under its canopy of flowers his whole stomach seemed to turn a somersault. It was as if his bowels had run to water. He knew who lay there before the first car came into sight. In his mind he saw her struggling to get out and at him. He felt sick, sick enough to want to vomit.

In the first car he made out the black-coated figures of Jimmy and Broderick and Arthur, and . . .

'Is this it, Hughie?'

He jerked in his seat as he looked at the screwdriver in Rosie's extended hand.

'No . . . no, no, Rosie; it's . . . it's a smaller one than that.'

As she bent her head he lifted his again. A second car had passed, and now in the third one, there was John, and Betty and a man he vaguely recognised as Michael from Cornwall.

He had just caught sight of Dennis and Florence in the next car when Rosie said, 'There isn't a small one, Hughie.'

'Hand me the tray up, will you, Rosie?' He could not keep his voice steady.

As she handed him the tray he exclaimed on a deep tired note, 'Oh bust! The lights are changing. Just leave it, I'll do it when we get to the top.' He fumbled at the gears, grating them before he got the car moving again. He had the urge now to go into top gear and race up the hill and out of the town. His whole body was trembling. God! If it hadn't been for that van in front, she must have seen them. There was somebody, somewhere, he thought, on his side. For that to happen at the fifty-ninth minute of the eleventh hour and yet not come off, assuredly there was somebody on his side.

When they reached the top of Craig Hill he was glad enough of the excuse to stop, and as he examined the knob of the screen wiper he said, 'I think it'll do, it only wanted a twist.'

When she made no remark he looked towards her, but she was looking out of the window.

From the top of Craig Hill there was a full view of Fellburn. The town lay between two hills. The other rising on the far side was the famous Brampton Hill, with its long gardens reaching down to the river. Away in the distance, towards the head of the valley, were the shafts of the two dominating pits, and significantly separating them a sloping stretch of ground, which when clear of snow was a landmark which still remained white . . . it was Fellburn Cemetery. As Hughie stared towards it he saw nearing it a thin black line sharply depicted against the snow. It was weird, weird. It was as if she was watching him to the very end. As he hastily went to start the engine again Rosie's hand came on his, and it caused him to jerk his head towards her. 'We're leaving Fellburn, Hughie,' she said.

'Yes, we're leaving Fellburn, Rosie.' And the quicker the better, he added to himself.

'I don't ever want to see it again, Hughie. . . . Not that it's ever done anything to me, but I just don't want to see it again.' She didn't say to him, I don't ever want to come home again, I don't ever want to see me ma again. These were sentiments that couldn't be put into words. You just covered them up with the name of a town.

'Well, you won't ever see it again if you don't want to, Rosie.'

Her hood had slipped back and was showing her hair, bright and unspoilt above the distortion of her face. As Hughie's eyes lifted to it, she turned her face slightly to the side. 'There's something I'd like to tell you before we leave, Hughie,' she said. 'Before we start out so to speak.'

'Aw now,' he put in quickly, 'there's no need to tell me anything more, Rosie. Don't distress yourself further . . . please. I don't want to know. . . .'

'. . . Not that I would have come away with you even before this happened?' She touched her cheek with her fingers.

'Rosie!' He turned slowly but fully round in his seat. 'Do you mean that?'

284

'Yes, yes. That's . . . that's why I talked to you the other night. I didn't know why I wanted to tell you until after I had told you, and then coming . . . coming on top of the London business I couldn't trust myself or my feelings. I thought I wasn't the capable judge of what I wanted. And . . . and I also want you to know I would have felt the same if . . . if you hadn't come into the money. . . . Believe me on that above all things, Hughie.'

'Aw, Rosie.' He lifted her hands and pulled them inside his open great-coat; then bending slowly forward he let his lips touch hers for the first time. It was a touch without pressure and had the gentleness of a salve on her tight painful skin. Yet it had the power to break through the dead weight on her mind, shattering it, leaving her feeling light and faint with an overwhelming sense of relief, and the touch seemed to exhilarate him. The cloak of meekness he had worn for years disintegrated. His eyes shining, he looked at her a moment longer; then swiftly grabbing the wheel he put in the clutch and swung the car into the middle of the road. But no sooner had he done this when a terrific blast of a horn made him pull the wheel sharply to the left again. As a huge lorry passed him and a big head came into his view, shouting, 'You askin' for trouble, mate?' all he could do was stop the car yet once again.

And now, leaning over the wheel, his hands gripping the top of it, his voice trembling he said, 'I never looked in the mirror.' He glanced swiftly towards Rosie to see what her reactions were to his obviously bad driving, and when he saw her actually attempting to laugh his body jerked with a spasm. Then again it came, until, his head going back, he burst into loud body-shaking, relieving mirth. Looking down at her, he gasped, 'What odds, Rosie, what odds eh? Let them all shout. It won't be the last mistake I'll make before we reach the end of the line. Who do they think they are, anyway? "You asking for trouble, mate?" ' He was mimicking the lorry driver. 'Yes, I'm asking for trouble, mate. Lead me to it.'

Now, Rosie was really laughing, and it was a painful business, as her hands pressed against her cheeks showed, and she cried, 'Oh, Hughie! Don't. Don't.'

He was still laughing when he gripped the wheel once again and started the car. He felt a god, able to cope with any situation. He could make the woman he loved laugh: even under these circumstances he had made her laugh. He had won. He hadn't to wait until months ahead. He knew inside for a certainty now he had won, and he cried with the whole of his being, 'I've won, Hannah Massey! I've won!'

THE END

THE GILLYVORS
by Catherine Cookson

A century or so ago there lived at Heap Hollow Cottage, situated near Fellburn in County Durham, a man and a woman and their six children. By all appearances they were a close and loving family. Yet across the happy façade lay a shadow that had lengthened and darkened with the passing years. For the father and the mother were not husband and wife, which meant that to the narrow and bigoted minds of the Victorian rural community the offspring of Nathaniel Martell and Maria Dagshaw were base-born gillyvors – in country parlance, bastards.

Anna, the elder daughter, was entering womanhood resolved to face the legacy of her birth and the challenges it must continue to bring her. Her journey through life would not be an easy one and only her inborn courage and zest for life would sustain her quest for fulfilment and happiness.

'Realistic and satisfying – Catherine Cookson is an incomparable storyteller'

Sunday Telegraph

'Turns our hearts inside out'

Mail on Sunday

0 552 13621 2